I Have Never

Sadie Gordon Richmond

Also by this author

Front Page News
Sins of Silence
Sticks and Stones
Shadow Lines
One in a Million

'I've found it and it's *perfect*.'

Jakob raised his eyes from the graphics he had been poring over to see Summer standing in the kitchen doorway, her laptop tucked under her arm. Clad in a plunging red halterneck dress with her dark hair spilling over her shoulders, she looked as if she was about to head out to a party or a nightclub, not sit at a kitchen table refining a script. Given the nature of the plot, it wasn't as if the outfit would help her get into character, and, with rain lashing the windows, she certainly wasn't dressed for the weather. He pondered this for only a moment before dismissing it and asking the obvious question.

'You've found what?'

'The location for the shoot,' she replied, joining him at the table. 'It's a sixteenth-century castle on a private estate that we can hire for the weekend. And there's a ruined chapel in the woods, which is where I want to film the murder scene.'

'A castle?' Jakob echoed. 'How much is that going to set me back?'

'It's not as grand as it sounds,' Summer replied, opening up her laptop and tapping in the password before turning the machine through forty-five degrees to give him a decent view of the screen. The building filling the display looked like little more than a big old stone house; the only features that set it apart were the tiny windows and a couple of full-height turrets.

'And this is the chapel,' she added, flicking rapidly through a selection of photographs showing beautifully made up bedrooms and big fireplaces to an image of a derelict stone shell, cloaked in ivy, whose original purpose was apparent only from the unmistakeable shape of three adjacent lancet window frames on what had presumably been the chancel wall. None of the glass nor the roof remained.

'Parts of the castle could work really well for some of the other scenes, too,' Summer continued, moving on to an image of a windowless stone corridor with a high, arched ceiling and dark recesses on either side. She paused for long enough for him to take this in before flicking to another picture, which showed the uneven stone steps of a well-worn spiral staircase, and, after another pause, to a photograph of a low-ceilinged room that Jakob could best describe as a vault. He had to admit that the place had potential.

'And, even better, there's a massive lake only a stone's throw from the chapel,' Summer said, selecting yet another image before sitting back in her chair, her pitch apparently over.

'How much?'

'Fifteen hundred a night.'

Jakob whistled through his teeth.

'I know, but it's only for a couple of nights and it's not like you're going to have to pay the actors.'

'I'm going to need more than a couple of nights. It's not just filming time – I've got to work out the lighting for each scene, and if you want to use the chapel we need to allow for the weather, as well.'

'Rain would only add to that scene,' Summer enthused. 'I don't mind getting wet.'

'You might not, my equipment will,' Jakob returned, shortly. 'And it's not as if we can do endless takes.'

'We can make it work,' Summer insisted. 'You know we can.' She stood and turned her back to the table before perching on the edge and lifting a leg over him. Sliding back down off the table, she straddled him and leaned down to kiss him, her long hair falling like curtains around his face. 'I get turned on just thinking about the final scene,' she said, kissing him again before lowering herself into his lap. 'Don't you?'

'Uh-huh,' he responded, leaning to kiss her neck as she tipped her head back.

'And you can't put a price on a dream.'

'Mmm.'

'Then just say yes,' she breathed, pulling away from him and dropping her head to meet his eyes. 'Just say *yes.*'

Two years later

One

Hearing the gentle burbling of the coffee machine, Rebecca looked into the kitchen to find Leighton gazing out of the window as he attempted to straighten the fingers of his left hand against the palm of his right, his features tense with the effort not to wince. Severe frostbite sustained during a night spent shut in a freezer container some months earlier had left him with inflamed joints and damaged nerves, and minus all his fingernails. The nails had since begun to regrow, but whether he would regain anything approaching a normal range of movement and function remained unclear. In light of the fact the doctors hadn't expected him to come through the experience with all of his digits intact, Leighton generally remarked to anyone who asked that it wasn't a bad outcome. Rebecca had no idea how he really felt about the impact the injuries were having on his life, or the fact they might have put an end to his career. Then again, she didn't really know how he felt about anything material – herself included.

They had met several years earlier as colleagues, and had quickly become friends. In recent months, their relationship had graduated to something more, but Rebecca wasn't sure exactly what that *was*. Leighton was apparently happy to have her in his life and his bed, but in many ways still kept her at arm's length, finding ways to change the subject whenever conversations risked getting too personal. And despite the fact he frequently burned or cut himself trying to manage everyday household tasks, he point-blank refused to let her do anything to help. Rebecca found it infuriating, not least because, had the situation been reversed, he would have gone out of his way to help.

She was also growing increasingly concerned about his solution to the fact his injuries left him unable to cook. He had always been unhealthily reliant on junk food, but now seemed to be more or less living on takeaways, instant noodles and biscuits. When he had rebuffed Rebecca's latest efforts to help, she had tried to put the offer into perspective by pointing out that she only wanted to cook the odd meal, not give him a sponge bath. As ever, when faced with a serious conversation he didn't want to have, he had made a joke, lifting his eyebrows mischievously and remarking, 'Shame.' Rebecca was fast running out of patience, and the only thing stopping her from tackling him about it was the fact that there was only twenty-four hours to go before the man responsible for his night in the freezer stood trial.

'Hey.'

Leighton glanced around with a smile. 'Hiya.'

'What are you thinking about?' She asked, not holding out much hope of getting a real answer.

'Pandora,' he replied. 'I don't think she's been home since I've been back. I assumed she was next door, but Margaret says she's not seen her since Friday.'

'Is the tag on her collar not in range?'

'Not from here. I'll go for a walk around the neighbourhood later, see if I can pick it up.'

Rebecca nodded. Had it not seemed an inappropriate time to joke about the matter, she might have remarked that it would make a change using the tracker to look for the cat rather than her lost collars. Over the summer, Pandora had been losing an average of one a week, prompting Leighton to order fluorescent ones printed with his mobile number. He had since made the acquaintance of several local residents who had found discarded collars in their gardens.

'Coffee'll be another couple of minutes, I'm afraid.'

Rebecca glanced at her watch. 'I'd better get dressed,' she said, turning for the doorway. As she did so, her nightshirt caught the corner of a page stacked among the bills, takeaway menus and other papers heaped at the end of the worktop, sending them cascading to the floor. She crouched to gather them together, then stopped short as the word *Downview* caught her eye. Drawing out the relevant document, she held it up.

'What's this?'

Leighton glanced around. 'Looks like a prison visiting order,' he remarked, casually, as if he was describing something as inconsequential as an advertising flyer.

'She nearly killed you, and you're going to visit her?' Rebecca exclaimed. 'Seriously?'

'She didn't nearly kill me.'

'As good as! Why on earth are you visiting her?'

'She asked me to,' Leighton replied, unconcernedly.

'So?'

'It doesn't affect you.'

Rebecca struggled not to retort that it *did*. She had lived through the two long weeks he had spent in intensive care in the aftermath of his incarceration in the freezer, and that would never have happened had a former colleague not directed him there. The colleague in question had always maintained that she had only ever intended to distract him from a line of enquiry that had looked set to reveal her guilt in a hit and run, and that the end result of her misdirection had come as a massive shock to her, as well as to everyone else. Rebecca had never believed her. She should have known Leighton would take a more sympathetic view.

'Were you even going to tell me?'

'I really hadn't given it any thought,' he responded, turning to take two mugs from the cupboard.

'Oh come *on*.'

Leighton sighed, turning back. 'It doesn't bother you when I visit Tom.'

'That's completely different. For one thing, he's your brother.'

'Yeah, well, he doesn't always act like it,' Leighton observed. 'But life's too short to waste time and energy being angry with him. I'm not going to write people off just because they make mistakes. I've done more than my fair share of stupid shit in the past.'

'You were a kid. And you didn't do anyone any harm.'

'That was dumb luck. And I might not have fully appreciated the impact of what I was doing, but I was under no illusions about the fact it was wrong. If I could go back and apologise to all the people whose cars I nicked, I would.'

'You can't seriously believe joyriding is comparable to sending someone to almost certain death!'

'Nobody *sent* me anywhere,' he countered, reasonably. 'All she did was give me a snippet of misinformation. It was my decision to go chasing after answers.' He moved to open the fridge. 'I think it's fair to say I got myself into that one.'

The last thing Martina had expected to see when she came down for breakfast was two of her housemates caught in an embrace. Her arrival seemed to take Irene and Jakob by surprise, too, and they immediately dropped their arms and pulled away from one another as she entered the kitchen.

‘Morning Tina,’ Jakob greeted her, cheerfully, as Irene turned towards the sink.

‘Morning,’ Martina echoed, feeling embarrassed to have intruded on – what exactly? Irene wasn’t what she would have described as ‘touchy-feely’, so presumably the clinch had been something more than a friendly hug. But any relationship the two might have embarked on couldn’t be very long-lived; it was scarcely two weeks since Jakob had spent the night with Maya.

‘See you later, ladies,’ Jakob said, breezily, as he made for the door.

‘Later,’ Martina responded, reaching to open the cupboard above the extractor fan and standing on tiptoes to retrieve the cheese grater. Irene still hadn’t spoken, and, as Martina leaned to wash an apple, she asked, ‘You ok, hun?’

‘Uh-huh,’ Irene replied, her words almost lost as she tipped a cereal box past a critical point and unleashed an avalanche of cornflakes. ‘Oh for fuck’s sake!’ She muttered, dumping the box on the counter and making a start on sweeping up the sea of flakes that had overflowed the bowl. Martina shot her a sideways glance. She couldn’t be certain, but it looked as if Irene had been crying.

‘Are you sure?’ She ventured, hesitantly, torn between not wanting to pry and concern for her normally undemonstrative housemate.

There was a moment’s silence. Irene swallowed, then glanced around. ‘Period,’ she excused herself, with a weak smile. ‘You know.’

Martina nodded sympathetically, despite knowing the explanation to be untrue. It wasn’t long since Irene had remarked, whilst borrowing painkillers, that their cycles had synchronised. And, right now, Martina was still more than a week away from coming on.

Irene turned towards the fridge and Martina made a start on grating her apple, then stopped as her housemate said something else. She hadn’t been able to make out the words over the sound of the grater, but Irene’s irate tone had been clear enough.

‘Sorry?’ Martina asked, glancing around.

‘How many times?’ Irene returned, holding up a plastic bottle containing barely half a centimetre of milk. ‘It’s more than a week out of date! If he’s not going to finish it, how hard is it to rinse it out and chuck it in recycling?’

‘I’ll do it,’ Martina offered, holding out a hand.

'You shouldn't have to!'

'Are there any more in there?' Martina asked, nodding towards the fridge as she took the bottle from Irene. It wouldn't have been the first time. A pint of milk lasted Tony three breakfasts; after that, whether or not the bottle was empty, he abandoned it and opened a new one. On occasion, one of his housemates would pilfer the dregs for a cup of tea when they found themselves out of milk, but more often than not the bottle ended up being pushed to the back of the fridge and forgotten about. Irene had tackled Tony about it several times, apparently to no avail.

'I don't think it's that he's inconsiderate,' Martina offered, hearing Irene swearing under her breath as she retrieved another bottle from the fridge. 'He probably just doesn't think about what he's doing.'

'Thoughtless and inconsiderate are the same thing,' Irene retorted, banging the bottle down on the worktop. 'Typical bloody man.'

'That's not what I meant,' Martina replied, reaching for the bottle and wondering why she was standing up for Tony after all he had said on the night of her party. Two weeks on, she still didn't understand *why* her infatuation with Ed had made him so angry. She might be making a fool of herself, but that didn't reflect on him. And he could have conveyed his conviction that Ed was never going to go out with her – something Martina had always been aware of, deep down – in a more measured and kindly manner. Describing Ed as a *closeted chubby chaser* who was embarrassed to be seen out with her had been rubbing salt into the wound.

His subsequent failure to apologise had only compounded Martina's sense of betrayal. She had trusted Tony with feelings she'd shared with no one else, and had never imagined that, all the while, he had been privately judging her. And if he was judging her, everyone else was surely doing the same.

'I expect he's just on autopilot first thing,' she added.

Irene shook her head, saying nothing.

'Are you still on for tonight?' Martina asked, after an awkward silence, thinking the best option might be to change the subject.

'Hmh?'

'Maya's stopping by for a nightcap after she's finished at the theatre.'

'Oh. Right. Yeah, I'll be here,' Irene confirmed. 'But – could you not say anything – about –' she hesitated before abandoning the sentence unfinished and continuing, hurriedly, 'I'm sorry, I know it's not fair to ask you to keep secrets, but –'

'It's ok,' Martina stopped her, with what she hoped was a reassuring smile. 'It's hardly as if it would mean keeping much of a secret. I don't really have any idea what's going on myself.'

Having determined that the signal from his cat's RFID chip was coming from behind a row of houses that backed onto the railway line, Leighton had returned home for a high-vis vest before walking to the end of the terrace. The slatted metal gate set into the fence between the road and the railway embankment was secured with two padlocks that he would normally have been able to pick within a matter of seconds. With stiff, painful fingers it was a different matter, and it took what felt like minutes to get the job done. Despite this, nobody seemed to take any interest in what he was doing, and, slipping through the gate, he pulled it shut behind himself and set off along the embankment.

It took less than a minute for him to realise that he had vastly underestimated how challenging the search was going to be. The slope running down from the train tracks was steep – he guessed the gradient was somewhere around 40% – and beyond an initial grassy bank was buried beneath an almost impenetrable jungle of buddleias, ivy, bindweed and brambles. It was hard going, and his progress was hampered by both the fact he couldn't use his hands to help him part the dense vegetation and the knowledge that, should he trip, putting them out to break his fall would be excruciating. But he pressed on, muttering the occasional expletive and following the weak RFID signal that the tracking device expressed by way of discordant beeps and flickering lights. He could only imagine how his father or brother would react if they learned the lengths he was going to for a cat.

Leighton hadn't planned on getting a furry companion. Pandora had turned up in his garden one evening, a few months after he had moved into his flat. She had been far more interested in his supper than in him, and had been so thin that he had taken pity on her and shared his tuna steak. The following day he had arrived home to find her sitting outside the back door, and had given in to her big green eyes and cobbled together another meal for her. A few days later, he had contacted a charity on her behalf, only to be told that they were overflowing with cats and that if she didn't have a microchip she would probably be put to sleep. After a quick trip to the local vet failed to locate a chip, he had bought some cat food with an eye to feeding her until he could find her a home. Before long, she had moved herself in and taken to curling up beside him on the bed at nights, and he had put off and put off the task of rehoming her, eventually abandoning the plan altogether.

He didn't want to acknowledge how much the little animal's current absence was worrying him. She rarely stayed out overnight when he was home, and if she did it was usually because she was next door with his elderly neighbour, Margaret. Pandora had long been operating something akin to a time share between the two properties, dividing her time on the basis of where food was available and – particularly during the colder months of the year – who was home. Given that Leighton's job as a forensic pathologist involved long and erratic hours, and that Margaret enjoyed feline company but didn't want the responsibility of a pet of her own, it had been a mutually beneficial arrangement. In recent months, Leighton had seen considerably more of Pandora, and, aside from being welcome company while he was off work, she had proved a great help in maintaining something approaching a routine. There is, as the Internet meme avers, no snooze button on a cat that wants breakfast. And, in Pandora's case, no way of ignoring a well-placed claw through the lip or eyelid.

The signal from the cat's RFID chip began to ramp up, and as the lights down the centre of the handset lit up and the beeping reached a crescendo, Leighton spotted a hot pink collar hanging amongst the barbed coils of a sprawling bramble bush. With a sigh, he bent to try to retrieve it, then stopped dead as he caught the musty, sweet and sour stench of decomposing flesh. Leaving the collar where it was, he stepped carefully over another tangle of brambles, desperately hoping the smell was emanating from something like a dead fox, and not his – or anyone else's – pet. Relief washed over him as he caught sight of a strip of brown fur poking through between two fence panels, but the feeling was short-lived. A few seconds and another couple of steps closer brought with them the realisation that what he was looking at wasn't fur. It was human hair.

*****

Detective Chief Inspector Lawrence Forrester had had no trouble locating the Fox and Hounds pub the Home Office pathologist had mentioned during their brief phone conversation, but it turned out to be on a red route, making parking anywhere near it an impossibility. Having driven around several of the surrounding streets more than once, he eventually managed to tuck his car between a Range Rover and a BMW with just a few inches to spare. He was adjusting his tie in the rear-view mirror when a tap came at the passenger window, and he glanced around to see the elfin face of Detective Sergeant Rebecca Palmer peering in at him. He immediately wondered how on earth she had made it to Clapham from Highgate in the short time it had taken him to drive from Battersea.

'Morning,' he greeted her, as he climbed out of the car. 'How did you get over here so fast?'

'Ah, that would be telling,' Rebecca responded, cheerfully, her diminutive frame enveloped in a thick woollen coat. 'How are you? Good weekend?'

'Yes, thanks,' Lawrence nodded, closing the car door and activating the central locking.

'I didn't envy you on Saturday,' she went on. 'It must have been freezing.'

'Just a bit,' Lawrence replied, having spent a frosty morning stamping his feet on the sidelines of a football pitch, watching his fifteen-year-old son playing for his school team. 'Next time I have kids I'm planning to get them into tennis.'

Rebecca smiled. 'How did Jimmy get on?'

'He played well, and they won their match, so he was on good form for the rest of the weekend.'

'I didn't think that was allowed. Hasn't he read the teenager's handbook?'

'As it involves reading, I'd say it's unlikely,' Lawrence remarked. 'How was your weekend?'

'Yeah, good, thanks,' Rebecca responded, adding, before he could ask anything further, 'So where are we headed?'

'To a bridge within spitting distance of the Fox and Hounds, I think Max said,' Lawrence replied, drawing his mobile phone from his pocket.

Rebecca looked surprised. 'I didn't think he was working today?'

'Maybe he didn't have a choice,' Lawrence said, checking the details Max had sent through and starting down the road. 'He really needs to get someone in to help cover Leighton's workload.'

Rebecca grunted in agreement.

'How's Leighton doing? Have you seen him recently?'

Rebecca nodded in answer to the second question before answering the first. 'I honestly don't know how he is,' she admitted. 'He's still having a lot of trouble with his fingers, but other than that he seems all right. Whether he actually is –' she shrugged.

'Has he talked to anyone about what happened?'

'Not as far as I know. They did suggest it at the hospital, but he said it wasn't necessary. And if I try to bring it up he just makes jokes and changes the subject.'

'How's he feeling about tomorrow?'

'He hasn't said much about that, either. Other than that he doesn't expect much to stick.'

It was probably the best thing to expect, Lawrence reflected. Attempted murder was a very difficult crime to prove, and, much as he had pushed for the charge to be brought, Lawrence had been surprised that the Crown Prosecution Service had been prepared to pursue it. The verdict would hinge on whether the defence team could persuade the jury that someone might reasonably believe death wasn't a foregone conclusion of being locked in a freezer container – assuming the prosecution could convince them the defendant had closed the container door in the first place. In the absence of anything but circumstantial forensic evidence, that would come down to whom the jury believed. In the normal run of things, Lawrence didn't doubt Leighton would fare considerably better than serial-offender Norman Healy under cross-examination, but there was no getting away from the fact there was a world of difference between giving evidence as an expert witness and as the victim of a traumatic crime.

'Assuming his hands improve, do you think he'll want to come back to work?'

'Until now, I would've have said I don't know.'

'And now?' Lawrence asked, thinking Rebecca's response rather strange.

'I think your answer's over there,' she replied, nodding towards something up ahead of them. Lawrence followed her gaze to see a familiar stout figure standing behind the blue and white police tape that had been used to cordon off a section of the pavement. Leighton's long, thick hair was loose over his shoulders and he was talking animatedly to the uniformed police officer on the near side of the tape.

In the past, Lawrence had often found himself at odds with the pathologist, who had a very different outlook and work ethic from Lawrence's own. In Leighton's absence, however, Lawrence had been surprised to realise that he missed working with him. Not that he would ever have admitted as much to anyone else.

'All right?' Leighton said, brightly, as Lawrence and Rebecca neared.

'Yes, thank you,' Lawrence replied, coming to a halt. 'And much as it's very nice to see you, you shouldn't be on that side of the tape.'

Leighton grinned. 'I've been expecting someone to say that for over ten years.'

'I'm serious. You're still signed off, and –'

'Yeah, yeah, I know,' Leighton conceded, holding his hands up in surrender, whatever damage might still be visible concealed by leather gloves. 'I didn't intend to wind up at a crime scene. And I promise not to play with any sharp implements.'

Lawrence sighed. 'Where's Max?'

'On his way.'

'And where's the body?'

'In a garden about forty metres that way,' Leighton replied, indicating the railway embankment behind him.

'A garden?'

'Yeah, there's a broken fence panel, and you can see some hair and an ear.'

'Can you see enough to take a guess at his age, or how long he's been there?'

'Not really.'

Lawrence frowned as a train trundled into view. 'What on earth are they doing still sending trains down the line?'

'I don't think anyone's requested that they stop.'

Lawrence's frown deepened. 'Well if Network Rail don't know the body's there, who found it?'

'I did,' Leighton admitted, rather sheepishly.

Lawrence looked to the steel security gate, to the multiple warning signs bolted to it and the surrounding fence, and back to Leighton. 'I'm not going to ask.'

Probably best,' Leighton responded, with a mischievous smile.

'Right, well the first thing we need to do is get those trains stopped,' Lawrence continued, turning to Rebecca. 'Can you get someone onto that?'

She nodded, slipping a hand into her bag, presumably in search of her mobile phone.

'You realise you're effectively shutting down Clapham Junction during rush hour, don't you?' Leighton queried.

Lawrence hadn't actually given any thought to where the lines were going to or from, mainly because it didn't change the need to suspend rail traffic until the crime scene officers could conduct at least a cursory survey of the area beyond the garden in question. The information did, however, give him a fair idea of the sort of pressure his superiors were going to be under from the rail companies to reverse the closure – pressure they would waste no time in passing on to him. He could only hope the media didn't immediately get wind of the fact the death might be something more newsworthy than a fatality on the line.

It had taken Rebecca and Lawrence only a couple of minutes to work out which front door they needed to knock on to gain access to the garden containing the corpse. Two of the residents were home, and, with the help of a handful photographs, the attending pathologist had quickly identified the deceased man as Tony Mercier, one of their housemates. Martina, the young woman who had provided the pictures, had gone to pieces the moment Lawrence broke the news, and Rebecca had made her a cup of tea while her surviving housemate tried, rather awkwardly, to comfort her.

Twenty minutes later, Rebecca was standing outside on the pavement blowing into her hands when someone called her name. She turned to see DC Eva Dixon approaching, her curly blonde hair capped by a dark green beret, her cheeks and nose flushed with the cold.

'Hiya,' Rebecca greeted her, with a smile.

'How was Nottingham?' Eva asked.

'Good, thanks.'

'Was it your brother you were staying with?'

'Visiting. I stayed in a B and B. I'm too old for sleeping on floors and sofas.'

'You and me both,' Eva responded, with an expressive lift of her eyebrows. 'Did you go anywhere else?'

‘Not really,’ Rebecca answered, not wanting to lie outright by saying *no*. She had driven up to Nottingham via Sheffield, where Leighton’s parents lived, and on learning that she was giving him a lift, his mother had invited her for lunch. Rebecca’s relationship with Leighton wasn’t yet common knowledge among their colleagues, but, even if it had been, she would have been reluctant to mention the visit to Sheffield, because that might have meant talking about the experience itself.

Lorna Campbell had extended the invite to Rebecca directly, and Leighton had been very dismissive of it, suggesting on several occasions that Rebecca spend the time with her brother instead. Rebecca had assumed he simply didn’t want her to feel obliged, and afterwards had kicked herself for not giving the situation more thought.

The scars of the abuse his father had meted out during his teenage years ought to have better prepared her for the experience, but Glenn Campbell’s relentless viciousness had still come as a shock. Rebecca couldn’t imagine how it must feel to have a parent regularly use words like *useless* and *waste of space*, or how Leighton managed to resist showing any visible reaction to the continuous taunts and put-downs. She wondered whether the man’s tongue had been as harsh in years gone by, when he had been in a position to use serious physical violence.

‘So what’s the story?’ Eva asked, nodding towards the house standing with its door open as crime scene investigators came and went.

‘At this stage I’m not even sure there is one,’ Rebecca admitted, feeling thankful for the change in subject. ‘The body’s behind the shed at the bottom of the garden, propped up in a sitting position against the fence. Two of his housemates were in when we arrived, and the one we’ve been able to get any sense out of says he’s not seen the guy in a couple of weeks. Best he can remember, that was at a party. There are no outward signs of trauma, so it’s possible we’re looking at nothing more than someone getting drunk and disorientated, passing out and dying of hypothermia.’

Eva nodded.

‘But given where he is, if it wasn’t an accident there’s a good chance at least one of his housemates had a hand in what happened to him, so Forrester wants us to pin them all down before they have any further chance to confer.’

‘How many of them are there?’

'Four. Not including the deceased.'

Eva's eyebrows rose. 'These places must be bigger than they look.' There was a momentary pause before she went on, 'Have none of them missed him?'

'Who knows.'

'I'd like to think I'd notice if one of my flatmates disappeared,' Eva remarked.

Rebecca nodded, wondering whether she herself actually would, given the amount of time she had been spending at Leighton's place. She had scarcely seen her flatmate – a chef named Perry – in recent weeks, and suspected that if he did disappear, the first she would know about it would be when things started going off in the fridge.

'Assuming he had a job, you'd have thought his work might have wondered where he was, too,' Eva added. 'I suppose we should take comfort in the fact we wouldn't go unmissed for more than about five seconds.'

Rebecca smiled. Lawrence was a stickler for punctuality and discipline, and Eva was far from the only one of their colleagues to make jokes and snide remarks about his diligent and principled outlook. The fact that Leighton was hopelessly disorganised – and outside Lawrence's managerial control – had been the cause of considerable friction on many an occasion. Rebecca herself had never found Lawrence particularly difficult to work with. He might have high expectations, but he wasn't unreasonable, and she always knew where she was with him. That certainly hadn't been true of some of the other DCIs she had worked under over the years.

'Mind you, there are those I'd be more than happy to miss,' Eva remarked, sardonically, indicating something behind Rebecca with a shift of her eyes and brows. Rebecca glanced around to see DC Noel Osbourne fifty yards up the road, and nodded in acknowledgement; she shared Eva's antipathy towards the young man. He was cocksure and pushy, and adept at playing mind games, generally succeeding in pushing his luck far enough to get under her skin, but not so far that she could challenge his behaviour without looking petty.

'What say you and I hold a party and tuck *him* behind a shed?' Eva suggested. 'We'd be doing women everywhere a favour.'

'Excellent plan,' Rebecca replied, as she turned back towards Eva. 'Have you got a shed?'

'Nah, I live on the third floor,' Eva returned, ruefully. 'You?'

Rebecca shook her head. 'No. Leaves us a bit nowhere, doesn't it?'

Two

Martina Keeling was dressed almost entirely in black, and Eva wondered whether that was out of preference or simply an attempt to slim down her rotund shape. Eva herself always opted for dark suits in the hope they might take an inch or two off observers' view of her size-eighteen backside and ample chest, although she had long since come to realise that tailored jackets, however good their cut, would never hang the way she wanted – the way they did on petite women like Rebecca. At least now she was no longer in uniform, she was spared the regular humiliation of having to wear a bulky stab-proof vest: possibly the most unflattering garment in history. And, unlike Martina, at least she had been blessed with a waist.

'Could you tell us a bit about Tony?' Eva asked.

'He was lovely,' Martina said, sounding slightly dazed. 'A really nice man.'

'Were you close?'

'Yes. He was one of my best friends.'

'Were you ever anything more than friends?'

Martina looked thrown by the question, a reaction Eva understood the moment she revealed, 'Tony was gay.'

'Ah.' Eva nodded. 'Had he been seeing anyone recently?'

'Until about six weeks ago.'

'Was it a long-term relationship?'

'Fairly. They were together for about eighteen months.'

'Do you know why it ended?'

'I think Ross met someone else, but I'm not sure. Tony didn't seem to want to talk about it.'

Eva nodded. 'When did you last see Tony?'

'At my birthday party. The night the clocks went back.'

'Over two weeks ago, then,' Eva said. 'Did you hear from him after that?'

Martina swallowed. 'No.'

'Was it usual for you see or hear nothing from him for so long?'

'No.'

'You described him as one of your best friends. Weren't you worried about where he was?'

Several seconds ticked by before Martina admitted, 'He said some pretty hurtful things to me the last time we spoke. So for a few days I was quite relieved not to bump into him. Then – when I realised he wasn't around – I thought he'd gone away. He'd talked about going to India for a few weeks to get away from everything – I just assumed –' she shook her head. 'I did text him a few times, and asked if he was ok, but he didn't respond. I figured he was still angry. Or that he didn't have phone reception where he was.'

'What was he angry about?'

Fresh tears came to Martina's eyes. 'I'd invited this guy I liked to my party – and he'd said he'd come – but he never showed up. When I got upset, Tony had a massive go at me. It got a bit –' she hesitated. 'Personal.'

'Do you have any idea why that made him angry in the first place?'

'He thought I was letting him use me. The other guy, I mean. But I don't know why he went off the way he did.' She raised a hand to dry her tears as one spilled down her cheek.

Eva made a guess at joining the dots: the man in question had slept with Martina when he had had nothing better to do, but had no intention of ever taking things further. She had watched more than one of her friends make the same mistake, and could understand Tony's frustration – but that didn't excuse his being nasty.

'A moment ago, you described Tony as *a really nice man*,' she observed. 'I don't think I'd describe someone that way if they'd behaved as you've just described.'

'I know,' Martina acknowledged. 'But that was really unlike him. He'd never spoken to me like that before.'

'So would it be fair to say he wasn't really himself that evening?'

'He certainly didn't seem it.'

'Did he fall out with anyone else?'

'I don't know. But it wouldn't surprise me. He made a snide remark about Jakob right after he had a go at me, so who knows who else he might have offended.'

'And what was that remark?'

'One of my friends had been in Jakob's bedroom, and when she came out Tony said something like he thought she had better taste.'

'Do you have any idea what that was in reference to?'

'None. Tony normally got on with all of us.'

Eva nodded. 'You said Tony talked about getting away. Was he not working?'

'Not since September. Until then, he worked for Akiko's company, React8.'

'Is that the same Akiko who lives here?'

'Yeah.'

'So what happened in September?'

'She fired him.'

'Why?'

'I don't know. He said he couldn't talk about it because of some confidentiality agreement.'

'Did it come out of the blue? Or had things been tense between them before the point she actually fired him?'

'I wasn't aware of anything, but generally Tony tried to leave work at work.'

'Does Akiko do the same?'

'Akiko lives and breathes her work,' Martina responded.

'Did she respect the fact that Tony didn't?'

Martina hesitated before saying, 'Not always.'

'Do you think that might have been part of the problem?'

'I honestly don't know,' Martina replied, shaking her head slightly. 'Tony and I talked a lot, and he did tell me things in confidence – but he was always really tight-lipped about his work. I never figured out whether that was down to the nature of the work itself, or whether –' she broke off, and there was an awkward silence before she apparently decided to finish what she had started. 'Or whether it was because of Akiko.'

Jamie wondered whether his intense dislike of Jakob Radeki was solely the result of the documentary maker's overbearing arrogance, or whether his judgement was suffering as much as he was from the fact that he was into his third day without a cigarette. He had tried vaping, but found it a poor substitute, and nicotine gum hadn't done much to dent his desire for tobacco, either. It undoubtedly didn't help that the decision to quit smoking had been made under the emotional equivalent of something approaching duress.

Jamie had spent years resisting pressure from his mother and sister – not to mention friends, exes and even his superior – to relinquish the vice. Xanthe, his current girlfriend, was the only one who had succeeded in doing anything more than winding him up. They had met some six months earlier, and it hadn't taken Jamie long to realise he wanted much more than the brief fling he had originally envisaged. Unfortunately, however, conflicting work schedules, combined with the 60-odd miles separating their respective homes in Enfield and Brighton, meant that opportunities for them to spend much time together had been few and far between. Neither of them was inextricably tied to a location by their choice of career, but leaving the Met's homicide and serious crimes unit was the very last compromise Jamie wanted to make.

Xanthe had mooted the possibility of relocating to South London – from which she would still be able to reach most of her clients – but said she would consider the move only if he stopped smoking. He suspected the condition was as much a test of his commitment to the relationship as a product of her dislike of the habit, but, given that she was offering to make a far greater sacrifice, he had reluctantly agreed. And, tempting as it might be, he wasn't going to risk trying to pull the wool over her eyes by continuing to smoke when she wasn't around. If his job had taught him anything, it was how easily seemingly small deceptions can get out of hand.

'Did you and Tony get along?'

'Yeah, mostly.'

'So not always.'

'Who gets on with their housemates all of the time?' Jakob returned. 'I'm not a saint.'

Jamie nodded, thinking of all the people he'd lived with over the years. Sharing a kitchen and a bathroom was a surefire way to push a friendship to its limits, and he had long made it a policy not to live with anyone closer than friends of friends. This thought took him on to his next question.

'Would you describe Tony as a friend?'

'Depends what you mean by *friend*,' Jakob replied. 'We rubbed along ok, but I wouldn't say I'm particularly close to anyone in the house. They're nice enough people, they're just not –' he paused, presumably searching for the right word, before concluding, rather unimaginatively, 'My kind of people, I guess.'

Jamie didn't imagine he would have much time for Jakob's *kind of people*, and wondered whether he might have found the other occupants of the house more likeable.

'Presumably you saw a fair bit of Tony, though?'

'Yeah.'

'But not in the past couple of weeks.'

'No, not since Martina's party.'

'And how was he that night?'

'I can't say I paid much attention,' Jakob remarked, offhandedly. 'I was otherwise engaged most of that evening, if you get my drift.'

Jamie did, and concluded from Jakob's self-satisfied smile that his own judgement of the man had been right on all along. Physically, if not personally, Jakob was extremely attractive, and it was clear he knew it.

'Who were you with?' Jamie asked, doing his best to make it sound like a box-ticking question in which he had absolutely no interest.

'Maya. A friend of Martina's.'

'And where did you think Tony was in the two weeks since then?'

'I didn't really think anything. I don't see everyone in the house every day.'

'Do you not have any mobile contact?'

'On occasion, but not regularly.'

'Did none of your other housemates remark on his absence?'

'Not that I recall.'

'How many bathrooms does the house have?'

Jakob looked thrown by the abrupt change in subject. 'What does that matter?' He asked, with a frown, after a moment's hesitation.

'Is it a secret?' Jamie countered.

There was a brief silence before Jakob yielded. 'One.'

Jamie nodded contemplatively. 'I work shifts, so I sometimes go days without seeing my housemates,' he revealed. 'But I generally know when one of them's not been home for more than a day or two from the way things do and don't move around in the bathroom. Toilet seat, towels, toothbrushes, et cetera. Same deal in the kitchen.' He paused for effect before saying, 'Did you really not notice anything was different?'

'I can't say I've ever noticed what people do with their toothbrushes,' Jakob returned, rather scathingly. 'Perhaps you have an unhealthy interest in other people's bathroom habits.'

'Perhaps,' Jamie responded, pleasantly. 'But I am amazed that four people could completely fail to notice someone's absence for an entire fortnight. Especially nowadays, when we're all practically glued to our phones. Between social-media updates, social plans and requests for someone to buy washing-up liquid, I don't think I ever go more than a few days without hearing from my housemates. Whether I want to or not.'

Akiko Nakahara's sleek new-build office had been fitted out with the sort of quirky furniture that always seemed hugely overpriced for what it was, immediately prompting Rebecca to question the woman's priorities. Almost in the same moment, she found herself wondering whether she was being unfairly judgemental; perhaps the desire to have a striking, Instagramable office didn't detract from the dedication that Akiko avowed to her research on React8's website. Rebecca had read up on the founder and CEO of the biomedical start-up during the drive down to Horsham, where the company was based. Akiko had apparently launched React8 almost three years earlier – at the age of just twenty-six – with the goal of eliminating autoimmune disorders. The company now employed nearly one hundred people, an achievement that was both impressive and a little intimidating. Anyone achieving such success so young made Rebecca feel inadequate by comparison.

Akiko herself was petite, with dark hair and eyes, and smartly dressed in a white blouse and black trouser suit. There was little on her glass-topped desk besides a mug, a smartphone and a sleek grey MacBook, leading Rebecca to wonder how much she really used the office. Perhaps its primary purpose was for receiving external visitors.

'Is this going to take long?' Akiko asked, as Rebecca and Lawrence sat in chairs reminiscent of ice cream scoops.

'It'll take as long as it needs to,' Lawrence responded, shortly.

Akiko looked as if she would have liked to object to this, but she said nothing further, merely folding her hands in her lap.

'We're here because a body was found in the garden of your home earlier this morning. I'm –'

'A body?' Akiko exclaimed.

'Yes. And I'm afraid the deceased has been identified as your housemate, Tony.'

There was a moment's silence before Akiko responded, seemingly in disbelief, '*Tony*?'

'Yes. I'm –'

'I thought –' she broke off, shaking her head slightly. 'Are you sure?'

'I'm afraid so.'

Akiko swallowed, saying nothing.

'I understand you and he lived and worked together for several years,' Lawrence continued.

She nodded.

'I'm sorry, you must have been close.'

Akiko nodded again.

'Are you all right to answer some questions for us?'

'Yes.' She forced a smile. 'Of course.'

'Perhaps you could begin by telling us when you last remember seeing Tony?'

'Um – a couple of weekends ago, I think.'

'Two weeks ago?' Lawrence exclaimed. 'Were you not concerned by the fact you'd not seen him in so long?'

'I've not been home much.'

'So where have you been?'

'Here, mostly,' Akiko replied, before adding, with a rueful smile, 'There never seem to be enough hours in the day.' It sounded like a casual enough remark, but Rebecca sensed something studied about its delivery.

'Until recently, I gather Tony was working here, too,' Lawrence said. 'I spoke to Jakob briefly this morning, and he mentioned that you terminated Tony's employment a month or two ago. Why was that?'

'That wasn't just my decision,' Akiko returned, sounding put out.

'Who else's was it, then?'

'Tony's,' she replied, as if it should have been obvious. 'He'd been involved in the company since early on, and he'd always had a lot of input, but we reached a point where we didn't have the same vision for the future, so we decided it would be better to go our separate ways.'

'Are you saying you didn't sack him?'

'No, I didn't.'

'Did he resign, then?'

'Effectively.'

Lawrence's eyebrows rose, but to Rebecca's surprise he didn't challenge Akiko on this, asking instead what Tony's job had entailed.

'Primarily, keeping tabs on what was going on in the field,' Akiko replied.

'And how did he do that?'

'By reading papers and talking to people.'

'Is that really a full-time job?'

'More than. Thanks to the Internet, the volume of literature has exploded. A lot of it isn't worth much, but without looking you don't know what you might be missing.'

'And was Tony good at that?'

'If he hadn't been, he wouldn't have been working here long.'

Lawrence nodded. 'When did he leave the company?'

'Mid-September.'

'So if you last saw him a couple of weeks ago, presumably that was at the house in Eversleigh Road?'

'Yes. We had a party. For Martina's birthday.'

'How many people were there?'

Akiko shook her head slightly. 'I've no idea.'

'Rough guess?'

'I don't know – twenty, twenty-five?'

'What kind of time did the party go on until?'

'Late. I went to bed after they turned the music down, at about midnight, but I think a few people were up 'til three or four.'

Lawrence nodded. 'Where's your bedroom in relation to Tony's?'

'Across the hallway.'

'Did you hear anything unusual during the night?'

'It was hardly a *usual* night,' Akiko observed. 'I had earplugs in, but I still got woken up a fair few times by people making a racket.'

'Can you expand on what that *racket* entailed?'

'People being loud,' Akiko responded, with a shrug. 'How people get when they're drunk.'

Rebecca wondered whether the woman was being intentionally unhelpful. Lawrence was evidently thinking the same, because he didn't say anything further, instead regarding Akiko expectantly. After a few seconds, the pressure of silence worked, and she said, 'Vocal. Clumsy.' There was another brief pause before she added, with an expressive lift of her eyebrows, 'Annoying.'

'Anything else?'

'Jakob and Maya.'

'What about them?'

'They were at it half the night.'

'Is Maya Jakob's girlfriend?'

Akiko smirked. 'No. She's a friend of Martina and Irene's.'

'And why does the idea of her being his girlfriend amuse you?'

'It's not the idea of Maya being someone's girlfriend that's funny,' Akiko replied, drily. 'It's the idea of Jakob having an interest in a girl that lasted beyond the next morning.'

Martina had obligingly provided Eva with a list of everyone who had attended the party at which she and Jakob had reportedly last seen Tony. Among them were two of the students living in the house next door, and, once the interview with Jakob was over, Jamie and Noel wasted no time in trying to pin them down. The bleary-eyed young man who answered the door, clad in a threadbare navy dressing gown and green and black striped socks, gave his name as Brad, and looked more than a little relieved when Jamie asked if Robin or Ellis was home.

Showing Jamie and Noel into an open plan kitchen–living area that wasn't far off squalid, Brad cleared some plates, an ashtray and a dirty sock off the grubby beige sofa to make space for them to sit down before heading upstairs to fetch Robin. The floor around the sofa was dotted with glasses, an empty rum bottle and a carton of chocolate milk, and the air was heavy with the smell of stale smoke. It didn't do anything to help Jamie's mood.

Robin appeared in the doorway a couple of minutes later, looking as if he'd just rolled out of bed, which Jamie suspected was exactly what he had done. A short, chubby young man with dark hair and glasses, he was wearing baggy shorts and a t-shirt, his feet bare. He looked cold, and Jamie wondered why he hadn't stopped to pull on a dressing gown or jumper before joining them.

'Robin Elphick?'

He nodded.

'We'd like to ask a few questions about a party you attended next door a couple of weeks ago.'

'Tina's party?' Robin asked, perching in an armchair.

'That's right. How well do you know her?'

'Not that well. But she was always gardening when we were out the back in summer, so we got chatting.'

'Do you know any of her housemates?'

'Only by sight, really. Why?'

'I'm afraid one of them was found dead this morning.'

'Dead?' Robin exclaimed, his eyebrows shooting up. 'What happened?'

'We're not sure at this stage.'

'Who –' Robin trailed off.

'Tony, if you know who he was?'

'Yeah,' Robin nodded. 'He seemed all right. The other bloke's a wanker.'

Jamie couldn't disagree. 'Can you remember seeing Tony since the party?'

A couple of seconds passed before Robin shook his head.

'Did you see much of him that night?'

'He was around,' Robin replied. 'I didn't really speak to him, though.'

'Was he involved in any serious disagreements during the evening, do you know?'

'There was a girl with pink hair who kicked off late on,' Robin recalled. 'She was having a proper go at him.'

'Have you any idea why?'

'No, but earlier on he mentioned that they'd had a threesome, so I guess it might've been about that.'

Jamie frowned. 'I thought you said you didn't really speak to him.'

'I didn't. A whole load of us were playing *I have never*.'

'The drinking game?'

'Yeah. You know, you say something you've never done, and anyone who has done it has to drink.'

Jamie nodded; he'd played the game enough times himself. 'Can you remember what else came up during the course of that game?'

Robin's smooth forehead wrinkled in thought before he made a start on listing topics, slowly counting them off on his fingers. 'Skinny dipping – one-night stands – stalking your ex on social media – eating curry for breakfast – dead bodies – shop–'

'Dead bodies?' Jamie exclaimed. 'What about them?'

'I have never seen a dead body,' Robin replied, guilelessly.

'And who said that?'

'Tony.'

'Did anyone drink to it?' Noel interjected.

'One of the girls did, although I'm not sure whether she meant to. She was joking about something more lighthearted he could have said, and I think maybe she just lost track of the thread.'

'Was she the only one to drink?'

Robin nodded.

'In the days and nights after the party, were you aware of any unusual activity in the garden next door?' Jamie went on.

'No.'

'Did any of your housemates comment on anything out of the ordinary?'

There was a momentary pause before Robin shook his head.

'I understand you went to the party with one of them,' Jamie replied. 'Ellis. Is he home?'

'He's at his girlfriend's.'

Very wise of him, Jamie thought, given the state of the house. Reaching into his pocket for his card as he got to his feet, he asked if Robin would have Ellis contact him as soon as he returned. Robin nodded obligingly, taking the card and turning towards the front door, presumably expecting to show them out. He looked completely thrown – and more than a little concerned – when Jamie asked if they might first see the garden.

The two officers dispatched to interview Irene Milligan had arrived at her place of work in Epsom to be told she wasn't on site that morning. She hadn't returned home, either, and lunchtime came and went without anyone managing to locate her. On the drive back from Horsham, Lawrence decided to take a detour via Xornex Pharmaceuticals in the hope she might since have put in an appearance. After a frustratingly long wait in reception, he and Rebecca were shown to a meeting room on the second floor, where, some minutes later, Irene finally joined them.

Lawrence had half expected her to be wearing a lab coat, but in fact she was dressed in black trousers and a long-sleeved shirt that wouldn't have looked out of place in any London office. She had a slender, boyish figure, and with her long dark hair scraped back into a high ponytail and her face seemingly devoid of make-up, looked rather androgynous. Lawrence's wife, Katie, was fond of pointing out that one shouldn't be *able* to see products like foundation and blusher if they had been applied correctly, but, given Irene's pallor, Lawrence guessed that wasn't the explanation – and that Irene already knew why they were there. He wondered which one of her housemates had broken the news. Assuming Tony's death was news to her at all.

Her response to Lawrence's introduction of himself and Rebecca confirmed that she had already heard about Tony's demise, although she didn't say from whom, instead asking what had happened.

'It's too early to say,' Lawrence replied, shortly. 'Have you lived with him long?'

'A couple of years.'

'And what was your relationship like?'

'Pretty good.'

'So you got along.'

'Most of the time. We had words about household stuff on a few occasions. But nothing serious.'

'What sort of household stuff?'

'Tony wasn't great at picking up after himself,' Irene admitted. 'He often left shavings in the bathroom sink, or didn't wipe down the kitchen counters after preparing food – I sometimes felt like I was living with a teenager. But the fact things like that annoyed me didn't mean I didn't like him as a person.'

'Did you consider him to be a friend?'

'Yes.'

'Close enough that you would have kept in touch if one of you had moved out?'

Irene appeared to consider her answer before saying, 'My automatic reaction is to say yes, but –' she broke off. 'There are a couple of people among my Facebook friends who I once thought I would always be close to, but now all I know about their lives is what they post online. And that's not because they've moved far away.'

Lawrence nodded. 'Did Tony's lack of – I'm not sure what you'd call it – house training, I suppose – bother anyone else?'

'Well, we can't all be like Martina.'

Lawrence raised his eyebrows. 'What do you mean by that?'

'She always sees the best in people,' Irene replied, with a small smile. 'I wish I could be like that, but I'm not. And neither is Jakob.'

'Are you saying it bothered him, too?'

'Yes. He's a bit of a clean freak.'

'How about Akiko?' Lawrence asked, thinking of the woman's spotless and minimalist office.

Irene shrugged. 'She's hardly ever home.'

'Is that because she spends most of her time at work?'

'Uh-huh. I think sometimes she even sleeps there.'

'I understand that Tony was working with her until recently.'

Irene nodded.

'Do you know why their working relationship ended?'

Irene hesitated before saying, 'Not really.'

'So you do have some idea,' Lawrence concluded.

'I think it was to do with ethics,' Irene admitted, at length.

'Which one of them was concerned with ethics?'

'Tony.'

'What did he say to give you that impression?'

'He didn't say anything to me, but I overheard him arguing with her, and he said something like *you can't break the rules when people's lives are at stake.*'

'Did you hear any of what she said?'

'No, she wasn't there. It was a phone call.'

'And what else did he say?'

'That was the only bit I caught that made much sense in isolation,' Irene admitted. 'The rest was more general stuff like *no* and *that's insane.*'

'That's insane?' Lawrence echoed. 'Were those the actual words he used?'

'Yes.'

'Do you have any idea at all what that related to?'

'No. Sorry.'

Lawrence nodded. 'Can you think of anyone else he had words with recently?'

Irene hesitated. 'I wish I didn't have to –' she broke off. 'She's my oldest friend, and I feel like I'm dropping her in it – but –' Irene swallowed. 'She and Tony had a blazing row – at Martina's birthday party – and just about anyone who was there is going to tell you that.'

'Who?' Lawrence pressed, when Irene didn't offer anything further.

'Maya.'

'What was the row about?'

'I don't know the ins and outs, just that he'd said something to upset Martina. And she was really upset.'

'Was that unusual?'

'Yes and no,' Irene responded. Martina's quite sensitive. Her being upset isn't unusual. But Tony was normally the one picking up the pieces and fighting her corner. They were like that,' Irene held up her right hand, her middle finger wrapped around her forefinger.

'So the fact he was the one to upset her was unusual.'

'Very.'

'Has she said anything about it since?'

'Not really. I know it bothered her that he didn't apologise afterwards. But she's said nothing about what he did to upset her in the first place.'

Lawrence wondered whether Tony had had the chance to apologise. Perhaps he'd died first.

'According to our records, she wasn't the only person he upset recently. A couple of months ago he reportedly told a Somali family to *go back home*. Do you –'

'Oh that was so ridiculous!' Irene interrupted. 'He did nothing of the sort! All he did was tell a couple of kids to go home before they caused an accident, because they were doing wheelies on the main road. It was perfectly clear he only meant back to where they lived. Then one of their mothers called the police and made it out to be a hate crime!'

'You say his meaning was perfectly clear, were you there at the time?'

'Yes. And he wasn't the only one worried about it, there were cars driving by hooting at them. Sooner or later, someone was going to get hurt.' She paused, then added, as if it had only just occurred to her, 'Chances are, it would have been one of those kids!'

Three

William Maxwell glanced at his watch. He hadn't planned on spending his ninth wedding anniversary in the mortuary, and he was now in danger of incurring his wife's wrath for the second time that day by being late for their daughter's ballet recital. It didn't help that the situation was, as Marnie had pointed out that morning, largely of his own making. His apology had been met with a now-familiar refrain: 'I don't want you to be sorry, Will, I want you to hire a bloody locum!'

When circumstance had first forced him to juggle two jobs, Marnie had been more than understanding, tolerating his frequent absences – and even his failure to make their May half-term holiday – without complaint. Over the summer, the pressure had eased, thanks mainly to the assistance of two visiting medical students, and he ought to have taken the opportunity to arrange some cover for the autumn. Instead, he had put off the task, in no small part because he was privately enjoying doing more of the hands-on work that he had had little time for in the years since he had taken over the running of the pathology unit. He had also hoped the recruitment process might prove unnecessary. But from the contents of the most recent occupational-health report to land on his desk, it was clear the problem wasn't going to be resolved any time soon. As a result, finding a locum had now made it onto his *to do* list, but with so many competing demands on his time, the task kept slipping to *tomorrow*.

He reached for his mobile to chase up the colleague he was waiting on just as Lawrence appeared in the meeting room doorway.

'Sorry, Max,' he began, sounding slightly out of breath. 'I got caught –'

'I don't need the details,' Max cut him off, knowing Lawrence wouldn't be late without good reason. 'I just need to be out of here ten minutes ago.'

Lawrence nodded, obligingly getting straight to the point as he sat down. 'Cause of death?'

'I can't give you an unequivocal answer, because after spending days out in the open the body isn't in great shape.

You're lucky it's been so cold, or I'd probably have struggled to give you much at all. But I'm fairly certain he suffocated.'

'Suffocated?' Lawrence echoed, sounding surprised.

'Yes.'

'Were there any injuries consistent with a struggle, or of his having been restrained?'

'It's hard to say, given the onset of decomposition and the postmortem damage from animal and insect activity,' Max handed over several photographs to illustrate his point, including a close-up of what remained of a finger, the bone partially exposed and scored by tiny teeth marks. 'He did have a hairline fracture to one of the cervical vertebrae, but I can only guess at whether that happened in the hours before or after death.'

Lawrence regarded the images with visible distaste before returning his attention to Max. 'If it didn't happen postmortem, could it have any bearing on his death?'

'There was no displacement of the bone and no sign of serious brain injury, so it's unlikely.'

'Is there any chance death could have been accidental? If he was under the influence of alcohol or drugs, I mean?'

'Postural asphyxia can occur in those circumstances, yes,' Max replied. 'But the body was moved after death, so whatever happened clearly gave someone reason to panic.'

Lawrence nodded. 'Are there any clues to where he might have died?'

'Not really. A few fibres that might help if we had something to compare them to, but nothing to suggest where that location might be.'

'And any signs of drug use?'

'No evidence of serious drug abuse, but the mucous membranes were too degraded for me to be able to pick up on casual or occasional use, and there were no obvious drug remnants in the digestive system. So until we get the toxicology results through I'm as much in the dark as you are.'

'Can we run a hair test, as well? That covers more than just the days leading up to death, right?'

'Yes, about three months. And I have ordered one, although given how short he wore his hair it's unlikely to cover more than about six weeks.'

'Understood,' Lawrence replied. 'Anything else you can give me right now?'

'Maybe. There was a tiny amount of something blue embedded in a ridge in the bottom of one of his incisors,' Max passed Lawrence another photograph.

'Which could have come off whatever was used to suffocate him,' Lawrence concluded.

'Possibly. But it could just as well be an artefact. People use their teeth to open packets and bottles, and to cut tape.'

'Can we get the pigment analysed?'

'We can try, although it's a very small sample. And any information we do get will only be useful if we have something to compare it to.'

Lawrence nodded. 'Ok.'

'Have you managed to track down his next of kin yet?' Max asked, as he stood and reached for his coat.

'He was a French national and his parents are in France, so I'm waiting on someone over there to get back to me.'

'Ok, well if they want to view the body, give me some notice and I'll try to make sure Jon's around when they come in.'

'Jon? Why?'

'Because he's bilingual, whereas my French is limited to what I remember from school, and that was a long time ago.' He leaned to flick the light off. 'I'm afraid that these days I'm probably incapable of doing much more than ordering chips and beer.'

Maya Onslow showed Lawrence and Rebecca through to the living room of her ground-floor flat and gestured towards the cluster of metal-framed armchairs gathered around the coffee table. The chairs looked to Rebecca as if they belonged in a garden rather than a front room, and the preponderance of scatter cushions strewn across them struck her as rather incongruous. Perhaps, she mused, the chairs served both the house and the garden: that would be a novel way to save on storage space. She took a seat, finding it more comfortable than she had expected, and Maya rested a heel on the edge of a chair the other side of the table before folding her willowy frame effortlessly into the space that remained, raising a hand to draw her faded pink hair away from her face.

'Martina told me about Tony,' she said, awkwardly. 'And I don't want you to think I don't care, or that I'm being rude, but I'll need to leave in about twenty minutes. On Tuesdays I'm the only registered first aider at the theatre where I'm working, so they can't move any of the props to start setting up 'til I get there.'

'What is it that you do?' Lawrence enquired.

'I'm an actress.'

Rebecca wondered what she was performing in, but, perhaps mindful of the time, Lawrence didn't ask, instead moving straight on to the question of whether she had known Tony well.

Maya conveyed something of her answer with a wrinkle of her nose before saying, 'Not really. I mean, we hung out a lot, because he and Martina were close, and she's my best friend, but we were more –' she paused, seemingly struggling to find the words with which to express herself. In the end, she concluded, 'More friendly than friends. If that makes sense.'

'Have you known Martina long?'

Maya nodded. 'About twelve years. We were at uni together.'

'And Tony?'

'Um – I don't know – two or three years? Since he moved into the house, I couldn't tell you exactly when that was.'

'Presumably you can tell us how long is it since you last saw him?'

'Yeah, a couple of weeks. At Martina's birthday party.'

'And how did he seem then?'

'All right,' she replied, before adding, hurriedly, 'But I didn't really see much of him.'

'You found time to have an argument with him, though, didn't you?' Lawrence responded. 'A couple of people have mentioned that you and he had – and I quote – *a blazing row* late that night. What was that about?'

'I gave him what for because he'd upset Martina.'

'How?'

'I don't know what he said to her, because she wouldn't tell me, but she was in floods. And she wasn't drunk enough to get that upset about nothing.'

'So it wasn't anything to do with your sexual relationship with him.'

'My *what*?' Maya exclaimed. 'Where the heck did you get that from?'

'Are you saying it's not true?'

'No, it isn't!'

'One of the other attendees of Martina's party told us Tony made reference to a threesome you and he had participated in. Why do you think he might have done that, if it wasn't true?'

Comprehension flooded Maya's face. 'Oh, that,' she almost laughed. 'We were playing a game and one of my friends let slip that I'd had a threesome. I was mortified – I barely knew half the people playing – and Tony made a joke about it to take the heat off me. I guess whoever you spoke to didn't know him well enough to realise that was all it was, because Tony was as gay as they come.'

Lawrence nodded. 'I understand you stayed over at the house on the night of the party.'

'Yes.'

'Where did you sleep?'

Colour rose in Maya's cheeks. 'Jakob's room.'

'During the night, were you aware of any noise or movement in the other rooms?'

'Not really. Jakob's room is on the second floor, and I think you hear more from above than below in those houses. All I remember noticing was Martina's snoring, and feeling relieved I wasn't sleeping in her room.' She paused before adding, 'That was originally the plan.'

'Did Jakob go anywhere at any point?'

'I don't think so. But I wasn't awake all night.'

'And what happened the next morning?'

'I woke up about nine – went downstairs for coffee – sat around chatting with Martina –' she paused. 'At some stage I had a shower, and Irene and Jakob joined us. The plan was for us all to go to the Fox – their local – at lunch time, to meet up with a few others. But Tony wasn't around, and Irene was too hungover, so in the end it was just me, Martina and Jakob who went.'

'Where did you think Tony was?'

'He'd said something to Martina about going on to a club after the party, so we assumed he'd pulled and gone home with someone.'

'Were you aware of his leaving the house to go to the club?'

'No. But Jakob and I were up in his room a lot of the time.'

'Do you know whether Tony's room was empty on the Sunday morning?'

'When we were preparing to go to the pub I asked whether we should give him a shout. Jakob said he'd looked in earlier to borrow a computer cable and Tony had already split.'

'So nobody else went into Tony's room that morning.'

'I didn't. I don't know about the others.'

'You clearly know all of the housemates fairly well. Can you think of any reason why any of them might have wanted Tony out the way?'

Maya shook her head. 'None. Akiko's hardly ever there, but the other four were like friends, as well as housemates.'

'Really?' Lawrence queried. 'Jakob gave us the impression he wasn't all that close to anyone in the house. He said they weren't his sort of people.'

'Well I can't speak for him, but that's not the impression I got,' Maya replied. 'I envied the camaraderie in that house. I often hoped one of them might leave so I could move in.' She paused. 'If I'd known it would be in a body bag, I'd have been a bit more careful what I'd wished for.'

Rebecca had spent much of the afternoon and early evening shuttling between appointments with attendees of Martina's party, none of whom had had much to add to what Tony's housemates had been able – or prepared – to tell them. By the time the evening briefing rolled around at nine, she was flagging, having not had a chance to eat since lunchtime and been loath to grab a snack that she knew would leave her feeling unsatisfied. After two late nights with her brother, followed by another with Leighton, she was looking forward to an early night in her own bed. If Perry was out when she got home, she might take over the bathroom and have a soak in the bath.

'I know it's been a long day, so I'll try to keep this brief,' Lawrence began, once everyone had gathered around. 'It's looking increasingly likely that Tony died at some time between the tail end of a party on the last Saturday in October and the following morning. His housemate, Martina, has provided some photos from the party, and in those pictures Tony is wearing the same clothing he was found in,' Lawrence indicated a photograph affixed to the board behind him. 'Thus far, nobody we've spoken to has reported seeing him since then, and, although we're yet to get his phone records, the phone company was prepared to confirm that the number Martina provided hasn't been used in two weeks. The last activity was a brief call, made shortly before one a.m. on the Sunday. If we're lucky, the phone will be among his belongings, and we won't have to wait on bureaucracy to look through his communications or find out who that call was to.'

'Given the hour, my money's on his dealer,' Jamie put in.

'Or drunk dialling,' Eva added.

'Quite possibly,' Lawrence agreed. 'As it seems likely he died in the immediate aftermath of a party, I suspect he was left at the end of the garden in the hope we might conclude he'd found his own way there after getting drunk or high. We're still waiting on toxicology, but cause of death looks to have been suffocation, and he was moved postmortem, making accidental death unlikely.

'Meanwhile we've got two housemates claiming they didn't notice Tony was missing for a fortnight, and two who say they thought he'd gone away. Given that they all seem to have known one another well, I don't find either scenario particularly convincing.'

'Martina seemed pretty genuine,' Eva put in.

'I don't think I could say as much for either of the women we spoke to,' Lawrence replied, looking to Jamie. 'What did you make of Jakob?'

'The guy's a dick.'

'Well that's not a crime,' Lawrence observed, as several people sniggered.

'I didn't buy his story,' Noel said. 'I generally know whether or not the people in the *other* flats in my building are home. You might not think about where people are day to day, but for almost two weeks is pushing it.'

'Yeah, I was initially of that mind,' Jamie replied. 'But –' he wrinkled his nose. 'Maybe if you're that self-centred, other people don't really register on your radar.'

'He sounds like a charmer,' Eva remarked, sarcastically.

'I got the impression from Akiko that he's something of a ladies' man,' Lawrence said. 'She also mentioned that he'd spent the night of the party with one of Martina's friends.'

'Maya,' Jamie put in.

'That's right,' Lawrence responded. 'And during the evening, she and Tony were both involved in playing a drinking game called *I have never*. Is anyone familiar with that?'

Rebecca's answer to the affirmative was one of a chorus. Guessing that Lawrence might not have come across the game before, she added, 'It generally starts out pretty harmlessly, with things like *I have never kissed a stranger* or *I have never gone commando*, but as it goes on it gets more risqué, and things start getting personal. People can reveal confidences they would never have divulged outright.'

'Sounds like a dangerous game.'

'I have seen it end in tears.'

'I'm not surprised,' Lawrence remarked. 'And if it involves revealing secrets, it stands to reason it could also end in murder.'

'Perhaps we should try to assemble a list of everything that came up during the game,' Rebecca suggested.

'Good thinking.'

'Assuming people can remember what happened later on, of course.'

'Of course,' Lawrence replied, drily. 'Alcohol always makes for a very convenient excuse when people are faced with questions they don't want to answer.'

'And when faced with things they need to apologise for,' Rebecca observed, thinking of her ex-fiancé, Elliot. His response to an episode of severe depression had been to eschew medication or counselling in favour of vodka and Jack Daniels, and in the final year of their relationship Rebecca had heard the words *sorry, I don't remember* more times than she had cared to count. Eighteen months on from their split, there were still times when she found herself wondering what she could have done that might have made a difference.

'Could you try to pull a list together?' Lawrence asked.

'Sure.'

'And find out who took part.'

Rebecca nodded.

'We also need to identify Tony's ex-boyfriend. His first name is Ross, but neither Irene nor Akiko was able to give us his surname. I don't suppose Martina knew?'

'Yes, Ross Tomlinson,' Eva said. 'She didn't have an address, but apparently he lives somewhere in the city, so it shouldn't be too hard to track him down. Whether he'll be there is another matter, she said he travels a lot for work.'

'Ok. Can you look after tracing him?'

Eva nodded.

'And we'll need to work our way through Tony's bedroom, once the CSI team are done. They've already flagged several things from the garden, most notably that there's no sign the body was dragged into position behind the shed. Considering the amount of clutter around there – not to mention the huge planters all but blocking the way – that suggests he was moved by at least two people.' Lawrence paused. 'Unfortunately what it doesn't do is give us any clues to which of the twenty-odd individuals at the party might have been involved.'

Four

'Jimmy, what would you like in your sandwiches? Ham or chicken?'

The boy didn't respond, and Katie spoke his name again.

'Jim, answer your mother,' Lawrence said, when his son still didn't move.

Jimmy gave a pointed sigh. 'I've told her, like, a *million* times not to call me that.'

'Sometimes we have to keep reminding you about things, too,' Lawrence pointed out.

'That's different,' Jimmy retorted.

Lawrence didn't respond, not prepared to be drawn into an argument. He would never have said as much in front of his son, but he could understand the boy's frustration. Despite Lawrence's repeated objections, his own mother had never stopped calling him *Larry*. Early on in their relationship, Katie had taken to doing the same, and at that stage he hadn't liked to correct her. By the time he had felt confident enough to do as much, the name had stuck, so more than twenty years on he was still tolerating it.

'Would you rather make your own sandwiches?' Katie snapped.

There was a pause before Jimmy sighed again and conceded, irritably, 'No.'

'Right, so what would you like?'

'Ham and pickle.'

'Ham and pickle what?'

Jimmy rolled his eyes. 'Please.'

'That wasn't so difficult, was it?' Katie remarked, as Jimmy returned his attention to the tablet in his left hand and reached for a spoonful of Weetabix with his right.

'Do you think you might put the MediaPad down while you're eating?' Lawrence said, as Jimmy dripped milk onto the table.

'It's for school,' Jimmy countered, making no move to relinquish the tablet.

'Homework?'

'No,' Jimmy replied, rather defensively. He was in the habit of leaving things until the last minute, and it was a constant battle to get him to adhere to the rule that homework always be completed by bedtime on the night before it was due in. Lawrence's observation that it would invariably need doing sooner or later, so it made sense to get it over and done with, had been met with the response that you never knew when the world might end. And, ridiculous as it sounded, it was hard to argue with that.

'It can't be that urgent, then, can it?'

'It's for first period.'

'I thought you said it wasn't homework.'

'It's not.'

'Were you supposed to do it at home?'

'Yeah, but it's not *work*. It's for careers.'

'Well that sounds interesting,' Lawrence replied, his desire to hear more trumping the temptation to tackle the boy's use of semantics to excuse leaving the task until the eleventh hour. 'What are you looking at?'

'How to become an astronaut.'

'Is that what you want to do?' Lawrence asked, feeling surprised. Whilst in recent months Jimmy had developed something of an interest in astronomy – thanks in large part to an enthusiastic physics teacher – his principal ambition had long been to become a footballer. And although the idea of going to space might be equally fanciful, Lawrence suspected the trajectory it was on would be furnished with considerably more promising and varied career options.

'Uh-huh. I wanna go to the space station.'

'So what do you need to do to get there?'

Jimmy handed him the tablet before giving the Weetabix his full attention, his limited enthusiasm for discourse apparently exhausted. Lawrence scanned the NASA webpage open on the screen before saying, 'It says you'd need a science or engineering degree.'

'Yeah, I know.'

'Is that something you'd be interested in doing?'

The boy shrugged. 'Maybe.'

'In what subject? Physics?'

Jimmy shrugged again, before adding, as an afterthought, 'Not chemistry.'

Lawrence smiled. 'That was never my favourite subject, either.'

'It's *dead*,' Jimmy returned. 'They've run out of stuff to do, so they're trying to make new elements in colliders. It's so lame.'

'I'm sure there's more to it than that.'

Jimmy grunted disbelievingly, and Lawrence looked back to the tablet. Several paragraphs in, he came across an unexpected – although, on reflection, perfectly logical – requirement of the job.

'Did you see that you'd have to learn Russian?' He asked, wondering how long it would be before Mandarin also become a necessity.

'Yeah, we can do that in sixth form.'

'At your school?' Lawrence exclaimed. 'Really?'

'Uh-huh,' Jimmy confirmed, pausing momentarily before adding, 'We could go there on holiday.' The idea was apparently of sufficient interest for him to finally give Lawrence priority over his breakfast, and he looked up as he said, 'Cyrus and his dad went on a tour of the metro stations in Moscow. It looked totally lit.'

This, Lawrence knew, was not a reference to the subway system's lighting, but an expression roughly synonymous with the word *awesome*. That wasn't the only application *lit* appeared to have, however, and other uses he was less clear on. When it came to teenage slang, he wasn't inclined to invite scorn by asking for translations or trying to use the terms himself, and relied mainly on context and tone to surmise their meaning. Making sense of the plethora of acronyms that had grown out of the ubiquitous use of digital messaging media was more of a challenge, so unless he had cause for concern he tended to let them pass him by. And if he did need to decode anything, the answer was generally just a Google search away.

Jamie had spent much of the morning cursing paperless banking as he dealt with the bureaucracy required to access Tony's financial records. When he'd first started in CID, the rigmarole had rarely been necessary; more often than not, at least the most recent of a person's bank statements could be found somewhere in their home. Nowadays, the data was all stored electronically, and even if Tony had gone to the trouble of downloading his statements, the security on his laptop was such that, as yet, nobody had been able to break it. Francine, one of the Met's forensic computer analysts, had summarised the situation first thing that morning with the words, 'Either he locked everything down simply because he could, or he had something big to hide.' They were still waiting to find out which.

It came as a pleasant surprise when the effort involved in obtaining the statements turned out to have been worthwhile, and Jamie gathered several of the printouts together before walking the few steps to Lawrence's office and knocking on the open glass door.

'I finally managed to get hold of Tony's bank records,' he revealed, when Lawrence looked up from his laptop screen. 'And he's been paying Martina five hundred quid a month since August.'

'Rent?' Lawrence suggested. 'Or bills?'

'Unlikely. He had several direct debits set up for less-exact numbers – those have all been running for over a year – and –'

Lawrence's mobile interrupted the exchange, and he glanced at the screen before answering. 'Eva, hi.'

During the ensuing pause, Jamie watched his eyebrows rise, then contract into a frown. 'Ok, when you get back up here, can you print those out?' He responded, at length. There was another brief pause before he added, with an unnecessary nod, 'Yes, all of them. I know it doesn't make for pleasant viewing, but we need to try to identify the ... yes ... ok. See you later.'

'What've they found?' Jamie asked, as Lawrence hung up.

'Child pornography. On an SD card the CSI team found hidden in the lining of Tony's bedroom curtains.'

Jamie nodded, at a loss to know how else to respond. There were some things that didn't get any easier with experience. And, where anything involving child abuse was concerned, he always feared he might say the wrong thing – particularly when talking to people who had children of their own. In the end, he opted for a practical question.

'Didn't he do some charity work with children?'

'Disabled children,' Lawrence replied, heavily.

'Christ.'

'I spoke to someone at the foundation this morning and I've arranged a meeting with their volunteer coordinator at two. Depending on where Martina is, we might be able to catch up with her in the interim.'

'Are you thinking blackmail?' Jamie asked.

'Well if she knew he had indecent images of children, that would have made for a powerful bargaining chip.'

'Yeah, it would. Do you want me to see if I can locate her?'

'Yes please.'

'And shall I look into whether she or any of Tony's other housemates were on social services' radar as kids?'

'Good thinking. Who knows how someone with a history of sexual abuse might react to coming across that sort of material. It's jarring enough for those of us who haven't been through it.' Lawrence paused, then added, 'And I'll see whether the French authorities have any records of that nature for Tony or his siblings, as well.' He reached for a pen. 'I don't like to pigeonhole people, but we can't ignore the statistics.'

Headscarves made it harder than usual to age people, but Lawrence tentatively put Assia Hassan, the Harvey Foundation's volunteer coordinator, in her mid-to-late forties. She was on the phone when he and Jamie were shown into the charity's cramped and cluttered office, and from the blinking lights on the desktop device Lawrence guessed there were more callers waiting. Gesturing towards the other chairs in the room, she swiftly brought the conversation to an end and dispatched two other callers before replacing the handset and turning her chair towards Lawrence and Jamie.

'Sorry about that,' she said. 'DCI Forrester?'

Lawrence nodded, presenting his warrant card and introducing Jamie before thanking her for taking the time to speak to them.

'It's the least I can do,' Assia replied. 'Tony did so much for us.'

'Did you know him well?'

'As well as I know any of the volunteers. He'd been coming here for almost two years.'

'And what did his volunteering involve?'

'Week to week, he worked on art projects with the children. Our aim is to provide fun and accessible activities while also giving parents and other carers a break. And if it involved paints and glue, Tony was usually in the middle of it. He was very creative. And fantastic with the children.'

'When you say week to week, do you mean he came at a regular time?'

'Yes. We run three-hour sessions morning and afternoon. Tony helped out on Wednesday afternoons.'

'So he must have taken time out from work,' Lawrence assumed, feeling surprised Akiko would have agreed to that and wondering whether she had even known.

'I suppose so. I can't say I ever asked.'

'When was he last here?'

There was a pause before Assia said, 'Three weeks ago today.'

'Did you see or hear from him at all after that?'

'Once, late one night a few days later. He called me – which in itself was unusual, because we tended to communicate by text – and he sounded upset. And drunk.'

'Do you have any idea what he was upset about?'

'Not really. He didn't make much sense. He was going on about Harvey and a bubble.'

'A bubble?'

'Yes. I've no idea what that was about. At the time I dismissed it as drunken nonsense. He'd woken me up, so I'm afraid I wasn't particularly accommodating.'

'How about Harvey? Is it possible he was talking about the individual rather than the foundation?'

'I doubt it. Harvey's a surname. Charlotte Gibson, the founder, set it up with her husband, Andrew Harvey, in memory of their son Maxim. They're not involved in the running of the centre, although they do occasionally come to fundraisers. I doubt Tony would have had any real contact with either of them.'

'And it's not the name of any of the children who attend the centre?'

'I don't think so. None of the current group, at any rate. But I can have a look at our records to see whether we've ever had a child of that name visit us.'

'That would be very helpful, thank you. And I'd be grateful if you could check your phone for the precise time and date of Tony's call, as well,' Lawrence said, placing a copy of his card on the table. 'A screenshot of the details would be very useful for our records.'

'Of course.'

'On a more sensitive note, did you ever see or hear anything to suggest Tony might have behaved inappropriately with the children?'

'Inappropriately?' Assia echoed, sounding shocked by the question. 'No, never.'

'Was he ever alone with any of them?'

'No,' she replied, emphatically, her eyebrows drawing into a frown. 'Why would you try to smear him with something like that? Not every man who enjoys spending time with children is a paedophile!'

'I realise that, and we're not looking to smear him,' Lawrence responded, firmly. 'But we have to consider every possibility.'

Assia didn't look mollified by this explanation, but voiced no further objection, and Lawrence moved on.

'Did Tony give you any idea of what motivated him to volunteer here?'

'He told me he'd had a brother who was disabled.'

'Did he talk much about that?'

'Not really. I didn't have a lot of contact with him – if I was around when he came in we shared the usual chit-chat – what the children were up to, weekend plans, that kind of thing – but otherwise he just got on with what he was here for. If people are reliable and I don't hear any complaints, then there's no reason for me to keep tabs on them.'

'But you mentioned earlier that you and Tony stayed in touch by text message.'

'Well yes, but I do that with most of the volunteers. It's an easy way for me to keep them in the loop about any news, schedule changes or upcoming events, and for them to let me know if they can't make a session. My text exchanges with Tony weren't of a personal nature.'

'Were you surprised when he didn't turn up to the last couple of sessions?'

'Yes. He'd never missed a session without notifying us before. The first week I wondered whether he was embarrassed about the phone call, but when he didn't respond to my messages I thought it must be more than that – a family emergency, or something. If I'd known him better, I might have tried harder to make contact, but it didn't really seem appropriate.'

'Is there anyone we might speak to who did work closely with Tony, and might have known him better?'

'Well, there's Sandie, who runs Wednesday's sessions. I can't call her out of this afternoon's one because of legal requirements on staff numbers, but I can give you her contact details. And you might want a word with Ellie, one of our younger volunteers. She and Tony weren't really working together, but he was helping her with her French.'

'For school?'

'No, Ellie's a student. But she's deaf, and Tony could sign in French as well as English. My sign language isn't up to much, I'm afraid, but if you'd like a chat with Ellie I can probably find someone to translate for you.' She moved to stand. 'And if not, you have people you can call on for that, right?'

Ellie was a petite brunette, and was clad in an eye-catching tie-dyed crochet jumper that reached almost to her knees. She didn't seem apprehensive about talking to the police, and gave a polite smile as she waved hello from her seat at a low table in the corner of what looked a lot like an infant-school classroom. The walls were plastered with artwork, the shelves stocked with books and toys, and a large area of the floor had been painted to resemble a racing track.

Dale, who had agreed to interpret for them, was several inches shorter than Lawrence, with a thin face and close-cropped mousy hair. As he folded his wiry frame into the small chair next to Ellie's, he said, 'Ellie can lipread. So you can address whatever you want to say to her and then I'll translate her answers.'

'Great, thank you,' Lawrence nodded, looking to Ellie and hesitating as he debated whether he should adjust the speed at which he spoke or whether she might find that insulting. He decided to err on the side of caution and speak normally; Dale could let him know if that was a problem.

'When were you last in contact with Tony?' He asked, after quickly introducing himself and Jamie.

Ellie's answer was more involved than Lawrence had expected, and he wondered whether that reflected the complexity of what she was saying or simply the intricacies of sign language.

'She last saw him the day he was last here,' Dale revealed, when she had finished. 'The afternoon session ended at four, and Tony and Ellie stayed on for half an hour to go over some French. Apparently he tried to call her the following weekend, but it was late, so Ellie was asleep.'

'Was that on the Saturday night?'

Ellie nodded.

'Did he leave a message?'

The flurry of signing that followed led Lawrence to suspect that Tony had said something of note, so it came as a disappointment when Dale said, 'He left several messages, but Ellie obviously couldn't listen to them, and the voice-recognition software she uses struggled to make much sense of what he'd said. Her dad had a listen and said it was just drunken gibberish.'

Much like Tony's call to Assia, Lawrence supposed, asking whether Ellie still had the messages.

Ellie shook her head and mouthed, 'Sorry.'

The topic of the French sessions Ellie and Tony had engaged in was more illuminating. Lawrence had imagined their having some sort of structure, covering specific subjects or exercises, but apparently the two of them had simply made general conversation. Through a series of questions and bursts of translation they learned, among other things, that Ellie knew Tony had had a boyfriend, but not about their break-up; that he had talked a lot about his brother, who had died several years earlier, prompting Tony's decision to move to London; that he had spoken fondly of Martina and Irene; and that he had hoped, in the not too distant future, to spend six months travelling around South America.

When Ellie finally finished listing everything she could recall them discussing, Lawrence asked whether Assia's mention of Harvey and a bubble meant anything to her. Ellie's eyebrows contracted in what looked like puzzlement, and she looked to Dale, perhaps needing the question to be spelt out. Glancing at Jamie, Lawrence noticed that he had made precious few notes, and tried to catch his eye, but the young man was watching Ellie intently. It wasn't the first time he had been distracted by a pretty girl, and Lawrence felt more than a little irritated.

'No,' Dale said, as Ellie stopped gesticulating.

'On another note, did Tony mention anything that was worrying him lately?'

Ellie seemed to consider this for a couple of seconds before shaking her head.

Lawrence nodded. 'I think that's everything, thank you,' he said, with a smile, before looking to Dale to thank him, too. Jamie spoke up before he had the chance.

'I've a quick question, if you don't mind?'

'Fire away,' Dale replied.

'Why did you edit some of Ellie's answers?'

Dale frowned. 'Sorry?'

'When DCI Forrester asked Ellie about Harvey and the bubble, you told us it didn't mean anything to her. But that's not what she said.'

'No,' Dale conceded. 'But after a moment she realised she was thinking of a storybook. I didn't think that was relevant.'

'And did you think the visit one of Tony's friends made to the centre last month was irrelevant, too?'

Dale shrugged. 'Ellie only mentioned it in passing. I was just trying to summarise things for you to save time.'

'Well, for future reference, we'd rather decide what to summarise for ourselves. Ok?'

'Ok,' Dale echoed, sounding taken aback.

'Great,' Jamie responded, perfunctorily, before turning to Ellie and saying, 'You mentioned before that Tony had a visit from one of his friends while he was working here. Could you describe him for me, please?'

'Well that was impressive,' Lawrence remarked, as he and Jamie walked back to the car.

'And there you were thinking I was just slacking off,' Jamie responded, with a grin.

'Something like that,' Lawrence admitted. 'When did you learn sign language?'

'Oh, years ago. My sister's deaf. But I didn't want to offer to translate because I'd have had no record of what was said.'

'As it turns out, that was a good decision in more ways than one. What did Ellie have to say after you challenged Dale?'

'Not much of any note. Tony's visitor could have been Jakob, from her description, but then tall and good-looking with dark hair doesn't exactly narrow it down.'

'No,' Lawrence agreed, digging his key fob from his pocket and disabling the car's central locking. 'Perhaps more pertinent is the question of why Dale kept it from us.'

'Assuming it wasn't just laziness,' Jamie replied, as he opened the passenger door.

Lawrence nodded, climbing into the car and waiting until both doors were shut before saying, 'Given that Tony called both Assia and Ellie the night he died, there was clearly something on his mind relating to the charity. But as he was three sheets to the wind, it's impossible to know whether it was anything important.'

'I guess he might also have called the woman who runs the sessions he helped out with,' Jamie said, removing his mobile from his jacket pocket before tossing the garment onto the back seat. 'She might have more idea what it was about.'

'Sandie, yes.' Lawrence pulled on his seatbelt and started the ignition. 'Can you give her a call later, see what you can set up?'

'Sure.'

'And let's arrange a meeting with Charlotte Gibson, the founder, as well.'

'Ok,' Jamie replied, turning his attention to his mobile. A moment later, he said, 'Oh, wait up, Becks has finished her *I have never* list.'

'Well that should make for interesting reading,' Lawrence remarked, hoping Rebecca would still be in the office when he returned. She had spent the morning in court for the start of Healy's trial, and he was keen to hear how Leighton had coped with cross-examination.

'You'd think,' Jamie replied. 'But number one on the list is *I have never been to Wales*, and next up is *I have never cried while watching Titanic*.'

'Oh good grief,' Lawrence muttered, glancing over his shoulder before pulling out into the road.

'I've never watched Titanic.'

'Spoiler alert. It's three hours of your life you won't get back.'

Jamie laughed, then fell silent. From the occasional grunt or snigger, Lawrence surmised that he was reading through Rebecca's list, a hunch that was proved correct when Jamie said, '*I have never broken into the wrong house while drunk*. I knew a guy who did that once. He broke into a vicarage.'

'A vicarage?' Lawrence exclaimed. 'What happened?'

'Not much, the place was empty. His folks had only moved out of it a few weeks earlier.'

'So, in actual fact, he broke into his parents' old home.'

'Yeah, but telling it that way doesn't make for such a good story.'

Lawrence smiled. 'No.' He flicked the indicators on as they approached a junction. 'What's next?'

'*I have never eaten someone else's lunch from the office fridge*.'

'I'd like to think nobody would dare do that in CID.'

'Well I certainly wouldn't, some of what's in there looks like a health hazard,' Jamie replied, before adding, in a different tone, 'Jeez. *I have never torched a church*.'

'Bloody hell.'

'There's got to be a backstory to that one.'

'Did anyone drink to it?'

'No. But that doesn't mean much. One line that always gets a lot of people drinking is *I have never lied while playing this game.*'

'Which makes one wonder at the point of playing it at all,' Lawrence remarked. 'Clearly the basic objective is to get drunk, but I can't help feeling there's something pernicious about it. People are bound to feel pressure to participate, in effect giving other people a degree of control over their drinking.'

'I guess.'

'Who came out with the one about the church?'

'Irene. But she might just be fond of taking things to extremes, because she also went for *I have never stolen a car,*' Jamie observed, before adding, 'Well we all know someone who's done *that.*'

Lawrence glanced sharply his way, seized by the fear that his colleagues had somehow got wind of the fact that Jimmy had been caught travelling in a stolen car a year or so earlier. Jamie didn't appear to be anticipating a reaction, however; his eyes were still on his phone, his expression one of concentration. The panic dissipating, Lawrence reflected that the remark had probably been a reference to Leighton's teenage exploits. Lawrence didn't know how much truth there was to the pathologist's sporadic jokes about joyriding, but he suspected they weren't entirely without foundation.

'How about Tony?' He asked. 'If anything's going to be relevant to his death, it's likely to be something he said.'

'Um ... besides *I have never seen a dead body*, there's *I have never stalked an ex on social media, I have never dumped someone by text message* and *I have never made a sex tape.*' Jamie dropped the hand holding the phone into his lap, remarking, sardonically, 'The ways modern technology has enriched our lives.'

'I only wish there was a surefire way to get the magnitude of the risks through to the kids,' Lawrence replied. 'Particularly given that what they're seeing online directly contradicts what I'm telling them. Lewd pictures and sex tapes ruin lives, but when D-list celebrities leak them, more often than not they're rewarded with endorsements and reality TV shows.' He sighed. 'And that's a powerful message to be up against.'

* * * * *

Ross Tomlinson seemed stunned by the news of his ex-boyfriend's death, and asked more than once whether they were sure the body had been correctly identified. He then sat in silence for some seconds before asking what had happened.

'We're not certain at this stage,' Lawrence replied. 'Could you tell us when you were last in touch with Tony?'

'Um – well I haven't seen him since we split up, so I guess about six weeks ago?'

'I gather it was your decision to end the relationship.'

'Yes.'

'Would you mind telling us why?'

'I just wasn't feeling it,' Ross responded, with a shrug. 'You know.'

Lawrence nodded, although he wasn't sure he really *did* know. It was easy enough to identify with a situation in which a break-up resulted from a specific incident, like a fight or infidelity, but to understand the more nebulous experience of falling out of love he suspected you had to have been there. Having married his first serious girlfriend, he hadn't been.

'Do you have any idea how Tony felt about the break-up?'

'He wasn't likely to tell me, was he?'

'Who do you think he might have talked to, if anyone?'

'Probably Martina. She was his bestie.'

'Did you know her well?'

'I guess.'

'And did you like her?'

'She's a sweetheart,' Ross replied. 'Although she has a lot of baggage.'

'Oh?'

'Her confidence is at rock-bottom, so she lets people treat her like crap and blames herself for their behaviour. And then she comfort-eats and ends up feeling even worse. It's a vicious circle.'

'How did Tony treat her?'

'He tried to build her up, but it often seemed like it was one step forwards, three steps back.'

'That must have been frustrating for him.'

'Yeah,' Ross acknowledged. 'He did sound off about it a couple of times.'

'Did he ever convey his frustration to her?'

'I don't think so.'

'And what did you think of Tony's other housemates?'

'I barely knew them.'

Lawrence frowned. 'Martina told us you and Tony were seeing one another for around eighteen months. Did you not visit him during that time?'

'Not often. I couldn't stay over, so mostly we hung out here.'

'Why couldn't you stay at Tony's?'

'Jakob had issues with Tony having men stay,' Ross revealed, lifting his eyebrows expressively as he spoke the word *issues*.

'Could you expand on that?'

'That's about all I know. It was already a thing by the time Tony and I met. I didn't ask for the details. Straight guys being knobs about gay sex isn't exactly news.'

'No, but I'm surprised it didn't bother Tony sufficiently for him to either challenge Jakob or move out,' Lawrence remarked. 'I'd take a dim view of being told my partner couldn't spend the night in my own home.'

'Yeah, well, you've maybe never had to think about whether anyone might have a problem with your relationships. That's not everyone's reality.'

Lawrence conceded the point with a nod.

'Besides, Tony wasn't really one for confrontation,' Ross went on. 'And I don't think Jakob ever said he *couldn't* have people stay the night. I think he was just weird about it, and it made Tony feel uncomfortable.'

'Yet, despite that, he and Tony seem to have got along reasonably well,' Lawrence observed. 'At least from what we've heard.'

'Well as I said, Tony didn't really go in for confrontation.'

'Are you saying he simply tolerated Jakob?'

'On the whole.'

In light of what Jakob had told Jamie about his housemates not being *his kind of people*, Lawrence wondered whether he had felt the same. 'Was Tony any more inclined to confront people when he'd been drinking?'

'Not particularly. Why?'

'The night he was last seen alive, he seems to have been quite hostile towards several people, including Jakob and Martina. And nobody –'

'With Tina?' Ross exclaimed. 'Really?'

'Yes. Thus far, nobody has been able to offer any explanation for that.'

'Well I'm afraid I can't help you there, either.'

'How about his other housemates? What did he say about them?'

'He seemed to like Irene. He sometimes bitched about her being anal when it came to keeping the kitchen straight, but having seen him in action around here I could see both sides of that one.'

'And Akiko?'

Ross looked momentarily puzzled before his expression changed and he said, 'Oh, yeah. I forgot she lives there. Tony only ever really talked about her in relation to work.'

'Saying what?'

'Not a lot. But until recently what he did say was generally positive. Aside from him getting pissed off when she called him on weekends.'

'So what changed recently?'

'The last couple of times I saw him they were arguing about a medical trial. She was determined to push ahead, and he was dead against it.'

'Did he say why?'

'He kept telling her they needed more data and asking her to wait for him to get it.'

'Have you any idea what sort of data he was referring to? Or why he thought it was necessary?'

Ross shook his head. 'He didn't discuss it with me. I only know what he said when they were on the phone.'

'How much do you know about what he was doing for React8?'

'Very little. Whenever anyone asked, he said developing drugs was tedious and unsexy.'

'Did you ever ask why he was doing it, if he found it tedious?'

'I don't think he meant the job itself was tedious, just that it didn't make for very interesting conversation. I guess there's only so much you can say when you can't talk about the drug itself.'

'Was that confidential?'

'Yes.'

'And was that the only kind of drug Tony was interested in? Or did he use illicit drugs?'

Ross hesitated, and Lawrence added, 'I'm not interested in what you get up to, just Tony's activities.'

Several seconds passed before Ross admitted, 'Sometimes.' There was another brief pause before he asked, 'Is that how he died?'

'Possibly.'

'After last New Year he swore he'd be more careful.'

'What happened on that occasion?'

'He collapsed in a club after taking something dodgy. We ended up seeing the new year in in an ambulance.'

'Well we're still waiting for some test results, but it seems likely that in this case someone else had a hand in what happened to him.'

'You mean someone killed him?' Ross exclaimed.

'Can you think of anyone who might have had reason to do that?'

There was a long pause before Ross shook his head, looking almost as shell-shocked as when Lawrence had first broken the news. 'He wasn't the kind of person people dislike,' he said, at length, before adding, with another shake of his head, 'Sorry, that sounds stupid. Like that's the only reason people get killed.'

'It's still a reason,' Lawrence replied. 'And it's helpful for us to build up as complete a picture of Tony as we can.'

Ross nodded.

'I'm sorry to have to ask, but we do need to know what you were doing on the evening of the last Saturday in October.'

Ross blinked. 'Um – I don't know –' he frowned, presumably in thought, before saying, 'I was at a bar in town, then I went on to a club.'

'Who were you with?'

'I met a couple of friends around nine.'

'Were you with them all night?'

''Til about midnight. Then I headed to the club.'

'What club?'

'The Pump Room. It's in Vauxhall.'

'What time were you there until?'

'Half two? Three, maybe?'

'And after that?'

'I came back here.'

'Alone?'

'No. But I'm afraid I can't give you much in the way of details for the boy I went to bed with.'

'Boy?' Lawrence queried, his eyebrows rising. 'How old was he?'

Ross sighed. 'It was a figure of speech. I meant a man, obviously.'

'Why obviously?'

'Because I'm not some kind of sicko!'

'So you've never viewed pornography involving minors?'

'What?' Ross exclaimed. 'I use an ambiguous word to describe a one-night stand with a consenting adult and next thing I know you're implying I'm a paedo? If I'd said boy*friend* you wouldn't have given it a second thought!'

'You haven't answered my question. Have you ever viewed that sort of pornography?'

'Hell no!'

'Did Tony?'

'*Tony*?' Ross echoed, incredulously. 'No! No way!' He shook his head. 'Why are you even *asking* me this?'

'We found pornographic pictures of children in Tony's possession,' Lawrence replied, bluntly, largely to see how the man reacted.

'You *what*?' Ross responded, appearing genuinely horrified by this revelation. 'I really don't –' he shook his head in lieu of finishing the sentence. 'Are you sure? That they were his, I mean. Are his fingerprints on them?'

'The images were stored electronically.'

'What, and you could just open them?' Ross exclaimed. 'If they weren't buried under fifteen layers of security, they're nothing to do with him!'

Given the difficulty the computer analysts had been having getting into Tony's computer, the memory card's lack of even basic password protection was something Jamie had already questioned. Whilst Lawrence was inclined to agree – hiding an SD card in the lining of a curtain was the kind of behaviour he would have expected of his parents' generation – he was also aware of the danger of assuming that anyone's actions were entirely consistent. People make mistakes, and often mistakes were what brought criminals to the attention of the police in the first place.

But even if the pictures didn't belong to Tony, that didn't absolve him of all responsibility. The photographs had been taken almost a year earlier. What had stopped him turning the SD card over to the authorities?

On arrival home, Lawrence looked into Jimmy's room to find him lying on his bed, propped up on his elbows, his laptop open in front of him. Lawrence had long since given up trying to persuade his son to use a desk, and, as the computer was often left abandoned on the duvet, had taken the precaution of installing a smoke alarm in the boy's bedroom. The computer's primary purpose was for schoolwork, but it also served as a personal television, and Jimmy was watching what appeared to be a music video. Lawrence had never understood the attraction; he could count on one hand the number he had come across in which enough happened to hold his interest for more than a matter of seconds.

'Evening.'

Jimmy grunted in response, his eyes remaining fixed on the screen.

'How was your careers session this morning?'

'Crap.'

'What was crap about it?'

'They only wanted to talk about boring stuff.'

'What sort of stuff?' Lawrence asked, reaching for the chair at the desk and turning it around before sitting down. Jimmy used the word *stuff* more than almost any other – often as the sole descriptor for whatever he was or had been doing – and it tended to be an uphill struggle to get him to reveal any further information.

Jimmy sighed heavily, presumably to convey his displeasure at the prospect of having to have an actual conversation, before rolling onto his side. 'IT and accountancy and stuff.'

'Common professions, you mean?'

'I guess.'

'Did you tell your teacher what you were interested in doing?'

'Uh-huh.'

'And?' Lawrence prompted, thinking, not for the first time, that conversing with teenagers had a lot in common with questioning a reluctant witness.

'She said I was taking the piss.'

'I assume that wasn't the word she actually used?'

'It's what she meant.'

'Well, if it's what you really want to do, I wouldn't let that stop you,' Lawrence replied, keen that any interest his son might have in science not be discouraged. 'There may not be many opportunities for space travel right now, but that doesn't mean there won't be in ten years' time.'

'Yeah, maybe,' Jimmy responded, without much enthusiasm.

'If you find out more about it, your teacher might take it more seriously,' Lawrence suggested. 'Have a look online and see whether there are any exhibitions or events that interest you.

The planetarium in Greenwich might be a good place to start. We could head over there the next time I have a weekend off.'

Jimmy appeared to consider this for a moment before saying, 'Or we could go to the space centre in Florida.'

'Could we now?' Lawrence remarked, with a smile. 'Well, we can talk about that if you're still keen this time next year.' He moved to stand. 'In the meantime, let's see what we can find closer to home.'

Five

Martina hadn't been answering her phone on Wednesday, and when Lawrence and Jamie had tried the house after their interview with Ross, she hadn't been home. She had finally responded to the messages they had left for her late that night, saying she had been to visit her grandmother in Tonbridge and had forgotten to take her mobile. According to Jamie, she had been very apologetic, but Lawrence wasn't convinced it hadn't been intentional.

She opened the front door to Lawrence and Rebecca on Thursday morning with reddened eyes, and, standing back to allow them to enter, gestured wordlessly towards the lounge. Lawrence accepted her offer of a coffee more to give her a chance to gather herself together than because he really wanted one, but when she rejoined them a few minutes later the delay didn't appear to have helped.

'We've been looking over Tony's financials,' Lawrence began, once she was sitting opposite them. 'And he made several sizeable payments into your bank account in the past few months. Would you mind telling us what those were for?'

'They weren't payments,' Martina replied, awkwardly.

'So what were they?'

'Loans.'

'What for?'

Martina swallowed. 'It's embarrassing,' she said, casting her eyes down. 'I got myself into a bit of a hole – financially – so Tony offered to lend me the money to help me out.'

'That was good of him.'

'He was a good person.'

'And how did you come to be in a position where you needed a friend to bail you out?'

Martina raised her pale eyes to meet his. 'What does that matter?'

'I don't know whether it does until you tell me.'

She lowered her gaze again. Several seconds passed before she admitted, in a small voice, 'Shopping.' She swallowed. 'I got – carried away – put too much on credit cards. It was stupid.'

'Had you and Tony worked out a potential repayment plan?' Lawrence asked, making a mental note to have someone pull up her financial records to check she really had needed the money.

'He said not to worry about it until I was in a better place,' Martina replied, before adding, hurriedly, 'Financially, I mean.'

'Even after he lost his job?' Lawrence queried. 'I'd have thought that might have caused him some concern.'

'He said it wasn't a problem,' Martina replied, with a weak shrug.

'Do you know whether Tony had any income besides that from his job at React8?'

'No. I don't.'

'From looking at his bank account, it doesn't appear that he was particularly flush,' Lawrence revealed. 'And given that he had no pay cheques on the horizon, I'm quite surprised he wasn't worried about the fact you owed him fifteen hundred pounds.'

'Well he didn't seem to be,' Martina said, her voice sounding strained.

'Did he give you any idea what he was planning to do about work going forwards?'

'He talked about consulting on cybersecurity. He was really good with computers.'

'Was he doing any of that sort of work for React8?'

'I don't know. He never talked much about his work. He said it was all confidential.'

'Really?' Lawrence asked. 'Akiko told us he mostly did research, reading up on new findings in immunology. I'm not sure how information that had already been published could be considered confidential.'

'I don't know,' Martina repeated, shaking her head slightly. 'He never went into any detail.'

'Do you think it's possible he kept it to himself because what he was doing was morally or legally questionable?'

'No,' Martina responded, clearly shocked by the suggestion. 'He'd never have done anything of that nature.'

Lawrence recalled what Irene had said about Martina always seeing the best in people, and wondered whether that had been a polite way of calling her housemate naïve. There was a world of difference between focusing on the positive and being oblivious to the negative. Leighton seemed to be able to find something to like in just about everyone, but he wasn't blind to people's flaws.

Conversely, Martina's opinion of Tony appeared to be veritably rose-tinted.

'You and Tony were clearly very close. Work aside, did he generally confide in you?'

'I think so.'

'How did he feel about your other housemates?'

'He got on with everyone.'

'I'm not asking if he got along with them, I'm asking how he felt about them. Did he like Jakob, for example? Or did he simply tolerate him?'

Martina didn't immediately reply, and Lawrence was just thinking that her silence was an answer in itself when she said, 'Somewhere in between, I think.'

'So you wouldn't describe them as friends.'

'I don't know,' Martina admitted, after another pause. 'There were times they seemed to get on really well, but sometimes things seemed a bit –' she hesitated. 'Awkward, I guess.'

'Is that because Jakob wasn't entirely comfortable with Tony's sexuality?'

'Maybe.'

'And how about Irene?'

'She was fine with it.'

'I was really asking how Tony felt about her.'

'Oh,' Martina nodded. 'He liked her. They were good at making each other laugh.'

'I understand that on occasion they fell out over the fact he didn't pull his weight with the housework.'

Martina sighed. 'I don't think he did it deliberately,' she said. 'He wasn't a morning person, and I think often he just wasn't thinking about what he was doing first thing. I tried to explain that to Irene, but she was already upset, so I don't think she was in the mood to hear it.'

'What was she upset about?'

'I don't know.'

'So how do you know she was upset?'

Martina hesitated before saying, 'She looked like she'd been crying.'

'Did you ask what was wrong?'

Martina looked uncomfortable. 'She said she had her period,' she revealed, her cheeks colouring.

'But you didn't believe her,' Lawrence concluded.

'No.'

'Why not?'

Martina reddened further. 'I knew it wasn't her time,' she revealed, awkwardly.

'When was this?'

'Tuesday. First thing – before we found out – about –' she trailed off.

'Perhaps she was upset because she knew something about Tony's death,' Lawrence suggested.

'What?' Martina exclaimed. 'No!'

'Are you sure? I know it's hard to believe that a friend could have had a hand in what happened to him, but it was your party he was last seen at, so one of your friends must know something.'

Martina didn't immediately reply. Eventually, she said, falteringly, 'I think maybe it was something to do with Jakob. That upset Irene, I mean.'

'And what makes you think that?'

'They're –' she hesitated. 'They're – kind of – seeing each other.'

'As this is the first we've heard of it, can I take it that's not common knowledge?'

'I'm not sure whether anyone else knows.'

'Presumably that's a relatively recent development, given that Jakob spent the night of your party with Maya?'

Martina shrugged. 'I really only know what I've already told you. I don't like to pry. They'll tell people as and when they're ready.'

'When they're ready to be the subject of gossip, you mean,' Lawrence observed. 'On that note, did anything come up at your party that someone might rather have kept quiet? I gather there was a drinking game that involved revealing secrets.'

'Yes, but there's no way of knowing whether everyone's being honest in that sort of game,' Martina replied. 'Unless you already know the answer. And then it's not really a secret, is it?'

Although he couldn't have put a name to the face, Lawrence had placed the man waiting in reception on sight, and paused for only a moment to instruct him to contact the press office before heading on towards CID. The man's response – that he had come to share information, not ask for it – was one Lawrence had heard countless times before, and he felt aggrieved that he was obliged to follow up on what would almost certainly turn out to be a spurious claim. Showing the man into a small meeting room where he would have no opportunity to eyeball any documentation or photographs pertaining to the investigation, Lawrence took a seat and, regardless of the fact his visitor clearly already knew who he was, introduced himself. A response in kind revealed the man now sitting opposite him to be an investigative reporter called Darryl Hayes, a name that proved to be as familiar as his face.

'So how is it you think you can assist us, Mr Hayes?' Lawrence asked, sitting back in his chair.

'I'm here about Tony Mercier,' Darryl began. 'He contacted me a month or so ago. Said he had concerns about a biotech company called React8 that he'd been working for.'

'And what were those concerns?'

'I don't really know,' Darryl replied, a touch apologetically. 'He wanted to discuss it face to face, so we planned on meeting up. But then he stopped responding to my messages. I assumed he'd changed his mind.'

'I see,' Lawrence observed, sceptically.

'I did a bit of digging into the company's affairs – or at least, I tried to, there's surprisingly little information in the public domain – and I managed to track down a couple of former employees, but they'd signed NDAs, so wouldn't talk to me for fear of legal action.' He paused. 'Then I heard about Tony's death. Given that his body was dumped behind his house and he lived with React8's CEO, I presume she's a suspect.'

'You can presume what you like,' Lawrence returned. 'But I'm yet to hear a word to suggest you're here on anything more than a fishing trip.'

The man held his hands out rather helplessly. 'I can't tell you what I don't know. But when people get in touch with me and then wind up dead, I struggle to believe it's a coincidence.'

Lawrence resisted the temptation to ask whether that happened often, saying instead, 'Perhaps you could tell me exactly what he said when he first made contact?'

'I don't remember his exact words, but it was something about ethical violations.'

'Ethical violations?' Lawrence echoed, recalling Irene's mention of ethics.

'Yes,' Darryl confirmed.

'So you spoke to him. Was that on the phone?'

'Yes. He called me.'

'On your mobile?'

Darryl nodded.

'From what number?'

The journalist dug his phone from his pocket, and after a few moments of tapping and scrolling recited an eleven-digit number. Lawrence checked it against the details on his own mobile before saying, 'That's not the number we have for him.'

'Well maybe he had another phone – or a burner – because he called me from that number on two separate occasions.'

'A burner?' Lawrence echoed. 'That seems rather far-fetched.'

'Does it?' Darryl returned. 'The guy was living with the CEO of a company he had concerns about, and within days of making contact with me, he was dead.'

'I'll bear that in mind,' Lawrence responded, coolly, as he moved to stand. 'In the meantime –'

'You *need* to look more closely at this,' Darryl pressed, urgently, getting to his feet and stepping in front of Lawrence to block his path to the door. 'Akiko Nakahara isn't all she appears to be.' He reached into his inside jacket pocket and pulled out a piece of paper that had been folded in half and in half again. Holding it out for Lawrence to take, he added, 'And I'm not at all sure her company is, either.'

Jamie glanced up in response to a cheerful, 'Howdy!' just as Leighton dropped into the chair at the adjacent desk.

'Hello stranger,' Jamie returned, with a smile. 'You do know you're supposed to skive off work to go to the pub, not the other way around, don't you?'

'I'm on my lunch break,' his friend came back, adding, as Jamie looked doubtfully at his watch, 'Late lunch.'

'Well I'm afraid the menu here isn't up to much.'

'So I see,' Leighton remarked, with a shift of his eyes towards the half-eaten sandwich and empty crisp packet on Jamie's desk. Apparently spotting the packet of nicotine gum, he said, 'Have you quit?'

'Trying,' Jamie responded, with a rueful lift of his eyebrows.

'Good for you,' Leighton said. 'And how's your lady?'

'Same,' Jamie replied, facetiously.

Leighton smiled. 'Was it her idea?'

'Yep.'

'Sounds serious. Have you told Forrester yet?'

Jamie shook his head. After many a mental debate about whether to divulge the fact he was romantically involved with someone he had met during the course of an investigation, he had decided not to explain himself until he had to. Lawrence had little time for gossip and wasn't inclined to pry into his colleagues' personal lives, so if Jamie was lucky that moment might never come. And, if it did, the more time that had elapsed, the better.

'What've you been up to?'

'Oh, you know – remodelling the country house, playing golf, test-driving Lamborghinis –' Leighton waved a careless hand through the air.

Given that Leighton's car had been written off some months earlier by his brother – who had taken it without permission – Jamie said, 'Have you got a new motor yet?'

'Nope. Still arguing the toss with the insurance company. They're refusing to pay out on the grounds Tom has a record for TDA, so I should have been more careful with my keys. The fact he wasn't supposed to be at my flat in the first place apparently isn't relevant.'

Jamie frowned. 'Did you not let him in?'

'No. He had some house keys from a previous visit, but he was on bail at the time and he'd been barred from the place, so I wasn't exactly expecting him to turn up.'

'So he wouldn't have been able to take the car without breaching his bail conditions?'

Leighton shook his head.

'Has he breached bail terms before?'

'I dunno. Probably.'

'Do you want me to find out?' Jamie asked, indicating his computer.

'No, ta, I don't want you getting pulled up for misuse of the PNC.'

'I was planning on getting someone to ok it first.'

Leighton smiled. 'I appreciate it, but you're all right. I'll ask Tom when I visit.'

'Are you going to see him?' Jamie exclaimed. 'That's big of you.'

'I can't really complain,' Leighton responded, with a shrug. 'If he'd not swiped the car, I'd probably be dead.'

Given that Leighton's failure to return a friend's car had been the impetus for the search that had dragged Jamie from his bed in the early hours of an April morning and culminated in Leighton's release – just in time – from a freezer container, he was probably right. But that had been by accident, not design, and if Tom had been barred from entering Leighton's home, Jamie guessed taking the car probably hadn't been the worst of his crimes against his brother.

'So what's on your shopping list if you can get a pay out?' Jamie asked. 'Another Aston?'

'Could be, although I wouldn't mind taking a spin in a couple of others before I make any decisions. I'll see what's out there if I ever get the cash. If I don't, I'll have to be a bit more creative.' He grinned. 'What d'you think to a penny farthing? I bet nobody's ever turned up to a crime scene on one of them.'

When Jamie's phone interrupted their conversation, Leighton stood and made for Lawrence's office. The glass door was open, and he tapped lightly.

'Hiya,' he said, as Lawrence raised his eyes from his laptop. 'Is Becks not about?'

'I don't think she'll be long,' Lawrence replied, sitting back in his chair. 'Come in.'

'Are you sure? I don't want to interrupt if you're busy.'

'You might actually be able to help me with something.'

'Oh?' Leighton queried, taking a seat.

'I've got a medical question. One of Tony's housemates runs a biotech start-up. He was working for her until –' Lawrence stopped as his laptop pinged, presumably announcing the arrival of a message. He turned his eyes to the screen, and, after several seconds raised his eyebrows. Looking back to Leighton, he said, 'Have you ever cheated in a test, or an exam?'

'Nope.'

Lawrence's eyebrows rose again, and Leighton guessed he had expected a different answer.

'There's no need to look so surprised.'

'Sorry.'

Leighton grinned. 'Cheating takes organisation.'

This drew a smile from Lawrence. 'Yes, I suppose that's true.'

'Jimmy?'

Lawrence shook his head.

'How's he doing?'

'Well, thank you. His latest ambition is to visit the International Space Station.'

'Wow. That's quite a departure from football.'

'Oh, I think football's still very much in the running.'

'Glad to hear it. Next time he's got a match, let me know, and I'll come along.'

'I'm sure he'd like that.'

'So who's been cheating?'

'The housemate of Tony's with the biotech start-up. The company's website says she read molecular biology at Cambridge – but conveniently omits the fact she never actually graduated. According to this,' he indicated his laptop. 'She was caught taking notes into one of her finals.'

'What's the start-up called?'

'React8. The blurb says –' Lawrence looked to his laptop again. 'They're working on bringing a technology to market that exclusively targets autoreactive cells and will make autoimmune disease a thing of the past.'

'That's a bold claim.'

'Unlikely to be true, you mean?'

'Perhaps. A lot of groups are looking for a way to target autoreactive cells – those are the ones that attack self tissues – but I think we're still a way from wiping out autoimmune disease.'

'So how do you think she'd have sold it to investors? Presumably they'd have medical consultants on hand to advise them?'

'I don't know,' Leighton admitted. 'But if you're still developing something you're unlikely to make the finer details public, so I suppose a lot of it comes down to how confidently you can pitch it. It certainly wouldn't be the first time someone succeeded in hyping up a concept that never became a reality. Elizabeth Holmes built a billion-dollar company on the back of a technology that didn't exist.'

'Who?'

'Elizabeth Holmes. The company was called Theranos. Holmes claimed to have come up with a way to run an incredible range of medical tests from just a drop of blood. She kept the charade up for years, in part by compartmentalising the company so that nobody else got the full picture, and by sacking people who challenged her over lies or inconsistencies.'

'That's interesting. Tony was working for the company until relatively recently. The CEO – Akiko – explained his departure away as being down to a difference in ideals, but she knows we can't ask for his side of the story.'

'Anyone else you could ask?'

'If so, we've yet to find them,' Lawrence responded. 'And it seems React8's employees are required to sign NDAs, so I'm guessing they're under strict instructions to keep schtum. What happened with the blood-testing company?'

'Oh, Holmes was charged with multiple counts of fraud. But Theranos is an extreme example. Ideas that come out of basic lab work might seem really promising, and then come up against barriers in the process of product development, meaning that projects launched with the best of intentions just don't work out. Against that backdrop, where there is intent to deceive it's probably hard to prove. And even if there is some evidence to support a case, it may be difficult to determine whether those involved did anything more than exaggerate their results and capabilities, and wind up believing the narrative they'd created.'

Lawrence nodded.

'If you don't randomise your studies, you also have some capacity to cherry pick your results, so the figures you can present aren't necessarily representative of what's going to happen in the clinic,' Leighton went on. 'One of the guys I did my master's with used to speculate about whether people ever stop cutting corners and fudging their results. He said that at GCSE level he'd assumed he'd do things properly at A-level, then at degree level, and so on. Given that he still wasn't doing things by the book for his master's thesis, he was questioning whether he'd finally go straight at PhD level, or when he was a postdoc with government or charity funding, or ever.'

'Did any of that resonate with you?'

'I didn't have any plans to do A-levels until I'd already finished my GCSEs,' Leighton admitted. 'And when I did, I can't say I thought very much further ahead.'

In fact, it was only thanks to his grandmother that he'd even completed his GCSEs. He had moved in with her – initially on a temporary basis – shortly after his sixteenth birthday. In the months after his elder brother's first conviction, life at home had gone from difficult to unbearable, and leaving school and getting a job had offered a way out. In response to an appeal from his mother, Meg Campbell had reluctantly agreed that, providing he kept out of trouble, he could stay with her for the remainder of the school year, no doubt assuming that his history of playing truant, joyriding and shoplifting was largely to blame for the strained relationship between him and his father. That she had

had no idea of the reality had become clear a couple of months later, when an asthma attack had landed him in A and E, and a concerned member of hospital staff had seen some of his scars and promptly called the police.

Having grown up in a community with a deep distrust of the law, and had it drummed into him that one of the worst things a person could do was snitch, Leighton hadn't been prepared to talk to anyone about his injuries. And, as he was, by then, an adult in the eyes of social services, there hadn't been much the authorities could do. Someone had clearly put Meg in the picture, however; she hadn't said a word to Leighton, but after the police had taken her aside her face had been white. A few days later, she had mentioned, casually, that she hadn't realised how much she had missed having company around the house, and added that, if he agreed to some ground rules, he would be welcome to stay indefinitely. After years of walking on eggshells day in, day out, he had been more than willing to abide by a curfew and a few other conditions in exchange for a home where the only thing he had to be mindful of was his language.

'How about in your job?' Lawrence asked.

'That's not really comparable. We're not pushing the boundaries of research, we're just running recognised tests.'

'But there must be times when you're hoping for one result over another.'

'Making that happen would be falsifying evidence. That's not shades of grey, that's black and white.'

'From where I'm standing it seems like just another point on a continuum of deception,' Lawrence observed, reaching for his glass. 'Even if the other end of that continuum involves self-deception as much as intent to deceive others.'

After several hours at his desk, Lawrence felt sorely in need of both a caffeine boost and a change of scene. Deciding to kill two birds with one stone by going for a walk to a local Italian café, he got to his feet and reached for his coat. He'd scarcely slipped one arm in when a knock came at his office door.

'Francine finally made it into Tony's computer,' Rebecca revealed, as he looked her way. 'And it turns out he was an extremely proficient and very busy hacker.' She presented him with several sheets of A4. A neatly typed list of what looked like company names ran the full length of the first page, and, taking it, he turned it over to find that the list continued on the reverse.

'He hacked into all of these?'

'Apparently so.'

'Bloody hell,' he raised his eyebrows, returning his coat to the stand in the corner. 'I wonder whether they'd have had any idea he was there?'

'Francine said it would depend on how they monitored online traffic, but at least some of them would have – although it's unlikely they would have been able to identify him, because hackers generally log in via the Tor network, which uses multiple servers and repeated encryption to conceal where an attack is coming from.'

'Do we have any idea what he was doing?'

'Francine said he doesn't appear to have been trying to install malware, so presumably he was intending to steal information rather than disrupt their systems. A lot of the companies are in biotech, so I'm guessing he was looking to find out what they were working on.'

'That sounds plausible,' Lawrence replied. 'I wonder whether he was doing that in addition to the research Akiko mentioned, or instead of?'

'My guess is instead of. His BSc was in natural sciences, which you'd think meant biology, but I called the university to check and it turns out to be a degree program encompassing a whole bunch of subjects. Weirdly, it includes computer science. That's got to be about as natural as a raspberry Slush Puppie.'

Lawrence smiled at this description. Elise was very partial to the icy turquoise drink, and although outlets selling it were mercifully few and far between, they seemed to turn up in the most unlikely places – like halfway up Mount Snowdon. The promise of a visit to the tiny café on the way back down had served as excellent motivation for the remainder of the climb.

'So Tony actually studied computer science,' he said.

'And maths.'

'Nothing that would have given him any grounding for interpreting immunology research.'

'No. And I don't think it's the easiest medical field to navigate. Leighton described it as *jargontastic*.'

'Chances are someone else was involved in evaluating Tony's findings from rival companies, then,' Lawrence observed. 'The question is whether that person was Akiko. Assuming she knew about it – and it seems hard to believe she didn't – he may have been trying to blackmail her in the wake of his departure from the company.'

'But if he'd exposed her, he would have been exposing his own activities, too,' Rebecca replied. 'The law would hardly have been on his side.'

'No, but she might not have wanted to risk calling his bluff.'

Rebecca nodded.

'Although someone must have helped her move the body.'

'Perhaps she and Tony weren't the only ones involved in whatever is going on at React8. Irene works in pharmaceuticals, presumably that has at least some crossover with immunology.'

'Good point. Let's see if we can pin both women down before the end of the day. But before we do that, can you sort out a warrant so we can get hold of Tony's company computer while we're down in Horsham?'

'Sure.'

'Did Francine find any sign of the photos and videos that were on the memory card the CSIs retrieved from his room?'

'Nada. I'm going through the contents of his hard drive again just in case, but so far all I've come across are the sort of friends and family pics most of us have.'

'How about his Internet search history?'

'He visited a few gay porn sites, but all legit stuff.'

'They must have been saved somewhere. Were there any memory cards or USB sticks in his bedroom?'

'There are none in our search inventory.'

Lawrence didn't miss the implication. Given how easily some novelty USB sticks might be missed – Jimmy had one disguised, very convincingly, as a double-ended eraser – he wondered whether it might be worth their sweeping Tony's room again.

'And there's one other thing.'

'What's that?'

'Tony didn't just hack into company computers. He had a nosy into some of his friends' machines, too.'

'He was spying on his friends?' Lawrence exclaimed. 'So much for being a nice guy.'

'I know,' Rebecca replied, with a lift of her eyebrows. 'And they weren't the only ones.'

'Who else was he snooping on?' Lawrence asked, guessing the answer before Rebecca even drew breath to reply.

'All four of his housemates.'

Six

Lawrence and Rebecca had a long wait to speak to Irene, and when chasing Xornex's reception staff had no visible effect Lawrence had demanded to speak to someone more senior. When Irene finally appeared, apologising profusely, she looked harassed, her long hair dishevelled. Lawrence wondered whether her explanation for keeping them waiting – that she had been running a time-critical experiment – was true. She looked as if she'd been doing something considerably more physical than lab work.

Lawrence got straight to the point as they sat down in the same small meeting room they had used on his previous visit, saying, 'How much do you know about React8's work?'

'Very little. Akiko keeps things pretty close to her chest.'

'Presumably you understand the ins and outs of the sort of work she does, though? You're both working in drug development.'

'That's like saying traffic cops must know all about counter-terrorism because it's all police work,' Irene returned, bluntly.

'Ok,' Lawrence acknowledged. 'Well could you give us some idea of the difference between what you and she are doing?'

'I work on small molecules, which are organic compounds small enough to get across cell membranes. Akiko's focus is on biologics, which are drugs based on living organisms or components of them.'

'Does anyone at Xornex work on biologics?'

'Yes.'

'And do you have access to that work?'

'Access?' Irene echoed, looking puzzled. 'What sort of access?'

'Access to the details of research projects. Files, experimental data, that kind of thing.'

'I've no idea,' she replied, seeming surprised by the question. 'I've never given it any thought.'

'So it's not something Akiko or Tony ever asked about?'

'No,' Irene said, her tone hardening. 'And if they had, I'd have told them where to go. I'm not in the habit of stealing intellectual property.'

'Were they?'

'I should hope not.'

'That doesn't answer my question.'

Irene shook her head. 'I really don't know. It's not something we ever discussed.'

'Did you not think it strange that Tony was working in drug discovery when he'd studied computer science at degree level?'

'I'm not sure I ever asked what he studied,' Irene admitted. 'But it doesn't strike me as particularly odd. Almost all businesses are reliant on IT these days, aren't they?'

'Yes, I suppose they are,' Lawrence agreed. 'However, Akiko told us a large part of Tony's job involved assessing new research being published in the field. Do you think someone would be able to do that without a background in immunology, or at least biology?'

Some seconds passed as Irene presumably weighed up her answer. 'I think it would be ambitious,' she said, at length.

'What we are in no doubt about is Tony's proficiency with computers. Is that something you were aware of?'

'I know he was good with them, but it wasn't something he talked a lot about. He did like the fact he could call people out if they were bullshitting, though.'

'How about hacking? Did he ever mention that?'

'He once mentioned catching a cheating ex by hacking into his email, but I didn't think he meant he'd actually hacked the guy's account, I figured he'd just guessed his password, or something.'

'So you weren't aware that he'd hacked into your machine?'

Irene's shock at this revelation was clear to see. She went to speak a couple of times before managing a coherent sentence. 'Why on earth would he have done that?'

'That's a good question,' Lawrence replied. 'Is there anything you can think of? Do you use the machine for work?'

'No. Most of what I do isn't the sort of work you can take home. My work email comes through to my phone, but my laptop's just for personal stuff. It's not even as if I'm particularly precious about it, if Tony had asked to borrow it I'd have lent it to him. Not that I'd ever have expected him to snoop, but –' she shrugged. Then, anger apparently taking over from shock, she added, 'I can't believe he'd do something so underhand! Devious bastard!' There was a momentary pause before she added, 'Sorry. I'm just at a loss to make sense of it. Not just because I don't know why he'd have bothered, but also because I can't imagine him doing something like that.' She paused. 'I trusted him, and all the while he was spying on me. That's really upsetting.'

'Martina mentioned that you were quite upset earlier this week, as well,' Lawrence went on.

'I think all of us were pretty upset.'

'I'm talking about before you received the news about Tony.'

'Oh. The other morning. Yes.'

'What was that had upset you?'

'Hormones,' Irene responded, shortly, averting her eyes.

'Martina seemed to think it was the wrong time of your cycle for that.'

'She told *you* that?' Irene exclaimed. 'Jesus.'

'Was she wrong?'

There was an awkward silence. Irene kept her eyes focused on the table that stood between them. At length, she drew a deep breath. 'I was late, ok?' She admitted, her voice wavering slightly. 'I thought I was pregnant, and my head was all over the place. I didn't know what I was going to do. I didn't even know what I *wanted* to do.' She swallowed, finally raising her gaze to meet his. 'And Martina doesn't agree with abortion, so I could hardly talk it over with her, could I?'

On Rebecca and Lawrence's second visit to React8, Akiko didn't receive them in her office. Instead, they were shown into a spotless modern laboratory, all gleaming surfaces and high-tech equipment, with glass screens partitioning the room into sections and huge ventilation pipes traversing the ceiling. Akiko was the only person in the room, and was in the process of transferring tiny amounts of liquid from a bottle to a row of tiny sample tubes using a bulky pipette not unlike those Rebecca had often seen Leighton using. She was wearing a white coat and safety goggles, but her long hair was loose over her shoulders, leading Rebecca to suspect her decision to receive them in the lab was more for show than because she was working on anything particularly important.

Seeing them approaching, she set the pipette down on the bench and stepped away from it, snapping off her rubber gloves and pushing the safety glasses up onto her head.

'If you'd called ahead, I could have worked around your visit,' she said, turning around and leaning against the bench.

Rebecca wondered whether their arrival had really come as a surprise; it was quite possible that Irene had already updated Akiko on their earlier visit to Xornex. 'We'll try not to take up too much of your time,' she replied, leaning against the opposite bench. 'We just have a few questions about a trial we gather you were planning to run. From what we've heard, it seems Tony was concerned about it because he didn't think you had enough data to proceed. Is that what led to his departure from the company?'

'No,' Akiko said, shortly.

'Really? It sounds as if he felt pretty strongly about it.'

'He did, and in the end he talked me round.'

'So you agreed to delay the trial?' Rebecca asked, trying to keep the scepticism out of her tone. There was no way to verify the claim, and Rebecca felt certain Akiko was taking advantage of that.

'Yes.'

'Where was Tony planning to get the additional data from?'

Akiko frowned. 'Sorry?'

'When we last spoke to you, you said his job involved keeping on top of what was going on in the field. In terms of the trial, what sort of data would he have been looking for in the literature?'

'It wasn't his job to look for the sort of data we needed for the trial,' Akiko responded. 'That would have been from work we're doing in house.'

'But from what we've heard, he asked you for more time to allow him to gather data.'

'Well whoever told you that must have misunderstood.'

'It wasn't data he was hoping to get from your competitors, then?'

'What?' Akiko exclaimed. 'You think he left React8 to be a spy?'

'Did he?'

'No!'

'No, I didn't think he did,' Rebecca replied. 'Because he was spying very effectively whilst remaining in your employ, wasn't he?'

'What?'

'We have evidence that Tony was hacking into the computer systems of other biotech companies. But given that he studied computer science, not immunology, someone else must have been reviewing the information he collected. Presumably that was you.'

'I know nothing about that.'

'So who do you suppose was involved?'

'I haven't the first idea, but I very much doubt it was anyone here. We have a very successful research program of our own.'

'What puzzles me is how Tony was able to do the job you described to us when he had no training in biology. I've had a look at some immunology papers, and I struggled to make head or tail of them. How could Tony have known enough to pick out the important advancements?'

'He was interested in the subject, so he'd read up on it.'

'And you employed him on the basis of that?' Rebecca responded, incredulously.

'It's not like I was taking a shot in the dark,' Akiko countered. 'I already knew Tony. He was a bright guy, and he was enthusiastic. That goes a long way.'

Rebecca didn't imagine it went nearly far enough. 'Can you show us some examples of his work? Notes on research papers he'd read, perhaps?'

'He didn't really make notes – he just printed out papers he thought I ought to see. Generally we discussed the work face-to-face.'

Rebecca was tempted to remark on how convenient it seemed that there was no way in which to verify Akiko's version of events, but instead said, 'We have a warrant to take Tony's work computer. If you could show us where it is, we'll get everything together and then get out of your way.'

'Of course,' the woman replied, pushing off from the bench and making for the door. 'But I think you're wasting your time. I've nothing to hide.'

Rebecca suspected the analysis of the machine *would* turn out to be a waste of time, but not for the reason Akiko had just given. Even innocent people tended to have concerns about handing over electronic devices, and Akiko's blythe reaction to the request indicated she was confident there was nothing for them to find on Tony's computer. Most likely the two of them had agreed that Tony would confine the hacking to his own machine, thus absolving the company of any responsibility should someone succeed in tracing him. Rebecca wondered whether he had ever even used his work computer. That was a question Francine would be able to answer, but precisely what information Tony had gathered from the companies he had infiltrated – and where that information was now – they might never know.

*****

Lawrence walked into the house just in time to hear a door slam upstairs. This was followed, moments later, by a bang from the kitchen, and he looked in to find Katie spooning rice out of a saucepan and into a Tupperware container.

'What was that about?'

'White carbs,' Katie responded, shortly, setting the spoon and the saucepan down.

'I beg your pardon?'

Katie repeated herself, turning around and leaning against the worktop before adding, 'Potatoes, pasta, et cetera.'

'What about them?'

'Madam's refusing to eat them. Apparently her gymnastics coach is giving out nutritional advice, now. Those girls don't have an ounce of fat to share between them, and the bloody woman's telling them to watch what they eat! I can't believe she could be so irresponsible! She'll be getting a piece of my mind first thing tomorrow!'

Lawrence nodded. His daughter, Elise, was in her first term at secondary school, and had made the gymnastics squad with little difficulty, but the team's competitive ethos had come as something of a shock after the relaxed approach taken at her primary school. And the competition didn't extend only to other teams; within the squad, the girls also seemed to be in competition with one another.

'Maybe it might be an idea not to make too big a thing of it,' he suggested.

'Are you serious?' Katie demanded. 'That woman has no right to –'

'With Elise,' Lawrence stopped her.

Katie sighed. 'Maybe. I don't know.'

'How's Jim?'

'He's playing a video game loosely based on Macbeth. As the play is one of their GCSE texts, he says it's practically homework.'

Lawrence smiled, thinking that Shakespeare's floating dagger and itinerant forest could have been written for a computer game. He turned back towards the hallway, saying, 'I'll just pop up to say hello and get changed, and then I'll see if I can track down a copy of *Police Quest*. Given that it's practically work, I don't see why we shouldn't play it in the office.'

Reaching the top of the stairs, Lawrence tapped on his daughter's bedroom door before easing it open and looking in. Elise was sitting at the end of her bed, her back against the wall and her knees drawn up, thumbs skittering over the keyboard of her smartphone. Until recently, she had owned only a basic phone – mainly in case of emergency – but Lawrence and Katie had reluctantly agreed she could have a *proper* phone when she started secondary school. Lawrence would have dearly loved to further delay the moment, but there had been no getting away from the fact that almost every other child in the year would have a smartphone. Besides, there wasn't really anything she could do with it that she couldn't already do on a computer, and, thanks to the march of the digital age, she had needed one of those for her schoolwork before her age was even into double figures.

'Hello ladybird.'

Elise looked up, raising a hand to flick her long strawberry blonde hair off her face. 'Hi Dad.'

'Did you have a good day?'

She shrugged. 'It was ok.'

'What are you up to?'

'Talking to Libby. Her mum's taking us ice skating at the weekend.'

Lawrence nodded. The hours Elise seemed to spend messaging her school friends reminded him of the long calls his sister, Carla, used to make, and their father's incredulity that she could possibly have anything left to say to her friends when they had spent all day together at school. Lawrence had resolved not to pass similar comment when he became a parent, but his determination to keep his mouth shut didn't stop the thoughts from coming to mind.

A movement in the corner of the room caught his eye, and he looked around to see Elise's hamster sitting on the pillow at the head of the bed, cheek pouches bulging, chewing on something gripped between her front paws.

'What's Ginger doing out of her cage?'

Elise glanced in the hamster's direction, her small exclamation of surprise indicating that she had forgotten the animal was loose. 'Oh, it's ok, she comes if I call her,' she replied, unconcernedly, holding a hand out towards the rodent. Ginger immediately scampered down the bed, undermining any argument Lawrence might have made about the risk of her running off and getting lost in the house.

'That won't stop her gnawing holes in your duvet again, will it?'

'I won't let her do that this time,' Elise responded, running a finger down the hamster's back.

'Well let's not take any chances,' Lawrence suggested, leaning to scoop the animal up and turning to deposit her in her tiered cage, ignoring his daughter's roll of her eyes.

'If you let me have a puppy you wouldn't have to worry,' Elise observed. 'Dogs don't need cages.'

'Neither do daughters, and I worry about you far more than I do Ginger,' Lawrence replied, with a smile, leaning to plant a kiss on the top of her head. 'Adding a dog to the mix might just finish me off.'

'How much do you reckon you spend per month on groceries?' Rebecca asked, as she and Leighton walked back to his flat from the local pub. 'Ballpark.'

'Depends. Do groceries include Chinese?'

Rebecca smiled.

'In all honesty, I couldn't tell you without looking at my credit card statements,' Leighton admitted. 'Why d'you ask?'

'I'm trying to make sense of something,' Rebecca replied. 'Tony paid Martina a chunk of money recently, which she said he'd lent to her after she'd run up debts getting carried away shopping. But the details of her financials came through just as I was finishing up, and although she does quite a bit of shopping on websites that come under the umbrella of women's fashion, she's also been spending hundreds of pounds a month in supermarkets.'

'Expensive taste in wine?' Leighton suggested. 'Or some weird raw-food diet involving punnet upon punnet of blueberries, steak tartare and chia-seed drinks?'

'Ugh,' Rebecca responded, pulling a face. 'I don't understand how anyone can stomach those, it's like drinking frogspawn.'

'Well that's frogspawn on toast off the breakfast menu, then,' he joked. There was a brief pause before he went on, 'How about scratch cards? I can't buy one of those without going back for at least another five.'

'Yeah, I wondered about that, but none of the entries on the statements are round amounts. Alcohol's also a possibility, but we've seen and heard nothing to indicate that she has a problem. And I can see how people on a really tight budget could struggle not to overspend on food, but blowing hundreds you can't afford in a matter of weeks seems like a different ballgame.'

Leighton nodded thoughtfully. 'Bulimia?' He offered, at length. 'Or binge eating disorder? The compulsion to binge could easily override the issue of affordability. And on top of the cost of food, there could well be things like laxatives and weight-loss supplements. Plus if you're losing or gaining weight and you need to dress smartly for work, new clothes might be a necessity. Eating disorders can get very expensive.'

'I'd never considered that,' Rebecca admitted.

'Not a very likely motive for murder, though.'

'No, Rebecca agreed, as they turned up the path towards Leighton's front door. 'But it helps to rule things out.'

'Maybe one of her friends might –'

'Well, if it ain't the Artful Dodger,' a voice interrupted from behind them. Rebecca looked around to see a lanky man with three-day-old ginger stubble and a black beany hat pulled down to his eyebrows leaning against the gatepost.

'Kai,' Leighton responded, coolly, after a momentary pause. 'Long time.'

'Ain't it just?' Kai came back. 'And you seem to be a bit of a celebrity these days. Me mam says she saw your picture on the telly yesterday.'

'Your mam still lives five doors down from mine, she saw me in person last week,' Leighton returned, irritably. 'What do you want?'

'That's not very welcoming.'

'Don't piss me about. You can't have come to reminisce about the good old days, we didn't have any. So either you want something, or Tom wants something. Which is it?'

'Are you no' in touch with him yourself?'

'What do you want?' Leighton persisted.

Kai didn't answer the question, saying instead, 'It don't seem like the papers know a whole lot about you.'

'Maybe they're not very interested.'

'Oh I doubt that,' Kai replied. 'I'm sure they'd love to hear about some of your more alternative skills.' He smirked. 'I expect your bosses would, an' all.'

'Don't threaten me.'

'Just an observation.'

'I'm not paying you to keep your mouth shut,' Leighton informed him, shortly. 'So if that's what you came for, you're out of luck.'

Kai shrugged. 'The papers'll pay me if you won't.'

'You do know you can get fourteen years for blackmail, don't you?' Rebecca put in, presenting her warrant card. Kai did a double take and took a step back before looking up from the card to Rebecca, then back to Leighton.

'I'd love to see your old man's face when he finds out you're screwing a cop.'

'I really couldn't give a shit what he thinks,' Leighton retorted. 'And I think we're done here. Good luck finding anything more than hearsay to take to the papers. Now fuck off!'

Seven

'Charming individual,' Rebecca remarked, sardonically, as she closed Leighton's front door behind herself.

'Yeah,' Leighton replied, carefully easing his left glove off.

'Is he a friend of Tom's?'

'I don't know. He used to be, twenty years back.'

'Was the Artful Dodger your nickname in those days?'

'In certain circles.'

'I'm surprised Tom and his friends were familiar with Dickens.'

This succeeded in drawing a reluctant smile from Leighton. 'They weren't the ones came up with it.'

'So who was?'

There was a pause before he admitted, 'One of the local plod.'

Rebecca raised her eyebrows. A couple of seconds passed before he yielded to her expectant look, saying, 'A bunch of us were hanging around in an old playground and they'd come to quiz us about one misdemeanour or another. I made some smart remark and he told me I should watch out, because even the Artful Dodger's luck ran out in the end.'

'And did yours?'

'No. But I get the feeling it's about to catch up with me.' He sighed. 'Probably deservedly. But if I'm going to be held to account I'd rather it wasn't to the advantage of an arsehole like Kai.' He turned towards the kitchen. 'D'you want a drink?'

'G and T?'

'Gin I can do,' he replied. 'Tonic –' he opened the fridge door and regarded the contents for a moment before concluding, 'Not so much. Would gin and orange do?'

'Sure. Thanks.'

Taking the carton of juice from the fridge, he elbowed the door shut and made for the cupboard containing the glasses. Rebecca hovered in the doorway for a moment before deciding to make herself useful by stacking the plastic takeaway containers littering the draining board.

'You don't have to tidy up after me,' Leighton objected.

'I'm not doing it because I *have* to,' Rebecca responded. Then, catching sight of the bowls in the corner of the room, she changed the subject with, 'Has Pandora shown up yet?'

'Nope.'

'Have you tried calling local vets?'

'I got her microchipped, so if she'd turned up at a vet's I'd have heard about it,' Leighton replied, before using his teeth to remove the cork from the Bloom gin.

Rebecca tried to think of something else to suggest, guessing he was a lot more concerned about the cat's absence than he was letting on. Leighton poured a generous measure of the gin into a glass, then flinched as he righted the bottle and lost his grip. The bottle took a chunk out of the tumbler as it landed, and Leighton made a grab for it, catching his fingers on the exposed glass as he did so.

'Bollocks!' He cursed, setting the gin down and making a start on gathering up the pieces of the tumbler, then stopping as the cuts began to bleed and reaching for a tea towel to wrap around his hand.

Rebecca moved to continue the job of collecting up the glass, glancing around to see whether there were any copies of the local paper to hand that she might wrap it in, but Leighton stopped her.

'I've got it.'

'Just sit down and let me do it,' Rebecca replied, firmly.

'I don't need you to mother me!' He returned. 'I can manage!'

'Repeatedly burning and cutting yourself is not managing! And nor is living on junk food because you can't cook anything! I'm not sure what –'

'I don't need a fucking lecture on healthy eating!' Leighton returned, angrily. 'I am already perfectly well aware it's not good for me to eat an entire bag of doughnuts inside ten minutes! Just give me a fucking break, will you?'

He left the room before Rebecca had a chance to reply. Moments later, she heard the front door slam behind him. She sighed, heading for the living room, where she flopped down onto the sofa.

It shouldn't have come as a surprise that he would be sensitive about his weight, given some of the cruel taunts his father came out with. During Rebecca's recent visit, Glenn had described the fortnight Leighton had spent in intensive care that spring as *the best diet he's tried yet*. Leighton had shown no visible reaction to the jibe, and Rebecca had marvelled that he managed to go on being civil to the man.

Lorna had been more obviously affected by the remark, but she clearly knew better than to say anything. From what Rebecca had seen of Lorna and Leighton's relationship earlier in the year, it had been evident that, emotionally, Lorna was very reliant on her son, and Rebecca wondered at what stage she had begun leaning on him. Maybe she always had done, and that was why Leighton was so good at looking after other people and so reluctant to let anyone return the favour. Perhaps looking after himself was all he had ever really known.

*****

Jakob watched Irene's eyelids fluttering as she dreamed, much of her face hidden by her hair, her hands tucked beneath the pillow. She always seemed to sleep with them in the same strange position, almost as if she was resting her head on them. How she didn't end up with pins and needles was anyone's guess.

His gaze travelled down to meet the bulbous eyes of the multicoloured gecko tattooed on her right shoulder, which was peeping out from beneath the duvet. Not for the first time, he found himself wondering whether the artist responsible for the inking had mistaken one group of lizards for another, and erroneously given the animal the garb of a rainbow chameleon. Of course, one might contend that accuracy didn't matter where art was concerned, but Jakob wasn't of that mind. Fantasy, be it in literature, film or design, often seemed to be merely an excuse for lazy composition; a creative pick'n'mix with an *anything goes* mentality. The fundamentals of science fiction narratives were often similarly discordant, and Tony's precious Star Wars was a perfect example. Despite its futuristic setting and fantastic feats of space travel, many of the characters' wardrobes looked to have been borrowed from Medieval peasants, while their terrestrial living quarters could have come straight out of Biblical Damascus. The whole thing was absurd.

He turned his eyes to the digital clock on his Bose sound system, wishing they had spent the night in Irene's room rather than his own. She had already voiced her intention to call in sick that day, so he had no excuse to wake her up. There was next to no chance of their having morning sex – you were lucky if you could even engage Irene in conversation before she'd had a coffee, and after the previous evening she would probably have a hangover to boot. Given the absence of a good reason to stay in bed, he would have liked to make a start on editing the video footage from the previous day's filming, but he couldn't do that with her around.

He reached for his phone. The only new messages were communications between other members of a squash-related WhatsApp group. He dismissed them unread and returned the device to the shelf at his bedside before sitting up and drawing the covers aside. He might as well get up.

As he got to his feet, Irene mumbled something, and he looked around to see that her eyes were half open.

'What was that?'

When she replied, he was fairly certain her words weren't a repeat of whatever she had said previously. 'I had that dream again,' she revealed, her voice wavering. 'About Tony.'

Jakob sighed. He could do without tears this morning. Sitting back down, he reached for the hand that had emerged from beneath the pillow. 'The reason you're having crazy dreams is because you're going to bed hammered,' he said. 'You promised me you'd dial it back.'

She swallowed. 'I know. I'm sorry.'

'Try to find something to do today so you're not just sitting around getting upset about things you can't change.'

Irene nodded slightly. 'We could walk down to the common later, if you're not busy?' She suggested, hopefully, after a moment.

'I'm working. I've got a load of video editing to do, and at three I need to be at the British Library to meet a historian from Portsmouth University.'

'What about?'

'Memento mori.'

'Memento what?'

'Mori. Portraits of the dead.'

Irene pulled away, her eyebrows contracting into a frown. 'Is that supposed to be funny?'

'No. It's research. Postmortem photography was big in Victorian times.'

'For real?'

'Yes.'

'Sounds grim.'

'Maybe, but it's the kind of macabre thing people are fascinated by, so it has great TV potential.'

'Does it? Do people really want to see photos of ancient autopsies?'

'It's postmortem as in after death. The pictures aren't grisly. It's often not immediately obvious that the people were dead, and in some cases there are other people posing with them.'

Irene grimaced. 'Oh that's horrible.'

Jakob shrugged. 'People weren't so squeamish about death in those days. Queen Victoria practically turned mourning into an art form. The pictures were – I don't know – like a memorial, I guess. Photography was expensive, so people didn't necessarily have any other pictures of their loved ones. Particularly children. And a lot of children died in infancy then.'

'Even so.'

'One of the most interesting things is the modern myths that have grown up around it,' Jakob went on. 'There are loads of historical pictures that people are falsely touting as memento mori. And even a few that have been photoshopped to make them look like the bodies are decomposing.'

Irene screwed her face up in disgust. 'You're making me feel sick. Can we talk about something else?'

'Sorry,' Jakob offered, with a rueful smile. 'I'm going to make some coffee.' He moved to stand. 'Would you like one?'

'Please.'

Jakob made for the door, hoping a caffeine hit might be sufficient to coax Irene out of bed. If it didn't, he would have to come up with somewhere else to go to process the footage he had gathered on his most recent shoot. Given the subject matter, it was hardly the sort of job he could do on a laptop in Starbucks.

When Rebecca's mobile had rung shortly after midday, she had hoped the call might be from Leighton. She had heard nothing from him since the previous evening, having opted not to wait around for however long it took him to cool off and return home. Whilst cleaning up the broken glass in the kitchen, she had come to the conclusion that the best way to convey her thoughts might be in a format he couldn't interrupt, so she had written him a note before heading back to Highgate. She was starting to fear that the silence that had followed her ultimatum – that he either let her into more than just his bed, or they call it a day – might be a response in itself.

In the event, the call had been from one of the crime-scene investigators, who was ringing to report some thoroughly unremarkable test results. She terminated the call with a sigh and returned her attention to the photograph occupying the most part of her laptop screen. It showed an unidentified mark on one of Tony's calves, a small half-moon shape with teeth at either end of the flat portion, almost like the head of a tiny spanner. She was regarding it closely when a voice filtered through her thoughts, and she glanced up to see Jamie standing beside her desk with a large box in his arms.

'Sorry?'

'Where d'you want this?' He asked.

'What is it?'

'I haven't a clue. It was over there, with the post.' He tipped his head in the direction of the mail tray.

'Oh. Ok – just put it down here.' She indicated the floor beside her chair. Jamie obliged, and, as he straightened up, she pointed to the photograph on the screen. 'Any idea what might have caused this?'

He leaned in for a closer look, and regarded it in silence for several seconds before saying, 'The back end of a cam bolt, maybe?'

'A what?'

'One of those little metal widgets you use to bolt things together at right angles. You get them in flat-pack furniture. The other side has a Phillips head, so you can screw it in.'

'Oh, I know,' Rebecca nodded. The fixings had probably been in every piece of furniture she'd ever assembled, but because instruction leaflets tended to be largely pictorial, it had never occurred to her that they had a name. Even as she was thinking this, it struck her as daft; everything had a name.

Jamie made for his own desk, and Rebecca minimised the image. Given how ubiquitous cam bolts were, she doubted the mark on Tony's leg was going to lead them anywhere unexpected. With a sigh, she turned her attention to the box Jamie had just delivered.

It had clearly come from an external source, and, given that she had no recollection of ordering anything, she wondered whether it was something unmemorably domestic. A couple of her friends got excited about things like soup makers and steam mops, but, as far as Rebecca was concerned, they were no more desirable than toilet brushes and J cloths.

Reaching for a pair of scissors, she set about scoring the tape that secured the box. She prised the cardboard flaps apart to find herself looking at a bundle of broccoli, carrots, sweet peppers and leafy greens, and after a moment's confusion realised that they had been gathered into a bouquet. An attached card named the company responsible for the arrangement as The Veggie Florist, and she opened it to find a printed note that read simply, 'Sorry for being a twat x'.

She smiled.

'What have you got there?'

Rebecca glanced up in surprise to find Lawrence standing a couple of feet away. 'Long story,' she replied, with a lift of her eyebrows, closing the box.

'Any news on Tony's work computer?'

'Yes and no,' Rebecca replied. 'I heard back from Francine about half an hour ago, but she found nothing remotely compromising.'

Lawrence sighed.

'In fact, there wasn't much on it full stop. Francine said it had often gone unused for weeks at a time.'

'Is it possible Akiko gave you the wrong machine?'

'I thought of that, but Francine said if it was a decoy it must have been used as one for a while, because there's no sign of any historical change to the login details.'

'Presumably, then, he did most of his work – if you can call it that – on his own machine.'

'And he probably did it from home. Otherwise there would have been a risk of the company being linked to his activities via its IP address.'

'Well we should be able to get an answer on that one way or another by talking to some of the other employees at React8,' Lawrence observed. 'What about his work email account? He must have had one.'

'Francine's going to let us have everything to look through, but it doesn't sound as if many of the communications are likely to be of much interest. She said it's mainly group messages and meeting invites.'

'And I'll bet there's not much in the way of the literature he was supposed to be reviewing on the hard drive or in email attachments.'

'I'll let you know as soon as I do.'

'Thanks.'

'I've also had a call from Clive Nicholls,' Rebecca went on, adding, when Lawrence's eyebrows contracted towards a frown, 'That friend of Martina's who we couldn't get hold of earlier in the week. Apparently he's been out of the country. He's back now, so I made an appointment for three o'clock.'

'Good work. Anything else?'

'No. Although I'm about to buzz out for a sandwich, if you want anything?'

'I'm all right, thanks,' Lawrence replied, turning towards his office.

'Ok. I won't be long.' Rebecca got to her feet and pulled on her coat before reaching for her mobile to write Leighton a message to thank him for the edible bouquet. No sooner had she hit send, she thought of something else to say, and tapped out a quick one-liner before tossing the phone into her bag.

'Stir fry @ your place tonight?'

Rebecca and Lawrence arrived at Clive's flat to find him dressed in an airtex t-shirt, shorts and trainers, presumably planning to head out for a run upon their departure. Lawrence hoped he might get home in time to do the same. For years he had tended to exercise early in the morning, when the chances of work getting in the way were relatively low, but he had changed tack since the summer because it greatly increased the chances his son would join him. Until a few months earlier, it hadn't been particularly difficult to get Jimmy up in time for a run before Lawrence had to leave for work, but over the long summer holiday he had slipped into the habit of sleeping late into the morning, and it was now a challenge just to get him out of bed in time for school.

'I gather you're an old friend of Martina's,' Lawrence said, once he had introduced himself and Rebecca. 'Did you know Tony well?'

'Not really. I saw him from time to time – Tina often brought him along to meet ups in lieu of a date – but we never got to know each other on more than a superficial level.'

'Did you see much of him at the party?'

'I suppose. I was there, he was there –' Clive shrugged.

'And how did he seem?'

'Earlier in the evening he was fairly chilled, but later on he was in a right mood. He gave Tina a hard time over something, and then he really laid into Jakob.'

'Do you think his temper – or the arguments – could have had anything to do with something that came up during the game of *I have never*?'

'I've no idea, I took that starting as my cue to go out for a smoke,' Clive responded. 'I've not been seeing Trish, my girlfriend, long, and I can do without her hearing about what I got up to before we met.'

'Did she go outside with you?'

He shook his head. 'No. She was passed out on a sofa by then. She was so hammered she'd already fallen in a bush by about half nine.'

'If she was that drunk, why were you concerned about her learning anything from the game?'

'Not everyone was out of it. And some people have big mouths.'

'Is that a dig at anyone in particular?'

Clive gave a non-committal shrug.

'So that's a yes,' Lawrence concluded. 'Who at the party did you not trust to keep things to themselves?' Then, when Clive hesitated, he added, 'We've no reason to divulge who told us what where basic background information is concerned.'

There was a brief pause before he said, 'Well Candice couldn't keep a secret if her life depended on it.'

'And how about Martina and her housemates?'

'I only know a couple of them. Besides Tina.'

'Perhaps you could answer the question as far as you can?'

He sighed. 'Tina's the soul of discretion. But Tony didn't always think before he spoke. Especially after a few drinks.'

'Could you give us any examples?'

'Well, one time he mentioned something really embarrassing one of his friends had done in front of a guy she had a massive crush on,' Clive replied. 'And on another occasion, he let slip that a mate was tracking his partner's phone without their knowledge.'

'That sounds like the kind of secret that needs to be told,' Rebecca remarked.

'Yeah, maybe. But it didn't seem like that was why he brought it up.'

'Do you recall any of what was said during his arguments with Martina or Jakob?' Lawrence asked.

'Not a lot. But I think with Jakob it might have been something to do with his work.'

'What gave you that impression?'

'Tony was going on about the kinds of films Jakob makes. And he kept saying *I know what you did to Harvey*.'

'Have you any idea who Harvey is, or was?'

'None. I don't think I've ever met anyone called Harvey. It sounds like the kind of name you'd give a cat.'

'And what was Jakob's response to that?'

'He told Tony he hadn't a clue what he was on about.'

Lawrence nodded. 'Anything else you can remember?'

'Other than Tony calling Jakob a *twisted fuck*, no.'

Lawrence's eyebrows rose. 'Strong words. What do you suppose that was in reference to?'

'I dunno, but he's made some pretty dark films. You could certainly describe necrophilia and cannibalism as twisted. And I know the fact you're making a documentary about something doesn't necessarily mean you're into it yourself, but –' Clive paused, wrinkling his nose. 'You must have some interest in it, mustn't you?' It seemed this was a rhetorical question, because, after a moment, he went on, 'And, arguably, you could question whether anyone should be documenting that kind of depraved behaviour for public consumption at all.'

Lawrence returned to the office mid-afternoon to find Leighton lounging in a chair chatting to Eva. They both looked his way as he approached, and Leighton greeted him with a smile and a cheerful, 'All right?'

'Twice in two days,' Lawrence remarked. 'Anyone would think you were missing us.'

'Well I'd hate to deprive you of my company, and I had a meeting with Max, so I was walking practically past the door,' Leighton responded, with a grin, getting to his feet and following Lawrence into his office. 'How's it going?'

'Good question,' Lawrence responded, slipping his jacket off and moving to hang it up. 'At the moment I'd have to say nowhere fast.'

'I've got some pictures that might be of interest,' Leighton said, sitting in one of the chairs on the near side of the desk.

'Martina tagged Tony in a Facebook post a week after he was last seen. And although –'

'Hold it,' Lawrence stopped him, raising a hand in emphasis. 'Much as I value your input, officially you're not a part this investigation, and I can't risk having you compromising it by digging around without authorisation.'

'Relax,' Leighton responded, sounding mildly exasperated. 'I didn't go digging. It's a public Facebook post. Anyone can see it.'

Lawrence sighed. Regardless of the Facebook post's availability, the fact Leighton had been looking at it in the first place meant he must have been following the investigation, at least loosely. And, if he was doing that, there was no knowing where curiosity might lead him. Lawrence wondered where Leighton had been getting his information from, guessing he probably still had access to the pathology unit's systems and making a mental note to ask Max.

'Ok, but going forwards you need to check with me before you go looking into anything,' he said, sitting at his desk. 'Clear?'

'Crystal,' Leighton replied. 'Anyway, Martina's Facebook. When you first look at the photos she's posted, it appears as if they were all taken at the same time, but I don't think they were.' He eased his mobile phone out of his inside jacket pocket with his right thumb and forefinger, then set the device down on the edge of Lawrence's desk to use the touch screen. His fingers were a patchwork of different pinks, and in places the skin looked tight and shiny, particularly over the swollen knuckles of the middle and ring fingers of his left hand. What were presumably surgical scars ran down the sides of a couple of his digits. Lawrence averted his eyes as Leighton glanced up.

'I've sent you an email.'

Lawrence unlocked his laptop and pulled up Outlook. He had to refresh his inbox three times before the message appeared, and opened it to find four photographs attached. In one, Tony was glancing up from digging a flowerbed; another depicted him and Martina standing side by side on the lawn, leaning on a large fork and spade, respectively. The third and fourth images featured a cold frame in position on the original flowerbed, in the latter instance with Martina kneeling beside it.

'Tony isn't pictured with the cold frame, which the post describes as having been put in that day. Martina's wearing the same clothes in these two pictures –' he indicated. 'But I think they were taken on different days.'

Lawrence regarded the photos closely, but nothing immediately stood out. By the time the cold frame had been installed, all there was to see besides the soil around it and the fence beyond was a cheerful-looking garden gnome, and the picture of Martina and Tony was taken from a different angle altogether and didn't contain any part of the flowerbed. He turned his eyes to his colleague. 'What am I not seeing?'

Leighton indicated the neighbouring house, which was partially obscured by scaffolding, in the background of the picture featuring Martina and Tony, then traced a forefinger over the reflection of the top corner of the house in the cold frame glass. 'No scaffolding.'

'Good spot.'

'I've only got copies of the images so I can't check the metadata for the dates they were taken, but hopefully someone can retrieve that information from Facebook. If not, it shouldn't be hard to find out what dates the scaffolding was in situ.'

Lawrence nodded. 'I'll get someone onto that. Thank you.'

'You're welcome,' Leighton replied, flashing a smile as he moved to stand.

'But I meant what I said earlier. You need to leave this alone. The last thing we need is for a perfectly good case to be thrown out by the courts simply because you've been meddling in it without authorisation.'

'Yeah, yeah, I copy,' Leighton replied, with a small salute, before turning to go. At the same moment, Rebecca appeared in the doorway, her mobile phone in her hand.

'Apparently, Maya's given name is actually Mary Ann,' she announced, without preamble. 'And one Mary Ann Onslow was arrested the year before last for assaulting her then-boyfriend with a stainless steel ladle.'

'Was she now?'

'He wound up with a serious eye injury. It didn't go any further, because he claimed it was an accident, and there wasn't enough evidence to bring charges.' Rebecca tapped her mobile against her free hand. 'But given that they're no longer a couple, it could be worth our while talking to him. He might be prepared to tell us what actually happened.'

Eight

Richard Manning worked at a gym in Hackney, and from the size of his biceps clearly spent a considerable amount of time lifting weights. Rebecca found herself wondering whether his reluctance to make a statement against Maya had stemmed from the fear he might face ridicule from friends or family over having been attacked by a pretty size-ten blonde. It was a problem she had come across more than once during her time in uniform, and wasn't helped by the fact that men were often afraid to defend themselves against domestic violence for fear of being labelled the abuser.

Having shown Rebecca and Lawrence into an unoccupied room that the sign on the door named as a physiotherapy treatment suite, Richard perched on the padded bench, glancing towards Rebecca and holding out a hand to offer her the lone chair parked beside a console table. Not wanting to wind up too far below his eyeline, she chose to remain standing, and leaned against the table, saying, 'We'd like to talk to you about Mary Ann Onslow. You might know her as Maya.'

Richard's dark eyebrows drew together suspiciously. 'What about her?'

'I understand you and she were involved in a physical altercation a couple of years ago.'

'So?'

'Could you tell us how that came about?'

'I didn't want to talk about it then, and I don't want to talk about it now,' he responded, shortly.

'We appreciate it's an unwelcome topic, but we're investigating a suspicious death, and your experience may –'

'Suspicious?' Richard interrupted, sounding incredulous. 'You're not suggesting she's killed somebody? You can't be serious!'

'Why not?' Rebecca asked. 'By all accounts you were lucky not to lose the sight in your left eye when she assaulted you. If someone can do that in the heat of the moment, chances are they're also capable of doing a lot worse.'

'She didn't assault me. It was an accident.'

'An accident that saw your neighbour call the police to report –' Rebecca checked her notes. 'Banging, crashing and screaming.' She raised her gaze. 'That doesn't sound very accidental to me.'

Richard sighed. 'She threw a few things at the kitchen wall and one hit me as it bounced off. It's not like she was aiming for me.'

'She must have been pretty angry to be throwing things.'

'It wasn't all on her. We had a row.'

'About what?'

'None of your business.'

'Your neighbour's account mentioned the football,' Rebecca replied, guessing she might have more luck with an indirect approach. 'What, were you fighting over the TV remote, or something?'

'Of course not.'

'So?'

There was a long pause before Richard yielded. 'I play five-a-side on Sunday mornings. I'd mixed my days up and said I could go to a breakfast thing because I thought it was on a Saturday, then realised I couldn't.'

'She got that angry over an honest mistake? Was that how she generally reacted when you rowed?'

'No,' Richard countered, too quickly to be convincing.

'Are you sure about that?'

He shrugged. 'Occasionally she threw things when she was angry. She's a passionate girl.'

'I suppose that's one way of putting it, but it's not the word I'd use,' Rebecca observed.

Richard didn't respond.

'How long were you and Maya together?'

'Six months, give or take.'

'And why did the relationship end?'

'It just wasn't working.'

'Nothing to do with her disproportionate response to arguments?'

'If we hadn't been arguing so much in the first place, that wouldn't have been a problem.'

Thinking of Maya's description of Martina as her *best friend* and Ross's use of a similar expression to describe Martina's friendship with Tony, Rebecca asked, 'Were any of those arguments the result of jealousy on her part?'

'One or two,' Richard admitted, uncomfortably.

'Do you think she was justified in feeling that way?'

Richard frowned. 'How d'you mean?'

It seemed like a straightforward enough question, and Rebecca suspected he was playing for time. She didn't remark on the fact, however, saying, 'Well, if you were flirting with another woman, it wouldn't be unreasonable for Maya to feel jealous, whereas if you were just talking to a female friend, that would be a different story.'

Richard nodded, but didn't immediately reply, and when he did it was clear he had been trying to come up with a way to avoid laying blame at either his own door or Maya's. 'I don't recall doing anything to provoke her, but that doesn't mean I didn't inadvertently make her feel insecure.'

Rebecca tipped her head to one side. 'You seem to be very reluctant to say anything against Maya. Is that because you're afraid of what she might do if she learns you've been badmouthing her?'

'I'm not afraid of Maya,' he replied, sounding weary rather than defensive. 'But the fact we're no longer together doesn't mean there's any bad feeling between us.' He paused. 'And if you want to put words into someone's mouth, you're talking to the wrong bloke.'

Although it was mid-afternoon when Rebecca and Lawrence arrived at Maya's home, she looked as if she was still getting ready for the day. She was dressed, but her anaemic pink hair didn't appear to have been brushed, and with the exception of what looked like the remnants of the previous day's eyeliner, her face was devoid of makeup. Despite her rather dishevelled appearance, Lawrence couldn't help thinking she looked better without it, and wondered, not for the first time, why so many perfectly attractive women insisted on slathering on a cosmetic mask before leaving the house every day.

She showed them in, apologising for the state of the living room. There might have been no makeup on her face, but the coffee table was liberally scattered with it, and Maya made a start on collecting up eyeshadows, lipsticks and the like as Lawrence and Rebecca sat down. Having tossed everything higgledy-piggledy into an iridescent vanity case, Maya offered them a drink, and, when Lawrence declined, perched on a chair opposite them.

'Perhaps you might start by explaining why you didn't give us your real name – Mary Ann – when we first spoke?' Lawrence opened.

'That's not my name anymore. I changed it.'

'By deed poll?'

'Yes.'

'And why did you go to the trouble of doing that?'

'To make life easier. When you're bouncing between theatre companies, making sure you get paid right is a lot easier if there's no confusion between your stage name and the name on your bank account and tax code.'

'So it didn't have anything to do with the fact your given name was on file as a result of your arrest for assault?'

'No.'

Lawrence nodded. 'We had a chat with Richard Manning about that incident this morning. How many other people have you lost your temper with and thrown things at?'

'I didn't throw anything *at* him,' Maya countered. 'I wasn't trying to hurt him.'

'That didn't stop it happening, though, did it?'

Maya didn't respond.

'You had a major falling out with Tony the night he died, did you throw anything in his direction?'

'*No*,' Maya insisted, before adding, tartly, 'Not that he didn't deserve it.'

Lawrence raised his eyebrows. 'So you think there are instances in which violence is excusable?'

'No, not really,' Maya replied, with a sigh. 'I shouldn't have said that. Look, what happened with Rich wasn't normal. I don't usually react like that.'

'Really? From what he said, it doesn't sound as if that occasion was a one-off.'

'I know, but –' she sighed. 'For a few months I was on medication that made me uncontrollably angry over really minor things. I've never experienced anything like that before. I stopped taking it after Rich got hurt.'

'What was the drug?'

The name Maya provided meant nothing to Lawrence, and, making a mental note to look it up later, he posed another question. 'Did you mention the anger to your doctor?'

'Yeah.'

'What did they say?'

'Supposedly it's not a side effect, but if you go online you find loads of people who've had the same problem.'

'And did the anger resolve after you stopped taking the drug?'

'Yes.'

'Have there been any occasions since then when you've felt angry enough to throw things?'

Maya shook her head.

'There's nobody who's going to tell us a different story?'

'No.'

'All the same, you did lose your temper with Tony on the night of Martina's party.'

'For good reason! And he deserved to be torn off a strip! But that's all it was, and anyone else who was there would tell you that, too!'

'People's accounts have been rather variable.'

Maya's eyebrows contracted into an uneasy frown. 'What does that mean? Has someone accused me of something? Because I yelled at Tony, but that's all I did.'

'So you didn't push him up against a wall?'

Maya shook her head slightly. 'I don't know. I might have. But it's not like he couldn't have stopped me.'

'Oh, that's all right, then,' Lawrence responded, sarcastically. 'DS Palmer here has self-defence training, do you think that makes it ok for me to push her around?'

'No, of course not, but it's hardly on a par with murder, is it?'

'That doesn't mean it couldn't lead to it.'

'Are you seriously suggesting I was responsible for Tony's death? How the hell do you think I'd have got his body all the way down the garden?' She held her hands out, fingers splayed, in a gesture that was presumably intended to draw their attention to her small frame.

'Whoever killed him, we suspect two people were involved in moving the body,' Lawrence replied.

This apparently gave Maya pause. Recovering herself, she said, 'And who do you suppose would have helped me? Jakob?'

'You tell me.'

Maya gave a derisive snort. 'He wouldn't put himself on the line for a shag! With Jakob, it's only ever about Jakob!'

There was a note of bitterness in her tone, and Lawrence suspected Maya had wanted more from Jakob than a one-night stand. Thinking of a line of questioning Rebecca had taken during their interview with Richard, he shifted the focus to another of her relationships.

'Were you jealous of Tony?'

'Jealous?' Maya exclaimed. 'Of what?'

'His friendship with Martina. On Saturday, you described her as your best friend. But she was close to Tony, too, wasn't she? Did you feel threatened by that?'

'Oh for God's sake, I'm not ten years old,' Maya returned, derisively. 'Both of us have other close friends besides each other. I've been friends with Irene since we were seven. And Tony was good for Martina.'

'How?'

'He had – I don't know what you'd call it – a way of making you feel special. He gave out a lot of compliments, and it's nice to hear those from a guy who you know isn't just trying to get you into bed.' She paused. 'And I guess it's even nicer when –' she stopped abruptly.

'When?' Lawrence prompted, when she didn't continue.

Maya sighed. 'This is going to sound really bitchy, and that's not how I mean it at all.'

'Go on.'

Maya closed her eyes briefly, and when she reopened them, kept her gaze on the floor. Several seconds passed before she said, awkwardly, 'When you're not used to hearing them at all.'

Max's office was deserted when Lawrence arrived shortly before five, an unopened bottle of Chianti standing on the desk. Lawrence was reading the label when his friend appeared in the doorway, and, holding it up, joked, 'Tough day?'

'You don't know the half of it,' Max responded, wearily. 'I've spent most of the afternoon trying to get an injunction against one of the tabloids.'

'An injunction?' Lawrence exclaimed, returning the bottle to the desk. 'What is it they want to publish?'

'You wouldn't believe me if I told you.'

'Did you succeed?'

'For the time being,' Max confirmed, as he rounded his desk. 'And with luck, by the time that changes the story will no longer be of much interest.' He sat down. 'How are things at your end?'

'Could be better,' Lawrence replied, taking a seat on the near side of the desk. 'Although I had Leighton in my office earlier, and he made a couple of useful contributions. I know there's a lot he can't do at present, but he clearly wants to be involved. Can occupational health not clear him for some light duties?'

'No,' Max returned, shortly. 'He's not fit to work right now, end of.'

'He seems on very good form.'

'So would you if you were high on oxycodone,' Max replied. 'And I can't risk having him messing around with sharps and chemicals when he's under the influence of powerful opioids.'

'I didn't realise he was still on such heavy-duty drugs,' Lawrence admitted, knowing better than to suggest Leighton be restricted to office-based tasks; the pathologist had never had much regard for rules, so trusting him to abide by any restrictions would be asking for trouble. 'Are there no alternatives?'

'Yes, there are, but an appropriate drug regimen can't be thrown together overnight. Besides, that's not all there is to it. I realise the fact the damage is largely limited to his extremities makes it easy to forget, but he's still recovering from some very severe injuries. If he'd sustained serious stab wounds I doubt we'd be having this conversation.'

Lawrence conceded the point with a nod.

'I'd love to have him back as much as anyone,' Max went on. 'But he is signed off for good reason. I can't force him to follow medical advice, and I can't stop him trying to work under the radar through you, or Jon, or Becky. But I would urge you to discourage it.'

'No, you're right,' Lawrence acknowledged. 'I tend to think of his injuries in terms of the impact they're having on his life, I hadn't really considered the physiological side of things.'

'I will ask that reception stops letting him into your building without someone to sign him in.'

'I'm not sure that'll stop him.'

'No, probably not.'

'Does he still have access to your systems?'

'Not since I found out he was using them, no.'

'When was that?'

There was a momentary pause before Max shook his head slightly. 'I don't remember. It was a few weeks ago. I doubt it made much difference, because he knows just about everyone and he could charm the skin off a snake, but I'm obliged to do what I can to keep on the right side of the health and safety executive.'

Lawrence nodded.

'Speaking of health and safety, this'll be what you're after,' Max went on, taking a document from the topmost of his stack of filing trays and sliding it across his desk towards Lawrence. 'Positive for alcohol and ketamine.'

'Enough to have killed him?' Lawrence asked, as he reached for the toxicology report, mindful of the fact Max hadn't been able to commit to a definitive cause of death.

'If you mean in terms of overdose, it's hard to say. It's a dangerous combination, but what constitutes a fatal dose varies from person to person. From an indirect perspective, ketamine can seriously impair motor function, so it could well have incapacitated him – and it would almost certainly have made it easier for someone else to overpower him.'

'And is there any chance he came by the ketamine medically? I'm sure I remember reading something about a new ketamine-based drug.'

'Esketamine,' Max replied, with a nod. 'It's been approved as an antidepressant, but it's only used in a clinical setting. Otherwise, ketamine's use is limited to anaesthesia, although not for want of trying.'

'What does that mean?'

'It's been the focus of a lot of pharma research. It's an analgesic, and it's –'

'Pharmaceuticals?' Lawrence exclaimed. 'Irene – one of Tony's housemates – works for Xornex. Is there any way – besides serving them with a warrant – of finding out whether they're looking at ketamine?'

'Off the top of my head, you could try asking them.'

'Yes, I could, but they're unlikely to want to confirm it when what I'm really asking is whether one of their employees might have been able to steal a controlled drug without their having noticed.'

'Oh, I see where you're coming from,' Max responded. 'I'll ask around, see what I can find out off the record.'

'Thank you,' Lawrence replied. 'What effect would the combination of alcohol and ketamine have on a person's behaviour? Would it make someone angry, or aggressive?'

'It could do. Would that tally with witness accounts?'

'People have mentioned that Tony's behaviour late on the Saturday night was out of character, and he seems to have been quite hostile towards a couple of his housemates. We've been trying to establish what might have been behind that, but we've not had much luck. If it was just an accident of chemistry, that might explain why we can't find anything concrete.'

'It's certainly possible,' Max responded. 'But that's not to say he didn't have anything to be angry about. He may just have kept a lid on it before.'

'Good point,' Lawrence acknowledged, feeling his mobile vibrate and drawing it from his pocket. Seeing the name on the screen, he answered it, shooting Max an apologetic look. 'Becky, hi.'

'Hi. We finally got Tony's phone data through from the service provider,' she revealed. 'And he sent a text to Irene a few days before he died that might be more than it seems.'

'What does it say?'

Rebecca related the one-line message and Lawrence nodded. 'That's definitely worth following up. I'll pick you up in fifteen and we'll head down to Clapham.' He bid her goodbye before hanging up and looking back to Max. 'It seems Tony was keen to do some shopping the week before he died.'

Max's eyebrows rose. 'What was he shopping for?'

'Cereal. Guess which one?'

When Rebecca and Lawrence arrived at the house in Eversleigh Road, the television was on in the lounge, and Irene showed them through to the large kitchen at the rear of the property. A long worktop ran the length of the inside wall, probably providing more surface space than was available in Rebecca's entire kitchen. It looked enviably clear, and, as a result, probably took all of thirty seconds to wipe clean. By comparison, the task of cleaning under and behind everything that didn't fit in the limited cupboard space of Rebecca's kitchen meant that it took far too long for her to do a thorough job anywhere near as frequently as she ought to have done.

Irene took a seat at the boxy wooden table that overlooked the garden, picking something too small for Rebecca to see off the tabletop. This was almost as bare as the worktops, and was in excellent condition, presumably on account of the stack of coasters and table mats that sat in the centre. As she sat in one of the matching chairs, Rebecca wondered whether the furniture had come with the house or whether it belonged to one of the housemates.

'In the week before his death, Tony sent you a text message asking if there was any chance you could pick up some Special K for him,' Lawrence began. 'You replied to say you'd see what you could do. Had you procured ketamine for him before?'

'What?' Irene exclaimed. 'No!'

'So why do you suppose he asked on that occasion?'

'He didn't! That's not what he meant!'

'Really? What was the text message about, then?'

Standing, Irene walked over to the washing machine, opened the cupboard above it and took out a packet of cereal. 'I'd said I was going to the supermarket after work, if anyone wanted anything,' she said, depositing the box on the table. Lawrence regarded it in silence for a moment before responding.

'If he was so keen to have this that he needed you to pick it up for him, why did he never open it?'

'How should I know? Should I have kept tabs on what he did with a box of cereal?'

Rebecca glanced at the open cupboard before saying, 'Why wasn't it in his cupboard?'

'Sorry?'

'We went through all of Tony's belongings on Wednesday, after the forensic team had finished. Including his kitchen cupboard.' She tipped her head in the relevant direction. 'That one. If the cereal was his, why wasn't it in his cupboard?'

'Oh, right,' Irene realised, aloud, seemingly unfazed by the question. 'We keep all the cereal in there. The boxes are too tall for the shelves in most of the cupboards.'

'Is there anything else in the house that Tony didn't keep in his room or his designated cupboards and shelves?' Lawrence asked.

'Well there's stuff we all use – like pans and bowls – that mostly belong to one or other of us. Plus there are certain things we buy between us, like olive oil, herbs, spices – otherwise we'd wind up with five of everything. And Tony usually had a box of Coco Pops in there, too,' she nodded towards the cupboard that had contained the Special K. 'But I guess someone must've finished them up.'

'Anything else?'

A couple of seconds passed while Irene apparently considered this before she said, 'Not that I can think of offhand. But if anything comes to mind I can let you know.'

'Perhaps you and the others could make a list,' Lawrence replied, in a tone that indicated it wasn't simply a suggestion. 'Going back to the Special K, postmortem toxicology shows that Tony took ketamine the night he died. Just a few days after he sent that text message.'

'Well if he did, he didn't get it from me,' Irene responded, her voice sounding strained.

'Have you ever worked with ketamine?'

Irene shook her head.

'Is anyone at Xornex working with it?'

'Not as far as I know.'

'Do you know whether Tony had used ketamine before?'

'No, but it wouldn't surprise me. He did poppers and nitrous oxide.'

'How about your other housemates?'

'I don't think so, but I could be wrong.'

'Given that you were aware Tony had used recreational drugs before, were you not concerned that might have been behind his uncharacteristic behaviour on the night of Martina's party?'

'I really didn't give it much thought at the time,' Irene responded, a note of exasperation in her tone. 'I wasn't exactly an independent observer. And it's not like people don't get into arguments when they've been drinking, is it?' There was a momentary pause before she added, apparently as it came to mind, 'In fact, someone's a lot more likely to throw a punch after they've had a skinful than a bulb of nitrous oxide. It's not called laughing gas for nothing.'

Despite the fact the working day was over, Martina looked very well turned out when she joined Rebecca and Lawrence in the kitchen soon after the conclusion of their interview with Irene. From her pale, opalescent gel manicure to her understated makeup and smooth, layered hair, it was clear she had put a considerable amount of effort into her appearance. Rebecca was reminded of something a friend had said earlier in the year; that large women were generally treated with less unkindness by strangers if they had made an effort with their clothing, hair and makeup. Perhaps that was Martina's experience, too. Rebecca wondered whether the remark would resonate with overweight men, guessing that it if did it would be to a much lesser extent. In her experience, public name-calling was a largely male pursuit, and she suspected a person's state of dress and grooming was far more likely to make an impression on the average man if the object of their scorn was female. Not that women weren't equally judgemental – if anything, they were probably more so – they were just less likely to hurl abuse at strangers on the street.

'We'd like to start with one of your recent Facebook posts,' Lawrence said, once Martina had joined them at the table, bringing Rebecca's thoughts back to the task in hand.

Martina looked nonplussed. 'Which one?'

'Ten days ago, you posted to say that *project cold frame* was finally complete, and put up some photos that were taken in October, alongside others dated a week after anyone last saw Tony alive. The post states that you were with Tony at the time.' Lawrence passed her a printed screenshot. 'Given that that clearly wasn't true, could you explain why you did it?'

Martina gave the printout her attention for a moment before saying, 'That's just how Facebook frames it when you tag someone.' She looked up, her expression anxious. 'I wasn't meaning to imply that he was with me there and then.'

'So why did you tag him?'

'Because he did the double-digging for me ahead of the cold frame going in, and because he was in some of the pictures,' Martina replied, a faint inflection of surprise in her tone. Her bemusement was understandable: much as they had needed to ask the question, Rebecca could have predicted the answer. She herself had tagged people – and been tagged by others – while not actually in their company. 'I was hoping it might prompt him to respond,' Martina added, sadly, after a moment.

'If you weren't trying to give the impression Tony was with you at the later date, why are you wearing the same clothes in both sets of pictures?'

'They're my gardening clothes.'

'Even the socks?' Lawrence asked, disbelievingly, presenting her with close-ups of the relevant pictures.

Martina leaned forwards to look at the images. 'I have several pairs with frogs on,' she said, as she raised her gaze. 'They were buy two, get one free. I can show you, if you want.'

'I think picture socks are the way to go when you live in a shared house,' Rebecca remarked. 'At one stage, I only bought black ones, because it made it easy to find two that matched, but I stopped doing that after a flatmate admitted to *borrowing* them. She used to pinch my socks from the laundry airers whenever she couldn't find a clean pair of her own.' Rebecca paused before getting to the point. 'Are any of your housemates so free and easy with other people's belongings?'

'No, not really. Tony sometimes borrowed the odd thing from my room when I wasn't around, but not if it meant going through my cupboards or drawers. And he would have been happy for me to do the same. Irene's quite precious about her things, so I'd never go into her room without asking. And Jakob's anal about his stuff. Nobody goes up to the second floor uninvited.'

'Do you think that might be –'

The first time Lawrence's mobile interrupted the interview, he silenced it without even removing the device from his pocket. When it almost immediately rang again, he drew it out, checked the screen and made a brief apology before heading for the door. As it closed behind him, Rebecca tried again.

'Do you think Jakob's protectiveness of his space might be because he has something to hide?'

Martina's eyebrows contracted slightly. 'I'm not sure it's fair to assume people have something to hide just because they value their privacy.'

'Perhaps not,' Rebecca replied. 'But if privacy is so important to Jakob, I can imagine he might not take it well if he found out someone had intentionally invaded his privacy.'

'I don't know. It's not something that's ever come up.'

'So you weren't aware that Tony had hacked into Jakob's computer?'

The revelation clearly came as a shock. After a moment, Martina shook her head.

'That must be a mistake. Tony wouldn't have done something like that.'

'I'm afraid he did. Rather frequently, in fact. He's been inside every computer in the house. Including yours.'

'Mine?' Martina exclaimed. 'Why?'

'That's a good question. Can you think of an answer?'

Several seconds passed before she shook her head, looking bewildered. 'No. There's nothing very interesting on it. You can have a look, if you like.'

Martina's response – bemusement as much as shock – was similar to Irene's, and Rebecca was beginning to suspect the answer to the question of why Tony had infiltrated their machines was as simple as *because he could*. She was about to pose another question when the door to the room reopened and

Lawrence looked back in, catching her eye and jerking his head in the opposite direction by way of a request for her to join him. She got to her feet, shooting Martina an apologetic look and heading for the door. Lawrence pulled it to behind her before saying, in a low voice, 'Elise has had an accident at the gym, so I'm going to have to get over to A and E. Can you finish up here?'

'Sure,' Rebecca replied. 'Is Elise all right?'

'At this stage, I really don't know,' Lawrence admitted, before turning and making for the front door. He glanced around as he opened it, pausing for just long enough to say, 'I'll update you when I can.'

Rebecca nodded, turning back into the kitchen. Martina was at the sink, filling the kettle, and said, 'Is everything ok?'

'Fine.'

'Would you like a cup of tea?'

Rebecca didn't much care for the drink, but accepted the offer regardless, thinking she might learn something from a more informal chat. Noticing that the American-style fridge-freezer by the back door was peppered with magnets and photographs, she moved closer to get a better look at the pictures. The largest one, which was held in place by four wooden ladybirds, was an eight-by-ten-inch image of Martina and her four housemates crowded around a table.

'Nice picture.'

Martina glanced around, then, seeing what Rebecca was looking at, nodded. 'That was last Christmas. Well, not Christmas Day – we did a house Christmas the weekend before, when everyone was here.'

'Who took the picture?'

'Jakob set it up and put it on timer. He's got a fancy camera.' She returned the kettle to its base and switched it on. 'I keep thinking I should take it down, but –' she shrugged. 'It'll come down when I move, anyway.'

'Is that on the cards?'

'Uh-huh. Maya and I are getting a place together.'

'Whereabouts?'

'I don't know, yet, we're going to see some places tomorrow,' Martina reached to open a cupboard. 'I've never lived with anyone who was a friend beforehand, it's always seemed like too much of a risk. But I don't think I could face living with strangers at the moment. And I wouldn't want to live alone even if I could afford it.'

'How long have you lived here?'

'Nearly three years,' Martina took two mugs from the cupboard before turning back around to face Rebecca. 'Earl Grey, camomile, peppermint or jasmine?'

'Jasmine, thanks.'

Martina turned back to the cupboard to reach for the tea bags before moving to open the fridge and taking a carton of oat milk from the door. Watching her pour a measure into one of the mugs, Rebecca found herself smiling. She recalled Leighton once saying he could tell the difference between a cup made by adding milk to tea and one made the other way around. Rebecca had thought he was winding her up until he had proved otherwise. When she had asked what the difference was, the answer had been something incomprehensible about proteins.

As Martina returned the lid to the carton, it slipped from her fingers, falling to the floor and rolling under the fridge. With a sigh, she crouched down to feel underneath the unit – something Rebecca would never have done without looking first for fear a large spider might be lurking just out of sight. And, she reluctantly admitted to herself, because it had been so long since anyone had cleaned under the fridge in her flat that it would almost certainly mean her fingers coming into contact with something sticky, fluffy and potentially disgusting.

'I hate to think what's under my fridge,' she remarked, conversationally, as, having retrieved the lid, Martina took hold of the worktop and heaved herself back up to standing.

Martina nodded. 'Tony helped me move some furniture around before the party and we found all sorts.'

'Whenever I've held parties, I've found the strangest things while clearing up afterwards,' Rebecca replied.

'Yeah, Jakob had a party last year and someone left a garden gnome behind.'

Rebecca smiled. 'Is he likely to be back soon, do you think?'

'I doubt it,' Martina replied. 'It's Friday night, so I expect he's out for the duration.'

Rebecca nodded, realising in that moment that she herself hadn't had a big night out in months. For much of her relationship with Elliot, a musician, weekends had been busy with gigs, parties and club nights. More latterly, when his interest in going out had nosedived along with his mental health, Rebecca had been far more concerned about him than the demise of their social life. In the aftermath of their split, she had increasingly filled her time with friends from work, much of it in pubs within walking distance of their offices.

Of all her colleagues, Leighton was probably the most gregarious, but in recent months his capacity for socialising had been stymied by the aftereffects of severe hypothermia and the impact of strong painkillers. By and large, Rebecca was quite happy with the new status quo, but it was clear Leighton was finding his limitations increasingly frustrating. As he had observed a few days earlier, the novelty of being able to sit around watching Netflix all day long had well and truly worn off.

'I was supposed to be going to see Maya's play this evening,' Martina went on. 'But I couldn't face sitting through three hours of Brecht.'

'I'm not sure I'd ever be able to face that,' Rebecca remarked, turning to lean against the worktop and then stopping as a Tupperware box beside the toaster caught her eye. It was filled almost to the brim with small plastic animals that looked reminiscent of toys from crackers or McDonald's happy meals. Rebecca wondered where they had come from, and, apparently noticing her interest, Martina said, 'They're flash drives.'

'All of them?'

'I collect animal ones,' Martina admitted, sheepishly. 'It's silly. It started with the penguin one, then someone bought me the polar bear – and it snowballed from there. Most of them were gifts.'

'I didn't know there were so many out there,' Rebecca replied, estimating that the box contained at least twenty animals. Among them were a crocodile, a koala and a fox. Spotting an odd-looking brown creature with bared teeth and a body reminiscent of a tree trunk, she fished it out and asked what it was.

'Oh, that's Chewie,' Martina responded, with a weak smile, reaching to take it. 'You know, from Star Wars. I got him for Tony last Christmas.'

'If it belonged to Tony, why is it in with all of yours?'

Martina shrugged. 'I'm not sure,' she admitted. 'I didn't realise it was. I guess someone came across it while tidying up and just assumed it was mine.' She returned the Wookiee to the box, then looked up, forcing another smile and adding, 'Either that, or we've got a ghost.'

Nine

Rebecca had received a one-line message from Lawrence on Friday evening to let her know Elise was all right, but she had heard nothing further, and wasn't sure whether he would be working on Saturday. Arriving at Scotland Yard to find him at his desk, she paused in his office doorway.

'Morning. How's Elise?'

'A bit sore, but she's ok, thanks.'

'What happened?'

'She fell off a beam doing a backflip. Katie got in a bit of a panic because they put her on a spinal board as a precaution, but fortunately the worst of the damage was a broken arm.'

'Ouch.'

'Elise cheered up as soon as she found out she could have a purple cast,' Lawrence responded, with a smile. 'And fortunately it's her left arm, so it's not going to be too limiting.'

'I was rather envious of friends with casts when I was her age,' Rebecca admitted, perching on one of the chairs on the near side of the desk.

'She is looking forward to showing it off at school on Monday.'

'I can imagine.'

'Although I'm sure she'll be sick of it by the end of the week,' Lawrence reached for his mug. 'Did you get much more from Martina last night?'

'Not directly,' Rebecca responded. 'But I was having a look around the kitchen and there's a photo of all five of them on the fridge. There's a tiny – I don't know what you'd call it – imperfection, I guess? In the picture. I've seen the same flaw before, in the pictures from the SD card we found in Tony's room. But Martina said the camera used to take the photo on the fridge belonged to Jakob.'

'He may not have been the only person to use it.'

'I know, but –' Rebecca paused, trying to put her thoughts into words. 'The flaw in the picture is a little white circle. Not a blob, a ring. In his call to Assia the night he died, Tony kept repeating something about Harvey and a bubble. I can see how the flaw might be described as a bubble. I'm wondering whether Tony might have known one of the children in the pictures or videos – maybe through the Harvey centre. If he didn't take the photos, and he'd only just come across them, that could explain why he was so upset.'

'Did the SD card have any fingerprints on it?'

'Only Tony's. But Martina was telling me the two of them moved some furniture ahead of the party and found various bits and pieces underneath things – if it wasn't Tony's card, that might be how he came across it.'

Lawrence nodded, pushing his chair away from his desk and getting to his feet. 'Let's have a look at this flaw,' he said, making for the door. Rebecca stood and followed him out into the open plan office, where he retrieved the folder containing the indecent images from a filing cabinet. After regarding the topmost picture for a couple of seconds, he tapped the mark Rebecca had noticed. 'Is this what you mean?'

'Yes. It's in the videos, too,' Rebecca replied, taking the folder and shuffling through it for some of the printed stills. 'Clive mentioned that Tony said something about films when he was arguing with Jakob – maybe these are the ones he was referring to.'

The videos featured an adult as well as a child, but, thanks to a Guy Fawkes anonymous mask, he was unrecognisable. One video began with a close-up of the man's right hand giving the camera a thumbs up, which appeared in the topmost picture Rebecca pulled out.

'Did we get anything back on whether there was enough detail for a partial print here?' Lawrence asked, indicating the picture.

'Not enough to run through the database, apparently,' Rebecca replied, as Eva leaned over the desk to get a look at the picture. 'And Tony's skin was too degraded to rule him in or out.'

'Surely a gay bloke would take more care of his cuticles?' Eva remarked, facetiously.

'I fear the CPS will require a higher burden of proof,' Lawrence returned, drily.

'What am I missing?' Jamie asked, as he joined them, a mug in one hand and a partially eaten Danish pastry in the other.

'We're revisiting the SD card images and videos,' Rebecca said, passing the image of the hand his way. 'We think Jakob might have taken them.'

Jamie leaned to put the pastry down on his desk to enable him to take the printout.

'I really don't think Tony was involved in abusing these kids,' Rebecca put in. 'He hacked into dozens of biotech companies, almost certainly to steal information, yet we've not found a shred of evidence outside the depths of his hard drive. If he was that careful about corporate espionage – and about keeping his computer secure – why would he leave incriminating photos lying around on an SD card? It doesn't make sense.'

Lawrence nodded. 'I'm inclined to agree.'

'And during the drinking game at the party, Tony came out with *I have never videoed a sex act.* I'm wondering whether he was directing that at Jakob.'

'Which would –'

'This is Dale Sanders,' Jamie exclaimed. 'From the Harvey Foundation.'

'Oh, yes, of course it is,' Eva responded, sarcastically. 'I don't know how we missed it.'

'I'm serious. I remember this scar,' Jamie traced his fingertip over the feature in the image, only narrowly avoiding spilling his coffee.

'That's oddly observant of you,' Eva remarked, still looking unconvinced. 'Or is it some sort of fetish you've yet to tell us about?'

'He was signing,' Jamie replied, sounding mildly exasperated.

'Signing what?'

'Using sign language. Interpreting for a deaf girl who works there.'

'That may be how Tony recognised him, as well,' Lawrence observed. 'Ok, I think we need to pull Dale and Jakob in, search their homes for any other indecent material and see whether we can find a connection – beyond Tony – between the two of them. Jakob's had plenty of time to get rid of anything he doesn't want us to see, but if he managed to lose that SD card in his own home, he's slipped up before. We only need him to have overlooked one other thing. Let's find it.'

In the normal run of things, Leighton would have been glad of the chance train travel offered to make use of what would otherwise have been essentially wasted time. Much as he enjoyed driving, he was almost always behind with something – or, more often than not, multiple somethings – and any opportunity to catch up was welcome, despite the fact that there was a good chance of his getting distracted and squandering it. At present, however, he had precious little to be distracted *from*, and all a train journey represented was more time he needed to find some way of filling if he didn't want to wind up with nothing to do but think.

This morning's effort to occupy himself with a newspaper had faltered at page three, where a picture of the Downing Street cat had offered an unwelcome reminder that he hadn't seen Pandora in over a week. The pages that followed hadn't provided much in the way of a diversion, either, as there had been little of interest that hadn't drawn his mind to the job he was currently barred from returning to. The sudoku puzzles hadn't taken him long, and he had felt relieved to arrive at his destination. Given where he was, he suspected he was very much in the minority.

The woman who checked him in to the visitors' centre had examined his Home Office ID closely before remarking that it no doubt made a change to be visiting a prison in a personal capacity. He had smiled politely; in reality, his elder brother's frequent run-ins with the law had meant Leighton was familiar with the process before he had even left school. What was unusual was the fact he was making the trip alone. It wasn't often that he visited Tom without his mother, and it was a relief not to have to worry about her fragile emotions.

Tom greeted him in typical fashion with a rude remark about his choice of t-shirt, and Leighton responded in kind with a comment on Tom's haircut before giving him a handful of pound coins with which to buy tea. On some occasions, visiting his brother felt like a chore, at other times – like today – he found himself looking forward to it.

When he had a drink inside him, Tom could be unpredictable and intimidating, much like their father. But sober, he was considerably more personable, and, at the end of the day, their shared history counted for a lot. There were things Tom understood that nobody else did; things Leighton didn't need to explain to him.

'You still skiving, then?' Tom asked, depositing two cups of tea on the table before taking a seat.

'Something like that,' Leighton replied. 'They won't sign me off to go back until they're confident I'm not going to inadvertently slice through the wrong artery. I wouldn't mind if I was a brain surgeon, but it's not as if I'm going to do anyone any harm.'

'Besides p'rhaps yourself,' Tom pointed out. 'What you gonna do if they don't let you back to it?'

Leighton almost smiled. It was a question he didn't doubt any number of people – his mother and Rebecca among them – would have liked to ask, if they'd not felt uncomfortable broaching the subject. It made a welcome change to not feel as if everyone was walking on eggshells around him.

'So, what, you gonna retrain as a GP, or summat?' Tom asked, when Leighton didn't immediately answer his previous question.

'God no. Can you see me sitting still in a consulting room all day?'

Tom smiled. 'Aye, fair point.'

'There are plenty of jobs in forensic science that don't involve postmortems and lab work, so I'm sure I'll be able to find something to keep me out of trouble. Assuming the Home Office doesn't designate me persona non grata, that is. I had a visit from Kai the other night.'

'Kai?' Tom echoed, seemingly in genuine surprise. 'What did that little scrote want?'

'Threatened to fill the papers in on some of my misdemeanours if I didn't pay him off.'

'I hope you told him to go fuck himself.'

'Words to that effect. But I doubt that'll be the end of it.'

'I'll put an end to *him* next time I get the chance,' Tom responded, darkly.

'Yeah yeah.'

'I'm serious. If he fucks with my family, he's got it coming.'

Leighton sighed, wishing he'd never mentioned his run-in with Kai.

'Talking of family, Mam sent us a picture from your last visit,' Tom went on. 'Your new bird's fit, in't she? I might even consider shagging the filth for a girl like that.' He smiled before adding, with a cheeky lift of his eyebrows. ''Specially if she was wearing a uniform.'

'Dream on.'

'I might say the same to you. She's well out of your league.'

Tom wasn't alone in thinking as much, and Leighton could have done without having his brother echo the refrain that regularly went through his own mind. He could just imagine what some of his colleagues would have to say about the relationship, were they to find out. Sooner or later, if he and Rebecca continued seeing one another, he suspected it would be unavoidable, a fact that would probably have concerned him more had he not been so preoccupied with the fear he might repeat his father's behaviour and hurt more than Rebecca's feelings. She had made it clear she didn't believe he had it in him to do her any real physical harm, and had more than once questioned why he was holding himself to account for other people's actions. He hadn't responded, not because he didn't have an answer, but because he very much doubted it would satisfy her. When it came down to it, letting his guard down just seemed like too big a risk to take.

Maya instinctively recoiled as something with too many legs to count shot out from underneath a plant that might have been coriander, but could equally have been flat leaf parsley. Cooking wasn't something she had much time for, and neither was gardening. She'd scarcely been at Martina's place ten minutes, and she was already regretting agreeing to help her friend dig up her extensive collection of herbs in preparation for a move that was still several weeks away.

The two of them had spent the morning flat-hunting, and had managed to secure a beautiful garden flat just a few minutes' walk from Clapham Common. Given that they were both locked into their current rental contracts for the best part of another month, there was no rush to pack, but Martina had been keen to get the plants into pots sooner rather than later. And with everything that had happened lately, her request for help with the herbs hadn't seemed like a big ask.

'Ugh,' Maya muttered, as the unidentified creepy crawly scurried under an attractive plant with a mixture of ice green and lilac leaves. She made a mental note to avoid digging that one up. 'Have you got any gloves?'

'The police took my gardening gloves for forensics,' Martina replied, apologetically. 'But we've some disposable rubber ones under the kitchen sink if you'd like a pair of those?'

'They'll do,' Maya responded, straightening up and making for the house. Anything was better than nothing when it came to keeping bugs off her skin and soil from getting under her fingernails. She raised a hand to open the sliding door that led onto the kitchen, then stopped short in surprise, which quickly turned to a very different emotion.

Ahead of her, Irene was sitting on the edge of the worktop, her legs wrapped around Jakob, who was standing in front of her, his mouth on hers and his right hand inside her jumper. For a moment, Maya couldn't breathe. That Jakob had wanted nothing more from her than a one-night stand had hurt, but, when it came down to it, he'd never made her any promises. Irene's betrayal was a different matter. She was Maya's oldest friend, and she knew full well just how much Maya liked Jakob. The fact she had clearly entered into some sort of relationship with him so soon after he had cast Maya aside hurt even more.

Jakob and Irene jumped as Maya pulled the door open, immediately turning to look her way. Irene's face flooded with a mixture of shock and horror, but Jakob appeared unconcerned, which only served to compound Maya's upset. Irene opened her mouth to speak, but Maya got in first.

'You bitch!' She exclaimed.

'I'm sorry,' Irene began, disentangling herself from Jakob. Maya didn't want to hear whatever excuses she might be about to make. She wished she could turn her back and walk away, but she wouldn't get far; there was no way out of the garden. Instead, she held up a hand to indicate she wasn't going to listen, averting her eyes and striding through the kitchen and on towards the front door, ducking quickly into the lounge as she passed to retrieve her handbag. Irene followed, grabbing Maya's arm as she stepped out of the front door.

'Maya –'

'Get your hands off me!' Maya yelled, twisting her arm away.

'I'm sorry, I –'

Maya turned on her. 'You're not fucking sorry! You're only sorry I found out!'

'I honestly never meant for this to happen, it's –'

'Don't give me that! This didn't happen *to* you! You made a choice! And you didn't choose our friendship!'

Irene shook her head, tears coming to her eyes. 'Please, Maya, give me a chance to explain and –'

'I think it's all pretty self-explanatory!' Maya threw back. 'It comes down to the fact you're a shitty friend!' She turned and started down the street, feeling relieved when Irene didn't follow her – and thankful that Irene had declined her invitation to relocate along with herself and Martina. At the time, Irene's decision to stay put in Eversleigh Road had come as a surprise to both Maya and Martina, but now it made perfect sense. She could hardly have kept her relationship with Jakob under wraps had she and Maya been living under the same roof.

* * * * *

After being forced to wait several hours for a solicitor to turn up, Lawrence had passed a frustrating twenty minutes attempting to interview Dale, who hadn't even gone to the trouble of saying *no comment* in response to questions, instead opting to say nothing at all. Eventually, Lawrence had parked him in a cell and headed back up to CID to see whether the search of the man's home had turned up anything that might provide some leverage.

Rebecca glanced up as he approached her desk, and got her question in before he had a chance to pose his. 'Any luck?'

Lawrence shook his head. 'I couldn't get a word out of him. How did you get on at his place?'

'We found masses of indecent pictures, but nothing to support a charge of producing or distributing, only possession. We might have more luck with the contents of his computer, though, Francine's working on it now.'

'Here's hoping, because I very much doubt the CPS will be prepared to proceed on the basis of our video footage alone. It just doesn't show enough.' Lawrence turned and made for his desk.

'I had a look to see whether we got any DNA off the original SD card,' Rebecca said, following him into his office. 'But it doesn't look like anybody requested the test.'

Lawrence sighed. It was at moments like this that he most missed Leighton. It wasn't a pathologist's job to follow up on inanimate evidence collected by police officers – or to track the ins and outs of a police investigation to gauge what might be *worth* following up – but somewhere along the line, Leighton had taken it upon himself to do both. When he had thought further tests were warranted, he had either put in the relevant request or, more often than not, done the job himself. The downside, which had for a long time been far more apparent, had been that the hours devoted to such tasks had come at the expense of timeliness elsewhere. Lawrence had found the need to continually chase for information infuriating, not least because when the pathologist hadn't been occupied with a crime scene or postmortem, he had tended to give the impression of being in no great rush to get anything done. It had only been in his absence that Lawrence had realised where much of his time had been going.

'Shall I have someone check it out?' Rebecca asked.

'Yes please. And well done for picking that up.'

'I can't really take the credit,' she admitted. 'I was talking it over with Leighton last night, and he asked if we'd managed to get any DNA from it.'

'I never thought I'd say it, but there are times when I miss his scattergun approach,' Lawrence said. 'Tell him to hurry up and get better, won't you?'

Rebecca smiled. 'I think he misses working, too. He's getting very bored.'

'I'm not surprised,' Lawrence responded. He could only guess at how he himself might fare if forced to take a prolonged break from work. He'd never been good at sitting around, and even the poolside holidays some of his colleagues – Leighton among them – were so fond of sounded like his idea of hell. Much as there were always more books he wanted to read than he had time for, he couldn't imagine spending entire days with his nose in a book – unlike Elise, who had to be separated from her tablet at bedtime to stop her from reading late into the night.

'If I had to spend six months at home I think I'd go mad,' he concluded, sitting at his desk and spotting a flashing light on his desktop telephone announcing the presence of a voicemail.

'It's only recently he's started climbing the walls. For the first few months he wasn't really well enough to do much.'

'Max is concerned he's not up to the work he's been trying to do lately,' Lawrence replied. 'It might be an idea to avoid discussing any active investigations with him for the time being.'

Rebecca frowned. 'He said the only thing stopping occupational health ok-ing him to come back was the fact he can't handle a scalpel safely.'

'I don't know, Becky, but I think there might be more to it than that. Just be careful.'

She nodded.

'Was there anything besides the SD card?'

'Oh – yes. We finally pinned Jakob down. Eva left him with the duty sergeant about half an hour ago.'

'Great. Can you find out what his situation is vis a vis legal representation? I'd like to interview him as soon as possible.'

'Sure.'

'With luck I won't have to spend the rest of the day waiting on another solicitor.'

*****

Jakob's loft bedroom had a large footprint, but the sloping ceilings meant much of the space was of limited utility. Perhaps as a result, the layout of the room was rather unusual. The kingsize bed stood in the middle of the floor, its headboard backing onto a shelving unit that faced the door, while the end wall – the only one that extended above waist height – was dominated by a huge flatscreen television. Large Velux windows ran along the street side of the room, with cupboards and shelving built into the eaves beneath them. Jamie was forced to duck to get close enough to open the cupboards, and couldn't help thinking it was far from an ideal living space for a man who stood more than six foot tall.

The base of the bed provided more storage, in the form of four shallow drawers. After a quick search of the contents – mostly sheets and towels – Jamie realised that by shifting the mattress he could reach between the wooden slats beneath it to access the space behind the drawers. It was no easy task, however, and between hefting the mattress around and leaning to feel along the underside of every slat, it felt like some kind of alternative workout. As it turned out, the exertion wasn't even worth the effort: he found nothing inside the hollow space besides a faded foam earplug, a plastic biro, a pound coin and a few dust bunnies.

'Who buys DVDs these day?' Noel asked, as Jamie straightened up. 'Why waste space when you can get everything online?'

'He's a filmmaker, isn't he, so maybe they're things he's worked on.'

'I doubt it,' Noel remarked, holding up a plastic case. 'This one's in Russian.'

'Well perhaps he couldn't get it online,' Jamie replied, making for the cupboards occupying the eaves at the back of the room. 'You can't stream everything, you know.'

'Most of these you can. *Minority Report, Tinker Tailor, The English Patient, The Big Short* –'

'Does it matter?' Jamie asked, opening a cupboard door to find it full of video and recording equipment. Perhaps, he reflected as he opened the next cupboard door onto more of the same, Jakob had opted to put up with the low ceilings in return for the opportunity to keep all of his equipment close to hand.

'Three-quarters of these are bog-standard Hollywood, the rest are in Russian,' Noel went on. 'I thought the guy was Polish?'

'That doesn't mean he can't speak Russian,' Jamie responded, irritably. Turning to see Noel reading the back of a DVD case, he held out a hand. 'Give me that.'

Noel passed it to him.

'Now do something useful, will you?' Jamie said, opening the DVD case and bending the two sides back to check there was nothing concealed behind the slipcover before snapping it shut and moving to return it to the shelf. 'I don't want to be here all day.'

'Do us all a favour and go for a bloody smoke,' Noel grumbled, reaching to open the adjacent cupboard.

Jamie ignored him, pulling out the next DVD case. He could still remember a time when DVD players had been prohibitively expensive, and it had been the cause of some excitement when the elder brother of one of his friends had bought one. On several occasions, a group of them had sneaked into his room in his absence to watch films their parents would never have allowed them to view, including *Pulp Fiction* and *American Beauty*. They had also rifled through the girlie magazines he kept hidden inside old copies of *Melody Maker*. Looking back, Jamie wondered whether the guy had had any real interest in music, or whether the selection had been based purely on the publication's large size. After all, you'd have no chance of concealing a copy of *Playboy* inside an issue of *Private Eye*.

Jakob had been in an interview room for the best part of an hour by the time Lawrence and Rebecca joined him, and was clearly irate at having been kept waiting.

'I don't have time to sit around here all day!' He objected, as Lawrence took a seat opposite him. 'I have a meeting at Channel Four first thing on Monday, and a shitload of work to do before then!'

'I gather you've declined the opportunity to seek legal advice,' Lawrence began, matter-of-factly. 'Are you sure about that?'

'Yes.'

'You're not under arrest at this stage, but you will be under caution dur–'

'Yeah, I already grasped that when she told me!' Jakob snapped, indicating Rebecca with a jerk of his head. 'You don't have to keep repeating everything, I'm not a halfwit!'

Lawrence glanced in Rebecca's direction. She obligingly started the recording device that was affixed to the end of the table, gave the details of who was in the room and delivered the caution before handing back to Lawrence.

'I gather that during Martina's party, Tony clocked your dalliance with Maya and said something to her along the lines of *I thought you had better taste,*' he said. 'Do you know what that was in reference to?'

'No.'

'No idea at all?'

'None. I don't know what got into him that night, he was being a right arse.'

'Is that why you and he had an argument?'

'We didn't have an argument.'

'More than one person has told us otherwise. We've been led to believe that the two of you had a very heated exchange late that night.'

'*Exchange* implies it was a two-way thing, and I said next to nothing!' Jakob returned, angrily. 'Tony was shouting the odds at me – like I said, he was being a jerk – but I haven't a clue what he was on about! He was pissed, and he wasn't making any bloody sense!'

'Could it have related to anything on your computer?'

Jakob frowned. 'What?'

'Our IT experts looked over Tony's computer, and it seems he hacked into your machine.'

'Hacked?' Jakob exclaimed. 'Why the fuck would he have done that?'

'I don't know, I was hoping you might be able to shed some light on it.'

'What, further than that he was a nosy cunt?'

In an era in which words deemed offensive just fifty years earlier were now part of the vernacular, Lawrence sometimes wondered whether it was wrong to judge people for their choice of language – but that didn't stop him doing as much. Not that he had been enamoured of Jakob beforehand; Jamie's succinct assessment of the man hadn't been wrong. Presumably, however, there was another side to him that they hadn't seen, given his apparent popularity with the opposite sex. Maya and Irene must have seen something in him.

'Can you think of anything on your computer that Tony might have objected to?' Lawrence continued.

'Plenty. I make controversial documentaries, not Disney films.'

'For example?'

'I've covered gang initiation rituals and people trafficking, and one of my current projects involves a bunch of interviews with white supremacists.'

'Do you agree with their views?'

'I'm half Polish and you're asking if I'm a Nazi?' Jakob demanded. 'Seriously?'

'Well, from what we've heard, you seem to have had issues with Tony's sexuality.'

'That's bullshit.'

'Really? Are you saying you didn't have a problem with his having men stay over?'

'Yeah, I did, but only because he brought random weirdos home, and one of them stole from me!'

Dislikeable as Jakob was, Lawrence couldn't argue with this objection; the risk of people bringing strangers home after a night out was, to his mind, one of the biggest drawbacks of communal living. It was also something he himself had never done – admittedly more as a result of circumstance than conscious choice.

'I understand you took this photograph,' he said, laying the picture of Jakob and his housemates during their Christmas celebration on the interview room table. Jakob glanced at it before answering.

'Yes,' he replied, his eyebrows contracting into a suspicious frown.

'It looks like there's something wrong with the lens here,' Lawrence observed, indicating the flaw in the top left-hand corner of the picture.

'Yeah, I lent it to someone and it got damaged.'

'Presumably you also recognise these?' Lawrence went on, placing a couple of the images from the SD card found in Tony's bedroom in front of Jakob. The young man jerked back from the table.

'Are you fucking out of your mind?' He exclaimed. 'That's disgusting! What the fuck is this?'

'You tell me,' Lawrence replied, tracing a finger over the flaw in the photographs. 'Because it looks like they were taken with your camera.'

'Not by me they weren't! Perverts who do that shit want their balls cutting off!'

'So if you didn't take the photos, who do you suppose did?'

'It could have been anyone! I sold the camera months ago!'

'When?'

'January? February, maybe? I can check the exact date if you want!'

'I don't think that'll be necessary, considering that these photographs were taken last year.'

'Well, until I sold it, I used to rent the thing out. So that still leaves a bunch of people.'

'How did you go about renting it out?'

'I used a website called Caged Magpie.'

'And how did the SD card containing these images – among others – wind up in your house? I can't imagine anyone renting a camera and then forgetting to retrieve a memory card with such incriminating photographs on it.'

'I don't know! But I did not take these fucking pictures!'

'In that case, I don't suppose you'll mind our taking a look at your computer.'

'You'd be welcome to, but you'll have to do better than your lazy-arse colleagues with finding it first!'

'I beg your pardon?'

'It got stolen,' Jakob responded, witheringly.

'When?'

'The week before last. Someone broke into my car.'

'How very convenient,' Lawrence remarked.

'It's the fucking opposite of convenient!' Jakob flared. 'There's nothing on it that'd be of any interest to you, and I've had to fork out for a new machine *and* a new window!'

'Leaving it in your car wasn't very bright, was it?'

'No shit,' Jakob retorted, sarcastically. 'I didn't mean to leave it in the car, did I? I was in a rush and I forgot it was there.'

'I presume you have the sense to have it backed up?' Lawrence said, using provocative language to increase the chances of getting an honest answer.

'Obviously. I'm not an idiot.'

'So you do have something we can take a look at. Great.'

'Not without a warrant, you won't.'

'You said we'd be welcome to look at your computer, if you had it. How does the backed-up version differ?'

Jakob glared at him, saying nothing.

'We'll come back to that,' Lawrence went on. 'Right now I'd like to talk about Dale Sanders.'

Jakob frowned. 'Who?'

Lawrence repeated the name.

'I've no fucking idea who that is.'

'No?' Lawrence queried. 'I tell you what, let's see if this helps refresh your memory.' He opened his laptop and positioned it so that Jakob could see the screen before starting the video that opened with Dale's thumbs up. Less than twenty seconds in, Jakob turned his head away and held up his hands.

'I'm not watching this filth!'

Lawrence paused the footage. 'There's no real need for me to play the rest of it, is there? You know what happens next.'

'Fuck's sake!' Jakob exploded. 'The closest I have ever got to this sort of shit is through a documentary about the perverts who get off on it! I've never watched it and I've never fucking filmed it! And when all this is over and done with, the first thing I'm going to do is sue you for showing me things I'll never be able to unsee!'

When Lawrence returned to the office, the first thing to catch his eye was the film footage playing on Jamie's computer monitor, its characters moving at an accelerated speed reminiscent of a early motion picture. Drawing level with the young man's desk, he noticed a handful of DVD cases printed with Cyrillic text stacked to the right of the monitor.

'Jim's talking about learning Russian,' he said, reaching for one.

'Well he won't learn much from these,' Jamie replied, pausing the activity on his screen and lifting the next case down on the pile. 'I noticed the details weren't stamped on the disc, like they normally are,' he added, snapping the case open and indicating the DVD. 'It's a sticker.'

'Pirate copy?'

'I wondered about that, too, but when I tried playing it, it wasn't in Russian and it didn't contain any submarines,' he flipped the box cover over to display the image on the front. 'I found someone who could translate the title and it wasn't the same as the one that comes up when you press play.'

'It's not along the same lines as the video clips on the SD card, is it?'

'Doesn't appear to be – so far it seems to be a rather amateur fantasy film. But I'll punt it on to the video analysts when I'm done in case it's concealing something else.'

Lawrence nodded.

'Talking of the SD card, I don't think Tony was referring to the Harvey Foundation when he called Assia and Ellie on the night of the party,' Jamie went on, reaching for his mobile phone. 'I think he was talking about a child.' Swiping the device open, he presented Lawrence with a portrait-style picture of a child who was immediately recognisable as the boy featured with the masked man in the video. 'This is Harvey Calhoun. His sister attends the centre.' Jamie swiped to another picture. The little girl in the image bore no obvious resemblance to the boy in the previous one, and Lawrence looked back to his colleague.

'How did you identify him?'

'When we spoke to Ellie, there were two things Dale omitted from his translation. One related to Harvey.'

'She said something about a book,' Lawrence recalled.

'Yes. I contacted Ellie for more information, and she named the book as *Harvey Goes Camping*. I couldn't find it on Amazon, so I asked around and it turns out to be a personalised book owned by one of the children who attends the centre. It originally belonged to her elder brother.'

'Harvey.'

'Yes. He's severely autistic. He's never attended the centre because he can't handle big groups of people. I guess Dale and Tony both came across him at some stage through his sister.'

Lawrence nodded. 'The question is how Dale got into a position where he was able to abuse the boy.'

'Presumably either he or whoever shot the video knows the family well enough for them to entrust Harvey to his – or her – care. Any advance on whether the videographer was Jakob?'

'Not really,' Lawrence admitted.

'What was his reaction to the photographs?'

'Explosive.'

'Protesting too much, do you think?'

'Perhaps. He says he used to rent the camera out via a company called Caged Magpie. According to them, it was rented out on the date the photographs were taken, but it seems it's quite possible to use the service without giving your real details, so we've no leads on who that renter was. And it doesn't help us to rule Jakob out, either, because the camera was returned to him that same day, and the only information Caged Magpie has is the date of return, they leave individuals to sort out times and places between themselves. The equipment's owner does check in to confirm that an item has been returned, but they can do that at their leisure. So the fact Jakob checked in that evening doesn't necessarily mean the camera wasn't returned in the morning.'

'Have we got the camera?'

'No, he sold it earlier this year. Or so he says.'

'We have got all the memory cards he had at home.'

'How many are there?'

'Eleven. I've had a cursory look, but some of them contain thousands of images, so I'm going to need some help sorting through them.'

'With that kind of capacity, you'd think two or three would be enough,' Lawrence observed.

'I dunno, my sister has something like four thousand pictures just on her phone. And they're almost all of her cat.'

Lawrence smiled, wondering how many pictures Elise had amassed in the few months she'd had her smartphone.

'Space-wise, they're not a bad way of storing pictures, when you think about it,' Jamie added. 'Memory cards, I mean. Now they're so cheap. Maybe he uses them for back-up.'

'Maybe,' Lawrence agreed.

They're pretty small, as well, so they're probably easy to lose track of. You buy another, then you find the old one –' Jamie shrugged. 'I've got four or five little combination padlocks knocking around at home, but every time I go away I end up grabbing a new one at the airport because I can never find any of them at the crucial moment.'

Lawrence nodded. 'I am starting to see how it might be possible for someone to lose one and not immediately realise,' he said. 'Initially it seemed extraordinary that someone would mislay a set of obscene pictures and not move heaven and earth to find it, but if you've got a handful of memory cards perhaps by the time you did realise one was missing, it would be too late to retrace your steps.' He turned towards his office. 'And if you don't feature in the pictures, it might be a safer bet to write it off than to try to hunt it down.'

Lawrence was no stranger to breaking bad news, but informing a single mother with two special-needs children that not only had her son been sexually abused, but that his ordeal had also been immortalised on film – and potentially widely shared – had ranked among the most difficult tasks of his career. He had kept the details and his questions to a minimum, and left the woman in the care of a family liaison officer.

Returning to Scotland Yard, he decided to try talking to Dale again before he headed home in the hope that the information the search team had provided might generate a response. After being kept waiting by Dale's solicitor for the second time that day, he finally sat down in an interview room shortly after nine.

'You've got quite a library of child pornography at home, haven't you?' He observed. 'Do you lend it out, or is it just for personal use? Because that's an awful lot of personal use.'

''S not –' Dale began, before his solicitor raised a hand to stop him.

'Not what? Yours?' Lawrence guessed. 'Well, I've got someone dusting for prints now, so we should know soon enough whether that's true.'

Dale shifted position in his chair, saying nothing.

'Let's go back to the video footage we discussed earlier,' Lawrence went on. 'We've identified the boy in the film as Harvey Calhoun. We've not been able to get much information from his mother yet, because she was understandably distraught when we broke the news. But I'm sure she'll be able to tell us a lot more in a day or two. So if you want to do yourself any favours by helping us out, now would be a good time to fill us in on who else was involved in making or distributing the film.'

Dale didn't respond.

'How about we start with who was behind the camera?'

'I can't help you,' Dale protested. 'I know you're convinced it's me in the video, but it's not. Someone must have spliced the first bit of footage in, or something.'

'And what reason would anyone have had to do that?'

'I don't know!'

'Ok, well then let's consider who might have done it. Someone filmed you giving the camera a thumbs up, who was that?'

When Dale didn't answer, Lawrence went on, 'It must have been someone with the know-how to seamlessly splice footage together, mustn't it? Someone like Jakob Radeki, perhaps?'

'Who?'

'Jakob Radeki.'

Dale shook his head. 'Don't know him.'

'So who?'

Dale sat with his eyes on the table for some time before saying, 'Tony.'

'What about him?'

'He filmed a couple of events we did for the foundation. I don't remember giving the camera a thumbs up, but I guess I must have done at one time or another.'

'If it was an event for the foundation, presumably you can tell us where the footage was shot?'

Dale didn't respond.

'And if Tony was involved, perhaps you could explain how he shot the film on a date that he was out of the country?'

Dale swallowed, but didn't speak.

'As I thought, he didn't,' Lawrence concluded. 'But he did uncover what you'd been doing, didn't he? Is that why he called you on the night he died?'

'What?' Dale exclaimed. 'I didn't have anything to do with what happened to him! I don't even know where he *lived*!'

'You didn't need to. All you needed to do was alert Jakob, and let him take care of the situation.'

'For God's sake! I don't know this Jakob you keep going on about!'

'Keep?' Lawrence echoed. 'I think I've mentioned him all of twice.'

'Well, I'm telling you, I don't know who he is!' Dale returned, hotly. 'And whatever he's done, it had nothing to do with me!'

Ten

Martina had spent much of the afternoon and evening in the pub with Maya, having more or less the same conversation over and over again, trying to comfort one friend while defending another. She hadn't been entirely truthful when Maya had asked whether she had known Irene and Jakob were seeing one another; she might not have been clear on the extent of their involvement, but she had known *something* was going on between them. Deep down, Martina was aware she was taking the cowardly way out in denying all knowledge, but she told herself that there was nothing to be gained from filling Maya in on the details – it would only have caused further upset.

It came as a relief when she could finally wave Maya off on the bus. The emotionally charged hours they had passed in the Fox and Hounds had been exhausting, and, on top of that, Martina was ravenous. Despite the knowledge that her size could leave nobody in any doubt that she ate far too much, she couldn't bear the thought of anyone seeing her eat, so her last meal had been at lunchtime.

Letting herself into the house, she headed straight for the kitchen, and the dilemma of what to have for her belated dinner – the Slimming World-compliant vegetarian casserole she had originally planned, or the cheese feast pizza lurking in the freezer. She got as far as taking the casserole out of the fridge before returning it and flicking on the oven. If Maya's meltdown wasn't an excuse to eat junk food, what was?

After pouring herself a glass of Pepsi Max and downing half of it, she made her way slowly up the stairs. Arriving on the landing to see a crack of light around Irene's bedroom door, she knocked gently, and then, when there was no answer, spoke her friend's name. Still receiving no response, she eased the door open and looked in.

Irene was asleep, fully dressed, on top of her duvet. An empty wine bottle and equally empty glass stood side by side on her bedside cabinet, and, from the purple splatters radiating out across her beloved Persian rug, it was clear one of the two had been knocked over at some stage. Martina sighed, turning towards the bathroom to fetch a cloth and some white vinegar.

Ordinarily, Irene was the only person to use the vinegar that lived in the cupboard under the sink; Jakob's repeated objections to the smell had long deterred Martina from using it whenever her turn to clean the bathroom came around. Why it bothered him so much was anyone's guess – as Irene had bluntly pointed out, he was more than happy to splash the condiment liberally over his chips.

Getting down onto her knees, Martina worked her way slowly across the rug, dabbing at the red wine stains and thinking Irene must have been thoroughly intoxicated to have made no effort to clean up the mess herself. Shuffling backwards, she knocked into the waste-paper basket that stood by the window. With a sigh, she turned to collect up the handful of items that had spilled out, feeling thankful that Irene kept on top of emptying it; her own bin would have generated a landslide of tissues, cotton wool balls and KitKat wrappers. As she returned the last of the rubbish to the basket, she stopped short, then reached back in for the crumpled blister pack she'd had in her hand a moment earlier. Flattening it out, she smoothed a section of the torn foil to allow her to make out the small black type before standing and stepping over the stained rug to reach the bed.

'Reenie?' She ventured, perching on the edge and resting a hand on her friend's arm. 'Reenie, wake up.'

Irene didn't stir, and Martina tried again, giving her a gentle shake. When this still elicited no response, Martina shook harder, starting to feel panicked. Irene's eyes finally opened, looking slightly out of focus.

'What?' She demanded, irritably and rather incoherently.

'How many of these did you take?' Martina asked, holding up the empty paracetamol packet.

'Huh?'

Martina repeated the question.

'I dunno. A couple this morning,' Irene replied, her lack of enunciation giving Martina some idea of how much she'd had to drink.

'Are you sure that's all?'

Irene grunted a response that could have been 'uh-huh' but could equally have been 'uh-uh', raising a hand to rub her eyes and pushing herself up onto one elbow. Martina still felt concerned, and was debating what to do when Irene clambered off the bed and made for the door. She staggered slightly as she crossed the room, and grabbed hold of the door frame on her way out. Moments later, Martina heard her vomiting, and, with a sigh, stood and headed for the bathroom.

Irene was in something approaching a kneeling position on the floor, with her right elbow resting on the edge of the toilet bowl and her right hand propping up her head. Martina joined her, reaching to gather Irene's hair away from her face as her body heaved.

'It's ok, hun.'

'It isn't,' Irene managed, before vomiting again. 'It's all my fault.'

'Maya'll get over it,' Martina replied, kindly.

'No,' Irene replied, shaking her head.

'Just give her some time.'

Irene continued shaking her head. 'Not Maya,' she said, at length, tipping her head to one side and resting it on the arm that lay along the rim of the toilet bowl. Martina realised she was crying. 'Maya hates me, but that's not what I meant.' She sniffed and gulped before saying, rather hopelessly, 'I meant *Tony*.'

Rebecca awoke in the early hours to find herself alone in Leighton's bed, and when, after a few minutes, he hadn't returned, she reluctantly peeled back the sheets and got up. She found Leighton sitting on the sofa in the dark, but the limited light from the street lamp outside was sufficient for her to see that he had his left hand held to his chest.

'What's wrong?' She asked, hurrying over.

'Nothing,' he responded, breathlessly. 'I'm ok.'

'You're not.'

'I'll be fine in a minute.'

Rebecca perched beside him. 'Are you sure? Maybe you should see a doctor –'

'I am a doctor.'

'You know what I mean.'

He coughed. 'I can do without a ticking off for being delinquent with my asthma meds.'

'Is that what it is?' Rebecca asked, noticing as she spoke that he had an inhaler in his right hand.

He nodded.

She hesitated before saying, 'I thought it might be anxiety.'

Leighton sighed. 'Bec, please don't take this the wrong way, because I do appreciate the fact you care, but I think you're more anxious about me than I am.'

'It just seems as though you're pretending everything you've been through this year hasn't happened,' she said. He had certainly never talked to her about his experience in the freezer container: she had learned more about it while he was on the witness stand earlier in the week than she had done in the previous six months. It had been hard to hear the answers to questions about what had gone through his mind during the hours he had been shut inside, and that he'd tried to estimate the volume of the container to work out whether he was more likely to die of carbon dioxide poisoning or hypothermia. His delivery had been almost clinical, and she suspected that it wasn't just everyone else he had been avoiding the subject with.

'You have to stop expecting me to fall apart,' he replied. 'Post-traumatic stress is not a foregone conclusion of having shitty experiences any more than lung cancer is a guaranteed outcome of smoking. Everyone is different. That's just biology.'

Rebecca didn't respond.

'And compared with sixteen years living with Dad, this year really hasn't been that bad.'

Rebecca might have dismissed the remark as an exaggeration, had she not seen physical evidence of the violence Leighton had grown up with. The worst of the damage had been disguised with an intricate tattoo of an owl coming in to land, which occupied two-thirds of his back, but at close range it was still possible to make out his scars, including a tangle of twisted skin fibres in the shape of an iron beneath his right shoulder blade. She often wondered at what age he had sustained that injury.

'I'm sorry,' she offered, awkwardly. 'I can't imagine what it must have been like growing up in that environment.'

Leighton didn't reply, and Rebecca felt torn, unsure whether his rather flippant remark had been made with the intent of closing the subject or whether, in light of what she had said in Thursday's note, he was trying to provide her with a way in. In the end, she decided to risk asking the question. It wasn't as if he was obliged to answer.

'Was there nobody you could confide in?'

Several seconds passed in silence before he said, 'It's not that there wasn't anyone. I was just too scared to talk to them.'

'Scared of what your dad might do?'

He shook his head. 'Of social services,' he revealed. 'Mum's biggest fear was that we'd be taken away.' He paused. 'She never said where to.'

Rebecca wished she could take his hand, but his fingers were often too sensitive, and she didn't want to risk anything interrupting the conversation.

'How did you cope?' She asked, at length.

'Mostly we kept out of the way.'

'You and Tom?'

'Uh-huh. Until he went down and Dad suddenly wanted to know exactly where I was and what I was getting up to every minute of the day.' There was a long pause before he added, 'I think he'd rather have been shot of me. Not that he was ever particularly fond of Tom. He just disliked him less.'

Rebecca resisted the natural urge to refute this observation: all platitudes were likely to change was his willingness to talk about the experience.

'Did he take his anger over Tom's incarceration out on you?' She asked, at length.

Leighton nodded. 'And then some.'

Rebecca absorbed this before asking how long Tom had spent in prison.

'A year.'

'Did things improve after that?'

'I didn't wait around to find out.'

Rebecca debated whether to ask her next question for some moments before she spoke. 'Have you ever talked to anyone about all this? Properly, I mean.'

'I don't need to re-live it.'

'You might still find it helpful.'

'It's not necessary.'

'But –'

'Jesus!' He exclaimed. '*This* is why I don't talk about stuff! Everyone always thinks they have the answer! I don't need to be told how to feel or what to do!' He stood and strode from the room.

Rebecca hurried after him. 'I'm sorry,' she offered, joining him in the kitchen, where he was filling a glass from the tap. 'I didn't – I just –' she stopped. 'I know it's not my place to tell you what to do, it's just –' she hesitated. 'I found it really hard spending just one afternoon in your dad's company. I love you, and I don't want his actions to hurt you any more than he already has.'

'I knew it would upset you, that's why I didn't want you to come,' Leighton responded, shortly. 'But you don't have to worry about me. I'm used to it.'

Rebecca doubted anyone could ever get *used* to hearing a parent describe them as *good for nothing* and *a loser*, but she didn't say as much. She was wrestling with what to say next when Leighton's attention was diverted by something outside the window. Smiling, he leaned to open it.

'What time d'you call this, then?' He asked. Pandora sauntered in off the windowsill as if she'd only been gone an hour or two and sprang up onto his shoulders. He raised a hand to stroke her and she rubbed her face against his ear, purring loudly. 'Breakfast time, huh?'

Leighton made for the cat's feeding station and Rebecca pulled the window shut, stopping short as a movement in the street caught her eye. Glancing at her watch, she hurried out into the hallway, grabbing her coat from the hook inside the front door and trying to remember where she had left her shoes. She wanted to know just where Akiko Nakahara might be going at quarter to four in the morning.

Eleven

Rebecca had spent some time trying to decide on the best way to share her knowledge of Akiko's late-night sortie with Lawrence without either lying about who had seen her or explaining what she had been doing in Clapham at that hour. She hadn't managed to come up with a solution by the time she arrived at work, and in response to the predictable question had ended up blurting out something about missing the last tube before immediately regretting it: it wasn't as if Lawrence wouldn't see straight through the lie. He had made a dry remark about Leighton's erratic timekeeping clearly being contagious before moving on to another topic, leaving Rebecca cursing herself and feeling thankful no one else had been around to overhear the exchange.

She hadn't even had a chance to pick up the phone to find out whether Akiko was at home or at work before reception called to inform her that she had a visitor. She threw on a jacket and headed for the lifts, wondering what Martina had to say that necessitated a visit to Scotland Yard on a Sunday morning.

As it turned out, Martina wasn't alone. She was accompanied by Irene, whose face was white, the mulberry-coloured stains on her lips an indicator of what she had been drinking the night before. From the look of her, Rebecca guessed Irene was seriously hungover, and her curiosity was piqued. She didn't imagine the woman would have dragged herself out of bed for anything that wasn't important.

Having shown the two women to a meeting room, Rebecca dispatched Eva to make coffee and, when her colleague returned, asked what had brought them in that morning. Martina looked to Irene, who was staring down into her coffee.

'Reenie?'

Several seconds passed before Irene said, haltingly, 'I think – I think it was – my fault.'

When she didn't say anything further, Rebecca said, 'Tony's death?'

'Yes. No. I don't know.' She swallowed. 'Was it the ketamine that –' she trailed off with a weak shrug.

'Did you supply the ketamine?'

Irene nodded. 'The stupid thing is that it was supposed to keep him safe,' she said, her voice wavering. 'Last year he took something cut with God knows what, and ended up in A and E. I got some pure ket so that wouldn't happen again. But I never let him have enough to fall into a K hole. I don't know what went wrong.' She looked up to meet Rebecca's eyes for the first time, tears in her own. 'Did he mix it with something?'

'Where did you get the ketamine?' Rebecca asked, ignoring Irene's question. 'Because it wasn't Xornex, was it? We've already checked, and none of their programs involve ketamine.'

'From a friend.'

'A friend at another pharmaceuticals company?'

Irene shook her head.

'A medic?'

'I'm not dragging anyone else into this. I was the one who supplied it to Tony.'

'Ok,' Rebecca replied. 'Run me through what happened.'

Irene's eyebrows contracted into a frown. 'I've just told you.'

'You've told me you supplied the ketamine Tony took the night he died, but not what actually happened that night. When did you realise something was wrong?'

'Sunday morning. I needed the iron and he'd been using it on the Saturday night. He didn't answer the door when I knocked, and I thought maybe he wasn't there – he'd said he might go to a club after the party – so I looked in.' She paused. 'Something felt wrong even before –' she swallowed. 'The curtains weren't closed properly, and he was so pale. Then I touched him, and –' she shrugged, pursing her lips. Martina slipped an arm around her.

'What position was he in when you found him?'

Irene looked thrown by the question, but answered readily enough. 'He was on his back. In bed.' She paused, then added, as if it had just occurred to her, 'He had one arm on top of the covers.'

'And what did you do after that?'

'I threw up,' Irene replied, taking the question unnecessarily literally. 'In the bathroom, I mean. I made it that far. Maya came to see if I was ok, and I told her I had the world's worst hangover.'

'Did you leave his body where it was?'

'No. I didn't know what I was going to do, but I knew someone might go in there, so once I'd got it together I moved him into the base of the bed.'

'When did you move him outside?'

'Not until late that night, after everyone had gone to bed.'

'Who helped you?'

'No one.'

'You're telling me you managed to get him to the end of the garden and over the massive planters by the shed all by yourself, without leaving so much as a scuff mark?'

'Yes.'

Rebecca uttered an exclamation of disbelief before saying, 'You must weigh, what, sixty kilos? And you expect me to believe you single-handedly carried a body weighing considerably more than that – and stiff with rigor mortis – through the house and down the garden, and then lifted it over all those shrubs without damaging any of them?'

'Yes.'

'Without a serious amount of weight training I doubt that would even be possible.'

'Well, I'm telling you it is.'

Rebecca regarded Irene in silence for a couple of seconds, then shook her head. 'Go on, then, take me through how that worked,' she said. 'Starting with how you got a body down a flight of stairs in the small hours without waking any of your housemates.' She sat back in her chair. 'Because that alone strikes me as quite an achievement.'

Lawrence was on the phone when Rebecca appeared in his office doorway, and he immediately guessed from her expression that she had something of note to impart. As he replaced the receiver, she said, 'Irene was the one who supplied the ketamine.'

'Has she admitted to it?'

'Yep. But she can't have been the only person involved. She says she found him lying on his back, and I struggle to see how he could have suffocated that way without there being anything lodged in his airway. She also claims she moved Tony's body by herself, which clearly isn't possible, but she's not budging.'

'And who do you think the most likely accomplice is?'

'Jakob or Maya. I really don't see it being Martina.'

'Ok, well let's get a full statement from Irene and charge her with supplying a class B drug, and then we'll focus on who else might have been involved. If we're lucky, she'll let something slip and save us the trouble.'

Rebecca nodded, turning to go before stopping and looking back around. 'Sir, about earlier –' she hesitated. 'Well – last night. I didn't miss the tube.'

Lawrence smiled. 'I didn't imagine you had. The Northern Line runs all night at weekends.'

'I don't know why I said that. It's just – I'm not really sure where anything is at – and it's difficult to explain something when –' she paused. 'When I'm not sure what it is I'm trying to explain.'

'You don't owe me an explanation, Becky. What you do in your own time is your business.'

'I just didn't want you to think it was – I don't know – personal, I suppose. I haven't really told anyone.'

'Well nobody's going to hear it from me.'

'I know, I didn't mean –' she shook her head.

'Don't worry about it,' Lawrence replied. 'We can pretend this conversation never happened.' He paused before adding, wryly, 'I'm just relieved to know you've not lost the ability to keep track of time.'

Having left Eva to take a full statement from Irene, Rebecca showed Martina to another room to answer a few further questions. It was clear that Martina was struggling to maintain her composure, and Rebecca felt for her. No doubt she had been putting on a brave face to support Irene, but now she was left to face the fact that her housemate was looking at serious prison time. To all intents and purposes, she had lost two close friends in the space of a week.

'I'm sorry to put you through any more questions,' she said, as she poured them each a glass of water. 'But does the name Dale Sanders mean anything to you?'

'Dale,' Martina echoed, seemingly considering the matter. 'No, I don't think so. Who is he?'

'He volunteers at the Harvey Foundation.'

A couple of seconds passed before Martina shook her head, saying, 'Sorry, it still doesn't ring any bells.'

'Does he look familiar?' Rebecca asked, placing a photograph that she had downloaded from the foundation's website on the table.

Martina dropped her eyes to the image and regarded it briefly, then shook her head again.

'Did you ever meet anyone involved with the charity?'

'A few times, at fundraising events.'

'And did your other housemates join you on any of those occasions?'

'Akiko didn't. But the others generally did.'

'Would you mind outlining what those fundraising events involved?'

Martina's eyebrows drew together into an uneasy frown. 'I'm not sure I understand why you're asking me this. Irene's told you what happened. Shouldn't that be the end of it?'

'This isn't directly related to Tony's death. We came across some evidence during that investigation which suggests a link to another case,' Rebecca responded. 'I'm sorry to be putting you through this, I really wouldn't be asking if it wasn't important.'

'I don't mind. I was just puzzled.'

There was a pause, and when Martina didn't say anything further, Rebecca prompted her with, 'Could you tell me about the fundraisers?'

'Oh – yes, sure.' She nodded. 'Well, there were the quiz nights, of course. Tony used to organise those, so he always twisted our arms to support them. And we went to a summer fete in June.' She smiled weakly, and her eyes filled up. 'We had a job dragging Irene away from the bouncy castle at the end of that afternoon,' she added, her voice wavering.

'So the fete was aimed at children?'

'Uh-huh,' Martina managed, reaching for the box of tissues on the table. She blew her nose and dried her eyes before continuing, 'A lot of the families with kids at the centre were there.'

Rebecca nodded, wondering whether that was how Tony had come to meet Harvey. 'Did Tony ever film any events for the foundation?'

'Film?' Martina frowned. 'I don't think so. He didn't really go in for that kind of thing, he used to say people were so busy documenting everything for Instagram that they missed half of what was going on.'

He wasn't wrong, Rebecca thought to herself. 'You mentioned the other day that when you and Tony moved some furniture ahead of the party, you found various odds and ends,' she went on. 'Can you remember what any of those were?'

Martina's eyebrows contracted in thought. 'Some of it was just rubbish – like chewing gum wrappers – and a couple things we had to bin because –' colour rose in her cheeks. 'We had a

Malteaser fight – a while back – and the stray ones we'd not found when we cleaned up had melted into a gooey mess. But we also came across stuff we'd lost or forgotten about – an Oyster card, a DVD, a lipstick –' she trailed off with a shrug.

'What sort of DVD?'

'I think it was *Out of Africa*,' Martina answered, clearly puzzled by the direction the interview was taking. 'It was one of those free ones that come with the Sunday papers. You know.'

Rebecca did; at one stage, her parents had periodically passed that kind of thing on to her. But since her laptop had died, she hadn't had anything on which to play them.

'Did you find any SD cards?'

Martina hesitated before saying, 'What are those?'

'Memory cards.'

'Oh, for cameras,' she nodded. 'Yeah, there was one down behind the corner unit inside the front door. It was a bit sticky, but otherwise it looked ok.'

'Another Malteaser casualty?'

Martina looked momentarily puzzled, then shook her head. 'No, it was more like it had had juice splashed on it.'

'Do you know who it belonged to?'

'We assumed it was Jakob's. He's the only one of us with a proper camera. Most people just use their phones.'

'Did you check what was on it?'

'I didn't. Tony might have, I suppose.'

'Have you seen it since?'

She shook her head. 'I'd forgotten all about it, to be honest. Jakob might know, though. I can ask him later, if you like?'

Rebecca politely declined the offer; she already knew Jakob's answer to that particular question, and she didn't imagine he'd be changing it any time soon. But then, given where the card – assuming it was the same one – had turned up, perhaps he was telling the truth. It wasn't unfeasible that a small, lightweight piece of plastic had been carried into the house with the camera, particularly if it had been sticky, when a renter returned the device. Had the camera subsequently been left atop the shelves in the entrance hall, the card could easily have fallen, unnoticed, down the back. In some ways, the explanation made more sense than the alternative. Anyone losing something so sensitive would more than likely turn their home upside down trying to find it. And the dumping ground of magazines, junk mail, gloves, sunglasses and other miscellany behind the front door seemed like an obvious place to look.

The film footage playing on Rebecca's monitor was reminiscent of a clip Lawrence had seen on the news a few days earlier. That had featured a rabble of protesters and looters smashing windows and ransacking shops, and had been shot in daylight. By contrast, the moving images on Rebecca's screen had clearly been recorded with an infrared camera, and the unfamiliar distribution of colours and shadows made the action considerably harder to follow.

'What've you got there?' He asked.

'One of the videos Francine flagged from Jakob's hard drive. There's nothing containing children, but there are several recordings of people committing other crimes.'

'Such as?'

'This one's criminal damage. Animal rights activists attacking a laboratory.'

'I can't see Jakob being particularly concerned with anyone or anything's rights but his own, so presumably it's footage for a documentary.'

'I'm guessing so,' Rebecca said. 'There are also a number of recordings that come under the umbrella of sex tapes. The sex looks to be totally consensual, but whether the women agreed to be videoed isn't clear.'

'There's a fair chance Tony's *I have never made a sex tape* was directed at Jakob, then, even if it didn't relate to the footage we first thought.'

'Yes.'

'Are any of the women identifiable?'

'I don't recognise any of them, if that's what you mean, but the footage is clear enough.'

'So Maya and Irene aren't on there.'

'No.'

'When did he last back up?'

'The day after Martina's party,' Rebecca replied. 'And Francine said it's the only back up on the drive. It was a brand new one.'

'Now there's a surprise,' Lawrence remarked, sarcastically. 'He gets a new back-up drive, then a day later his laptop gets stolen.'

'That's about the size of it.'

'Did you have a chance to check whether he reported that?'

'He did. And the broken car window. But there's no actual evidence – it was on a residential street, and there wasn't any CCTV.'

'Of course there wasn't.'

'I checked the window had really been broken, too,' Rebecca added. 'He got it fixed at a local garage a couple of days later.'

'Even if he didn't fake the theft, it doesn't take a genius to work out that if you leave a MacBook lying in full view on a car seat it's going to disappear faster than a rat up a drainpipe.'

'No,' Rebecca agreed.

Lawrence paused for thought, then glanced up as he heard heavy, rapid footfalls approaching to see Jamie bounding down the corridor that ran the length of the office.

'I just got a call from one of the video guys,' he imparted, breathlessly, as he neared. 'And those films in the Russian boxes are dodgy as fuck.'

'Child porn?' Lawrence queried.

'Nope,' Jamie replied, as he slowed to a stop a few feet away. 'Snuff movies.'

'*Real* ones?' Rebecca exclaimed.

'I don't think there's any other kind,' Jamie observed. 'But who knows whether they're genuine. That's the million-dollar question.'

'Are all six purported to be in that category?' Lawrence asked.

'I'm not sure. Ramesh said two of the titles are logged as being of interest, I've requested a dark web search for the other four.'

'Keep me posted on that.'

'Will do,' Jamie replied. 'D'you reckon it might be worth our while watching them?'

Lawrence smiled. 'It might be, but I don't think I can sanction that during working hours. You're welcome to take one home this evening, though, if you like.'

Lawrence had expected this to dent Jamie's enthusiasm, and was surprised when he responded with, 'Yeah, I'm up for that.'

'Me too,' Rebecca put in.

'I'll see if I can find a few other takers,' Jamie added. 'D'you want in?'

Lawrence could think of few things he would like to do less at the end of a long day than watch a film purporting to show a genuine homicide, and shook his head. 'I think I'll pass, thanks. But don't let me deter anyone else.' He turned towards his office, then paused to add, 'Just make sure everyone's clear it doesn't qualify as overtime. The powers that be would never let me hear the end of it.'

Jakob looked tired and dishevelled after his night in a cell, but the experience didn't seem to have dented his attitude at all. Before Lawrence had even had a chance to sit down, the man reiterated that he had had no involvement in producing the *filth* they had shown him the previous evening, and threatened to sue for wrongful arrest. Lawrence responded by asking why, if he had nothing to hide, he had not only managed to lose his laptop since Tony's death, but also appeared to have no back-up history prior to the 24 hours before the machine was supposedly stolen.

'I knocked a beer over my old hard drive.'

'Rather careless with your electronic devices, aren't you?' Lawrence returned.

'It was an accident,' Jakob snapped. 'I was rather preoccupied at the time.'

'What with? Worrying about what Tony knew of your activities?'

'With Maya.'

'Of course,' Lawrence returned, drily. 'On that note, we've been over your new back-up drive, and you have a number of recordings that show you having sex with women. The women don't seem to be aware that they're being filmed. If that is the case, you've committed a criminal offence in making those recordings.'

'No I haven't,' Jakob replied, calmly. 'It's only an offence if I filmed them so that I could view the footage to get myself off, or if I share it around.'

This response came as a surprise to Lawrence, who had expected Jakob to simply deny that the recordings had been made without consent. Raising his eyebrows, he said, 'If that's not why you did it, what was the purpose of filming the liaisons?'

'Insurance.'

'You're going to need to expand on that.'

'I'm not having some girl accuse me of rape just because she regrets having a one-night stand. I've seen that happen to far too many other blokes.'

'Are you psychic?'

Jakob frowned. 'Eh?'

'What makes you so sure accusations made against other men are spurious?' Lawrence asked. 'Given that you presumably weren't present when the alleged offences occurred?'

'There've been enough cases where women have been shown to be lying for it to be a legitimate concern,' Jakob returned.

Lawrence wasn't going to waste time arguing with the man, and, making a mental note to have someone check that none of the videos had been played more than once or twice, moved on.

'Did Tony know about those recordings?' He asked. 'Is that what he tackled you about on the night of Martina's party?'

'I don't *know* what that was about!' Jakob snapped. 'He was wired and he wasn't making sense! When I asked what he was on about, he just said something like *oh, right, we'll pretend you don't know*.'

'How did the argument end?'

'It wasn't a fucking argument, it was a one-way rant!' Jakob exclaimed. 'You can't *argue* with someone when you don't have a clue what they're talking about!'

'All right,' Lawrence held up a hand for emphasis. 'Diatribe, onslaught, whatever you want to call it. How did it end?'

'I went up to my room to try to get some peace, but he came after me. He forced the lock on the door and was getting really aggressive, so I headed back downstairs. He followed and slipped on the stairs, which finally seemed to knock some sense into him.'

'Did he bang his head?'

There was a momentary pause as Jakob presumably either thought back or pretended to do so before he said, 'I don't know, I didn't see. He crashed down behind me and practically knocked me flying.'

'From the word *crashed* it sounds as if it was pretty heavy fall.'

'I guess.'

'Was he all right?'

Jakob shrugged. 'He was a bit stunned for a moment, but he seemed ok.'

'Why didn't you mention this before?'

'It didn't seem like a big deal,' Jakob responded. There was a momentary pause before he frowned and added, 'Why? Did he die from a head injury?'

'Were there any witnesses?' Lawrence asked, wondering whether the fact he was only now hearing about the incident was because it hadn't actually happened.

'I don't know. Most people were downstairs, but I don't remember exactly who was where.'

Lawrence nodded. 'We know Tony hacked into your computer, so his anger may well have derived from something he found in there,' he said. 'But it's also possible your computer wasn't the only thing he snooped around in. And you've got an interesting selection of films in your DVD collection. Could you explain why a number of them don't match the boxes they're stored in?'

'To stop anyone who might be nosing around uninvited from borrowing them without asking,' Jakob returned, pointedly. 'Too often you never get things back.'

'Printing labels out for the discs themselves seems quite a length to go to,' Lawrence replied.

'Is there a law against it?'

'No. And I don't actually need you to tell me why they were so carefully disguised, because I know they're purported to be snuff movies. That being the case, I'd like to know how you came by them.'

'I got them from a guy in a market.'

'All of them?'

'Yes.'

'Given the lengths you went to to conceal them, you were presumably aware of their reputation when you purchased them?'

'Yes.'

'So why buy them?'

'Research. I was looking at doing a documentary on the topic.'

It was an easy and predictable answer, and explained why Jakob had hung onto the DVDs while conveniently losing his laptop and back-up drive. There was no law against owning videos that were simply rumoured to feature actual homicides: that was a claim anyone could make.

'From the way you said that, it sounds as if you decided not to,' Lawrence observed.

'It was hard to find anyone who was prepared to talk about participating in that kind of thing,' Jakob replied, with a casual shrug. 'It often is when you're dealing with something illegal. But that's not to say I won't ever be in a position to put a program together on the subject.' He sat forwards. 'As far as I'm aware, none of that's illegal. And as I've been here almost twenty-four hours, you either need to find something to charge me with, or you need to release me. Which is it going to be?'

It was eight forty-five by the time Rebecca let herself into Leighton's flat. She could hear the sound of a sporting commentary emanating from the lounge, and looked in to find Leighton lying on the sofa watching a football match with Pandora asleep on his chest. He glanced up with a smile as she appeared, reaching for the remote control to mute the television.

'Sorry I'm late,' Rebecca said, slipping off her coat.

Leighton checked his watch. 'Crumbs, is it really almost nine?'

'I'm afraid so. And I've got homework. Do you mind if I borrow your laptop?'

'Go for it.'

Rebecca reached for the MacBook on the coffee table, set it down in her lap and flipped it open. 'What's your password?'

'Owls – capital O – one eight six seven,' he responded, distractedly, his attention diverted by a player's attempt to score. He tutted as the goalkeeper succeeded in intercepting the ball.

Rebecca typed it in, smiling as she recalled a former colleague's use of his football club as the basis for his tablet passcode. That had been in the days when device PINs were limited to four digits, and the man in question had been the subject of relentless teasing after someone borrowing the tablet had asked what the code was and he had unthinkingly spelled it out W-H-A-M. She dug the DVD from her bag before checking each end of the laptop, only to find nowhere to insert the disc.

'Does this not have a DVD drive?'

'Huh?' Leighton looked around. 'Oh, no. Apple stopped doing them years ago.' He sat up slowly, tipping Pandora down into his lap. The cat sprang up onto the sofa back and stalked away, clearly put out at being disturbed.

Rebecca sighed.

'I'm only guessing, but I suspect a film with a title like *To Slay an Angel* won't be your cup of tea,' he remarked, indicating the DVD case in her hand. 'Mind you, given how you feel about tea, it might be exactly that.'

Rebecca glanced down with a frown before looking back to him. 'Don't tell me you can read Russian?'

'Uh-huh,' he replied, casually, taking the case from her and indicating the line of text beneath the title. 'A demonic assassin stalks the fringes of the subconscious.'

Rebecca stared at him in astonishment. After a moment, he broke into a grin. 'The sum total of what I know of the Russian language fits on a vodka bottle. I just recognise the picture on the box.' Handing the DVD case back to her, he added, 'I watched it with subtitles a year or two back.'

Rebecca smiled and rolled her eyes.

'How's that homework, anyway?'

'It's not. The film in the box isn't the one *on* the box. And rumour has it that the replacement is a snuff film. Jakob had a handful of them, all disguised as Russian films.'

'Put it on, then,' Leighton said. 'There's a DVD drive to the left-hand side of the screen.' He indicated the television.

'Do you not want to see the rest of the match?'

'Nah, it's just a random game I put on for something to watch.'

Rebecca hesitated before saying, 'Ok, but you'll have to keep it to yourself. Max has been on at Forrester, saying you need to take it easy and I should stop involving you in work.'

'How much easier is it possible to take it than sitting on the sofa watching TV?' Leighton asked, as Rebecca stood and moved to insert the disc.

'I know,' she acknowledged. 'Just keep it zipped and save me some grief, ok?'

'Yeah, yeah, all right.'

Rebecca slid the DVD into the slot before joining Leighton on the sofa. For ten seconds or so, the screen remained blank; then the name *In the Shadows* appeared in gothic font as the picture slowly faded in. It was shot in black and white, and opened with a slow zoom in on a young woman sitting crosslegged on the ground beneath a tree, threading daisies together. She was trussed up in a corset, and the daisy chain snaked across the full skirt of her dress. The camera was still panning in when Leighton sat forwards abruptly.

'Run it back.'

Rebecca glanced his way. 'What?'

'Run it back,' he said, adding a hand gesture for emphasis.

Rebecca sighed, reaching for the remote and rewinding to the moment the picture began to appear. As the field of view slowly contracted around the actress, Rebecca studied it intently, trying to work out what it was that he'd spotted. The image was periodically obscured by the credits, which announced that it was *A Eunice Oxtern Film* before naming its star as Emily Munster. Rebecca wondered whether she was the woman currently occupying the screen. The name melted away and was replaced, a couple of seconds later, by the words *Produced by Kojak D. Beria*.

'Stop there,' Leighton instructed.

Rebecca hit pause. The letters on the screen had started to fade out again, giving them a slightly ghostly appearance. 'What?'

Leighton reached for a pencil and a torn envelope that lay atop the coffee table, and began scribbling something. After several seconds, he passed the envelope to her. Rebecca cast her eyes over the handful of words and arrows in front of her before looking to him in astonishment.

'I can't believe you figured that out in the time it takes to blink,' she said. 'How is that even possible?'

Leighton shrugged. 'Years of cryptic crosswords?'

Rebecca shook her head. 'Your brain is on a different plane from mine.'

'Yeah, you remember to pay your credit card bills on time and don't get hit with late charges,' he responded, ruefully.

'Just set up a direct debit.'

'You make it sound so simple,' he replied, with a wry smile.

Rebecca was inclined to respond that it *was* simple, but before she had a chance Leighton changed the subject.

'Let's watch the film,' he said, at the same moment Pandora meowed loudly from her position by the back door. Leighton immediately moved to stand.

'She has you wrapped around her little paw,' Rebecca remarked, with a smile.

'Uh-huh,' he agreed. 'But it's probably best she doesn't watch this with us, anyway.'

'Why, because she's under eighteen?' Rebecca joked.

'Well there is that, obviously,' he replied, as he opened the back door. 'But more importantly, we don't want her getting any ideas!'

Twelve

Lawrence was waiting in reception when Max arrived at work, shortly after eight on Monday morning. Max didn't look as if he'd had a relaxing weekend, and the strain of his recent workload was beginning to show, which perhaps explained why his mobile had been switched off the night before. Lawrence had known him for almost twenty years, and although Max was a decade or so older, Lawrence had never really thought he looked it. This morning, he did.

'How do,' Max greeted him, without much enthusiasm.

'Morning,' Lawrence responded, getting to his feet. 'You look shattered. Tough weekend?'

'You could say that,' Max replied, wearily, using his card key to open the first of several doors into the pathology unit and holding it open for Lawrence to follow.

'As and when you have the time, we should grab a pint,' Lawrence suggested.

Max nodded before saying, facetiously, 'Is now too early?'

He didn't temper the remark with a smile, prompting Lawrence to ask whether everything was all right.

'Not really,' Max admitted, opening another door. 'Marnie said yesterday that as all I seem to need these days is a hotel, I ought to move into one.'

Lawrence didn't know how to respond to that. From the little Max had shared, there was no way of knowing whether Marnie had simply been expressing her frustration or whether she had actually wanted him to move out. The scenario was also rather too close to home. Katie's tolerance of the hours Lawrence's job demanded had fluctuated considerably over the years, and the subject was probably the most common cause of arguments between them. For a couple of years, Jimmy had been in constant trouble at school, and on more than one occasion with the law, and Katie had made it quite clear she held Lawrence – or, at least, his frequent absences – largely responsible. Thankfully, the boy's behaviour had improved considerably over the past year, much to the benefit of Lawrence and Katie's relationship.

'That seems a bit harsh,' he observed, at length. 'You didn't plan on being a member of staff down. And it's not like you got any notice.'

'No, but I haven't exactly gone out of my way to fix the situation.' Max responded, digging the keys to his office out of his pocket. 'Marnie thinks that's because I'd rather spend time at a crime scene or in the mortuary than with her and the girls. In actual fact, it's because I'd rather be at a crime scene or in the mortuary than drawing up schedules and budgets. The trouble is, those things still need doing.' He stopped walking as they drew level with his office. Unlocking the door, he added, 'So it is largely my fault I spent the night at a Premier Inn.'

Lawrence followed Max into the office, debating what to say next. 'It's a bit early for a drink, but I can make half an hour for a coffee, if you like?' He offered.

'Thanks, I appreciate it, but I really don't have the time.' Max slipped his coat off and flung it over a chair. 'And apologies for not getting back to you last night. What was it you wanted to ask?'

'It's about the fracture in Tony's neck. Is it possible that could have happened as a result of his falling back against something?'

'Very possible.'

Lawrence nodded thoughtfully. 'I know you said it was hard to ascribe a definitive cause of death,' he said, at length. 'What are the chances the fracture killed him?'

'Very small. There was some soft tissue damage, but no displacement of the bone, and no evidence of damage to the disks or ligaments. He could have been in serious trouble if he'd gone on walking around like that and something had shifted, but as far as those sorts of injuries go, he was lucky.'

Lawrence sighed.

'Sorry,' Max added. 'Not the answer you were looking for?'

Lawrence answered wordlessly with a change in expression.

'It is possible it killed him indirectly,' Max offered.

'How so?'

'Well, aside from pain, the after-effects of a cervical fracture can include stiffness. The pain could well have been masked by the ketamine in his system, but if his neck was stiff he may have had trouble moving it if he ended up face down on the bed.'

'So along with ketamine being a risk factor in its own right, that gives us two potential causes of suffocation that don't involve anyone else.'

'Is accidental death looking likely?'

'I'm not sure about likely,' Lawrence replied. 'But Jakob claims Tony slipped on the stairs and fell backwards. He said he might have hit his head, but he's not sure, because Tony was behind him.'

'From my perspective, nothing about that sounds implausible. Do you think he's genuine?'

'I don't know,' Lawrence admitted. 'We've no evidence he had any involvement in making the child pornography – we've found nothing of that nature on his mobile or any of his SD cards, and zero evidence of a connection between him and Dale. They've had no contact by phone or email, and, with the exception of Tony, it doesn't seem as though they have any contacts in common. So that leaves us short on any obvious motive for murder. But how we'll ever know for sure whether what happened was accidental, I don't know. All we seem to have is ambiguous evidence and one man's word to go on. And the fact I don't much like him doesn't make him guilty.'

Max nodded. 'I'm afraid there's not much more I can offer you,' he said, apologetically. 'Given the elapsed time between death and the discovery of the body, there are big grey areas, and there's probably little to be had from the postmortem that will be beyond reasonable doubt in court.'

Lawrence sighed.

'I'll ask someone else to take a look over everything, see whether they spot anything I've missed,' Max added. 'But I suspect the outcome of this case is going to hinge on your work, not mine.'

Lawrence nodded. Unwelcome though they were, his friend's words came as little surprise. 'I was afraid you might say that.'

'Morning.'

Lawrence looked up to see Rebecca leaning against his office doorframe, one hand wrapped around a mug featuring a picture of a cupcake, a piece of paper in the other.

'Morning Becky. How are you?'

'Good, thanks,' she replied, moving to sit down before saying, with a rather smug smile, 'I've come to turn in my film review.'

Guessing from her expression that she had something worthwhile to share, Lawrence leaned back in his chair and said, 'I'm all ears.'

'It was gothic horror. A beautiful young woman alone in a remote castle seemingly being hunted or haunted by a cloaked, hooded figure. A lot of it's filmed in a library, with her thumbing through old texts accompanied by a voiceover of her explaining how she came to be isolated and alone. Then at the end, she holds some sort of ceremony in a falling-down chapel and sacrifices her stalker on a stone sarcophagus.'

'Did it look realistic?'

'Very. And if it was, there'd have been evidence everywhere, because she slit his throat and there was blood all over the shop.'

'And the rest of the production?'

'Professional. It was clearly shot by someone who knew what they were doing.' She paused momentarily before adding, 'And I think that someone was Jakob.'

'Really?' Lawrence exclaimed. 'What makes you think that?' He didn't imagine Jamie would have overlooked something as basic as checking the names of the film's cast and crew when he had first gone through the DVDs. Besides, if it had been that simple, Rebecca presumably wouldn't have used the words *I think*.

Rebecca set her mug down on his desk to allow her to take hold of both sides of the piece of paper that she had laid in her lap when she sat down. Holding it up, she indicated the words *Produced by Kojak D. Beria*, which were superimposed on an image of a woman sitting under a tree. 'This is an anagram of his name.'

Lawrence leaned to take the printout. 'That's one hell of a spot,' he remarked, admiringly, mentally rearranging the letters to confirm it for himself.

'Not my spot,' she admitted, sheepishly.

Lawrence raised his eyebrows. 'Leighton?' He guessed.

She nodded.

'Let's go and talk to Jakob to see whether there's any possibility it really is a snuff movie. If that's nothing more than a rumour, he should be able to give us the actors' details. If he can't do that, we'll have to take a closer look.'

'And if we can work out where it was filmed, we can see whether there's any forensic evidence.'

Lawrence nodded. 'If need be, we'll apply for access to his financial records, check his SatNav history, et cetera. But let's talk to him first.' He reached for his mobile phone and moved to stand.

'I've also had a call from the lab about the original SD card,' Rebecca said, as she got to her feet. 'Martina said that when she and Tony found it, it was sticky, as if someone had splashed a fizzy drink or some juice on it. Turns out, it was semen.'

'Nice,' Lawrence remarked, drily. 'Did they manage to get any DNA?'

'They did, and it's not a match for Jakob. We're still waiting on Dale's DNA test. Oh, and I've managed to get an address for Dale's mother.'

'In that case, our chat with Jakob can wait,' Lawrence replied, checking his pocket for his car keys. 'Let's get round to Mrs Sanders' place before the magistrates let Dale out on bail and he beats us to it.'

*****

When asked for his mother's address, Dale had refused to provide it on the grounds she had dementia and that a visit from the police would serve no purpose other than to upset her. But, given that she lived within five miles of his own home, there seemed a reasonable chance that her flat was the site of the room used to shoot the indecent photographs and video footage. It certainly wasn't a possibility they could ignore.

Rebecca and Lawrence arrived at the Ealing address Rebecca had obtained from the local council to find that Eugenia Sanders' home was on the second floor of a relatively smart council block with pebbledash walls and new-looking windows. The front door was opened by a carer, who confirmed that she knew Dale and that he stayed at the flat a couple of nights a week. When presented with a photograph of Harvey, however, she shook her head apologetically, saying he didn't look familiar. She made no objection when Lawrence asked if they might have a quick look around the flat, and it took them only a couple of minutes to establish that none of the property's five rooms was a match for the one in the video. Rebecca paused by the kitchen window, which overlooked what an estate agent might have described as a car park, but was really just a handful of parking spaces and, beyond them, a row of garages.

'Do we know whether those garages belong to these flats? Lawrence asked, as he joined her at the window.

'Possibly some of them, but not this flat, according to the council,' Rebecca replied.

Lawrence sighed.

'Is Dale in some kind of trouble?' The carer asked, hesitantly, from the doorway.

Lawrence had scarcely drawn breath to provide a stock answer when a crash from the adjacent room diverted the woman's attention and she disappeared. Rebecca looked around herself, wondering whether the kitchen had been in place since the building's construction. The avocado-green formica cupboard doors must have been older than she was, and the white, stand-alone cooker reminded her of the one her grandmother had owned; the old-fashioned grill had cooked crispy bacon better than any appliance Rebecca had ever used.

She started as Lawrence touched her arm to get her attention. He nodded towards something behind her, and she turned to see an old Kenwood mixer, and, above it, a painted wooden key rack. It looked to be home made; a couple of the variously coloured wooden strips mounted on the rectangular plaque were slightly askew, and, instead of hooks, the keys were suspended from nails. Alongside several sets of keys attached to generic plastic tags was a keyring that looked as unique as the rack. Sealed inside a plastic bubble was a child's drawing of a fish and the letters SANDE, written in uneven black felt-tip pen. It reminded Rebecca of one she had seen in Tony's room featuring a yellow blob with lines radiating from it, presumably representing the sun.

'The woman who runs the sessions Tony helped with at the Harvey Foundation is called Sandie,' Lawrence said, in a low voice. 'I wonder whether they make things like this at the centre?'

'Probably. Tony had one with a kid's drawing in it, too.'

'Did he?'

'Yes. Where does Sandie live?'

'Near Gunnersbury Park. Probably only about a mile away.' Lawrence pulled his mobile phone from his pocket and took a photograph of the keyring before continuing, 'She has Mondays off. If we're lucky, she might be home now.'

Sandie's living room was dominated by an enormous tropical fish tank. The hexagonal structure stood in the middle of the room, topped with a spotless glass cover that looked as if it might double as a coffee table. Colourful fish darted in and out between plants and rocks, and Rebecca had a job keeping her attention on the woman sitting across from her.

Sandie was older than Rebecca had expected – at least fifty, probably nearer sixty – with greying corkscrew curls that verged on frizzy. She was clearly fond of bold accessories, and was wearing chunky drop earrings that rattled when she moved her head, and eye-catching glasses with multicoloured frames. Rebecca felt surprised that the woman didn't find having something so busy at the periphery of her field of view distracting, in the next moment realising that the reverse of the frames probably wasn't similarly kaleidoscopic.

'We've a few questions about Dale Sanders,' Lawrence began, after declining Sandie's offer of a drink.

'Dale?' Sandie echoed, sounding surprised. 'I don't think he and Tony really knew one another.'

'You may well be right,' Lawrence replied. 'How about you, do you know Dale well?'

'Yes, very. He and Gareth – my late husband – were great friends.'

'He has a set of keys with what looks like your name on them.'

Sandie's eyebrows contracted in concern. 'Is he ok?'

'He's fine. Are the keys yours?'

'Yes. When I go away he keeps an eye on my fish. Small problems can get out of hand very quickly in a tropical tank, and it's devastating to come home to find everything dead. Dale comes over this way every two or three days to see his mum, so he offered to look in on them at the same time.' She smiled. 'He even sends me pictures. It's nice to have that connection with them when I'm not around.'

Rebecca resisted the urge to raise her eyebrows in disbelief. People having a connection with a cat or a dog she could understand, but she couldn't imagine how one *connected* with a fish even while in its company, let alone from afar.

'It's actually a photograph that brings us here,' Lawrence replied. 'We're trying to identify where it was taken. Would you mind giving us a quick tour of the house?'

Sandie's eyebrows pulled into a frown. 'Can you not just show me the photo?'

'I'm afraid not. It won't take us five minutes to have a look around.'

'I'd really rather have a chance to tidy upstairs first,' Sandy said, anxiously.

'We're not here to judge you, Mrs Corcoran.'

With a sigh, Sandie nodded her acquiescence, standing and heading for the door.

Immediately across the entrance hall was a large room that had presumably once served as a dining room. A folded mahogany table was pushed up against the window, with six chairs stacked two by two in front of it, one of each pair upside down on top of the other. Where once the room might have been dominated by the table, its centrepiece was now another fish tank, which appeared to be an integral part of the long cabinet on which it rested. Fluorescent yellow and electric blue fish tacked and veered around a network of corals, and Rebecca could hear a low hum that was presumably emanating from the pump responsible for the bubbles rising through the water at the rear of the tank.

Rebecca half expected to find another fish tank in the kitchen, but, with the exception of a couple of garish abstract paintings, there was nothing remarkable about the room.

Looking to Sandie, Lawrence pointed to the closed door to what Rebecca guessed was a utility room.

'Oh – that's Gareth's studio,' Sandie said, making no move towards it. 'He was an artist.'

'May we have a look?'

There was a brief silence before she said, with a heavy sigh, 'If you must.'

Lawrence depressed the handle and pushed the door open. Even before she had a chance to follow him into the room, Rebecca was aware of the sudden influx of light. The rest of the house was decidedly gloomy, but the room in which she now stood had glass doors that spanned the full width of what would otherwise have been the end wall, and, above them, skylights set into the sloping roof. The space was almost completely unfurnished, containing only a couple of easels, a stool and a small wooden table. On top of the table – and perhaps what Sandie hadn't wanted them to see – was what Rebecca could only describe as a shrine. A framed photograph sat in the centre, with candles burning on either side and a handful of crystals scattered in front. Behind the candles were, on one side, a large pine cone and, on the other, an animal skull scarcely bigger than Rebecca's fist. Several moments passed before she managed to tear her eyes away to take in the rest of the room, and, instinctively, she looked up.

*****

'Well that was painful,' Lawrence observed, as he pulled on his seatbelt. And painful felt like an understatement. Telling a woman whose husband of almost three decades hadn't yet been dead a year that his art studio had featured in articles of child pornography had been bad enough without the follow-up realisation that the man had almost certainly been in on the abuse.

Having matched a hairline crack visible in the photographs and video footage to that on the studio's back wall, Lawrence's first question for Sandie had related to her whereabouts on the date the photographs had been taken. After looking out the previous year's diary, she had established that a visit to her sister had taken her to Dorset. Gareth had stayed at home, ostensibly to paint – so the chances of anyone else having had the opportunity to use the studio without his knowledge seemed remote. The only likely alternative Lawrence could think of, which would hardly have offered the woman much comfort, was that Gareth had remained in London for some other reason he had chosen not to share with her – presumably, an affair.

The original scenario quickly came to look like the correct one, however, when it became apparent that Sandie often provided respite care for special needs children, and had looked after Harvey and Louise Calhoun several times, on one occasion overnight. Lawrence hadn't been particularly surprised to learn that Gareth had been happy to let them play in his studio, despite normally being very precious about the space. But given that there was no chance of charging a dead man, having to put the woman through anything further had seemed nothing short of cruel.

'And on top of being hit by all that, she's now got people going through everything she owns,' Rebecca replied, summarising his own thoughts.

Lawrence nodded. In an ideal world, he would have left Rebecca to supervise that particular operation, because he knew she could be relied on to do it sensitively. But he was wary of relying too heavily on Rebecca for such tasks because it would almost certainly result in someone – probably Eva – objecting on the grounds that assigning the bulk of *touchy-feely jobs* to a woman who hadn't signed up for a career as a family liaison officer was nothing short of sexist. And perhaps there was some truth to that, although Eva herself was about as sensitive as a sledgehammer. More importantly, the fact Rebecca wouldn't have complained didn't mean she wouldn't have minded.

'Part of me hopes there won't be anything to find,' Lawrence admitted.

'I suspect that would be cold comfort at this stage.'

'You're probably right.'

'And no doubt she'll blame herself for not realising,' Rebecca added, drawing her mobile out of her handbag. 'He gets off scot free and she ends up paying the price.' She dumped the bag into the passenger seat's footwell. 'Life really is a bitch.'

Jakob didn't do much to disguise his displeasure at finding Lawrence and Rebecca on his doorstep early on Monday evening. Showing them into the front room, he dropped down into an armchair with the words, 'What now?'

'We'd like to talk a bit more about your collection of snuff movies,' Lawrence replied, sitting opposite the man.

Jakob practically rolled his eyes. 'That won't take long, there's not a lot more I can tell you.'

'No?' Lawrence drew out Rebecca's printout from *In the Shadows* and presented it to the man. 'This is an anagram of your name,' he observed. 'Quite a coincidence if you weren't involved in filming it, I'd say.'

'That's not a snuff movie,' Jakob responded, managing to sound exasperated and bored at the same time.

'It's being circulated as such on the dark web.'

'So? The Internet's full of bullshit.'

'You don't deny being involved in this film's production, then?'

'No.'

'Why didn't you put your real name to it?'

'Because I've made a name for myself in documentaries, and I'd rather keep the two separate. Plenty of journalists use a pen name when they write fiction, it's no different.'

'And why is it disguised with a Russian coverslip, like the purported snuff movies?'

Jakob sighed pointedly. 'I explained *that* yesterday,' he said. 'I use those when I don't want people to take things without asking.'

Lawrence nodded. 'It looks like you shot it in a nice spot,' he observed. 'Where did you do the filming?'

'In Scotland, in the middle of nowhere.'

'Which part of Scotland?'

'I haven't a clue. I didn't pick the location, and I slept most of the way there.'

'Really?' Lawrence responded, disbelievingly. 'Who did pick the location, then?'

'My ex, Summer. It was her baby – she wrote the script – I just did the filming and editing for her.'

'We're going to need her full name and contact details,' Lawrence said, drawing his notebook from his jacket pocket, turning to a clean page and setting it and a pen down on the coffee table in front of Jakob.

'I can give you her name, but I don't have any other details,' Jakob replied, reaching for the pen.

'Don't push your luck.'

Jakob held his hands out. 'She's my *ex*. We've not spoken in over a year.'

'And let me guess, she was responsible for hiring the actors, and you've no idea how we can get hold of them, either?'

'She *did* most of the acting.'

'Did she use a pseudonym, too, then? Because the credits name the lead actress as Emily Munster.'

'Which is an anagram of her name,' Jakob returned, as if it should have been obvious, scribbling in the notebook before sliding it back across the table.

Lawrence picked it up and flicked back a few pages in search of the name of the man whose character, at least, had been sacrificed in the final scene of the film. 'Does that mean Henry Love is also an anagram?'

Jakob shrugged. 'I don't know. I'd never met the guy before we started filming. He was someone Summer knew.'

'Well presumably you either used that name during filming or you didn't,' Lawrence observed, irritably. 'Or did you direct him with *oi, you* throughout?'

'He used a nickname. Ace.'

'Why Ace?'

'Fucked if I know,' Jakob returned. 'I didn't care what the guy's name was, I was more concerned with the fact he was bloody hard work to direct!'

'Any particular reason?'

'Yeah, he was whacked out half the time.'

'On what?'

'I don't know. Weed? Jellies? Smack, maybe? Something that zoned him out.'

'That would have been handy if you had wanted to finish him off, wouldn't it?'

'Well, I didn't.'

Lawrence nodded. 'If the sacrifice scene at the end of the film wasn't real, perhaps you could run us through how you made it look so realistic?'

'The same way anyone creating a murder scene for a film does,' Jakob responded, sounding exasperated. 'Latex, fake blood, makeup.' He shrugged. 'I didn't pull it all together, that was Summer's handiwork. But it took hours to prep and all of about a minute to destroy.'

'Considering how few people were involved in making this film, you seem to be very sketchy on the details,' Lawrence observed. 'You don't know the actor's name, you don't know where the film was made, you don't know how the effects were achieved –'

'And *you* seem to be determined to pin something on me, regardless of the fact you've no actual evidence,' Jakob returned, irritably.

'Well perhaps you can help us to help you,' Lawrence replied. 'If we can work out where the murder scene was shot, we can send a couple of crime scene investigators along, and if they don't find anything, we won't have to trouble you any further.'

'I already told you, I slept most of the way there.'

'How about on the journey home?'

'It was late and it was dark,' Jakob retorted.

'If the murder scene in the film wasn't genuine, presumably Ace was also with you for the return journey? I should hope he wasn't driving, if he was on drugs.'

'No,' Jakob responded. 'He and Summer stayed another night. I needed to get back for a flight.'

'Right,' Lawrence replied, disbelievingly, guessing the addition of this detail was intended to distance Jakob from whatever might have happened to Ace. 'So if you didn't drive, and Summer wasn't with you, how exactly did you get back from *the middle of nowhere*, as you put it? Teleportation? Or was there someone else involved?'

'I got the train.'

'Oh, so you *do* know about where you were.'

'Not really, it was over an hour's drive to the station, and I'm dyslexic, so I'm no good with all the weird long names up there.'

Lawrence raised his eyebrows. 'If you can't read road signs, I'm not sure you should be driving, either.'

'I didn't say I couldn't read them,' Jakob snapped. 'I said I'm not good with weird long names. They don't mean anything to me. But I wasn't driving. Summer dropped me off.'

'Presumably you did at least know where the train was going?'

'Glasgow. I got a train back to London from there.'

'Where were you flying to?' Lawrence asked, thinking Border Force might be able to help them to narrow down the date the film had been made – assuming that at least some of what Jakob had told them was true.

'How can that possibly be relevant?' Jakob demanded. 'You might have all day to ask pointless questions, but I don't have time to give you my life story! I've got a deadline to meet and a five-part series to research!' He paused momentarily before adding, 'That was supposed to start with a look at contaminated drinking water, but I'm wondering whether I shouldn't go for something closer to home. Perhaps I'll make my next documentary about police harassment!'

It was raining heavily by the time Rebecca and Lawrence left Jakob's home, and Rebecca pulled her scarf over her head before stepping out into the deluge. They jogged down the road and around the corner to where they had parked the car, diving into the vehicle's interior the moment Lawrence had released the central locking. Lawrence slammed his door shut before exclaiming, 'Arrogant son of a bitch!'

Rebecca didn't immediately reply, and after a moment he glanced her way, sighing heavily and adding, 'Sorry.'

Rebecca dismissed the apology with a shake of her head. 'You're not wrong.'

'I didn't believe a word that came out of his mouth,' Lawrence went on, as Rebecca peeled her sodden scarf away from her hair. 'But we've no body, no crime scene and no missing person, and I'm going to have a hell of a job persuading the powers that be to launch an investigation off the back of an Internet rumour.' He sighed again. At length, he drew his notebook from his jacket pocket. 'We need to run a search for Summer Tilney,' he said, opening it and passing it to Rebecca. 'Given that they're no longer in a relationship, we might be able to play them off against one another.'

Rebecca took the notebook. 'I suppose we could also try making anagrams from the name Henry Love and run the results through the misper database.'

'That's not a bad idea,' Lawrence replied, starting the ignition. 'Are you seeing Leighton this evening? That sounds like a task that would be right up his street.'

'No,' Rebecca replied. 'But there's sure to be a website that can do it.' She rummaged around in her bag for her mobile.

'Good point. All we need after that is a website that can solve crimes, and we can all go home.'

Rebecca smiled, typing *anagram generator* into Google, then selecting the first one that came up. She wasn't expecting that many results for a name just nine letters long, and the outcome of the search took her by surprise.

'Wow. I get nearly eight hundred results.'

'For making anagrams?' Lawrence asked, glancing over his shoulder before pulling out into the road.

'No, for anagrams of the name Henry Love.'

'Crumbs.'

Rebecca began scrolling down the list. 'Although most of them aren't viable combinations if you're looking for more than random combinations of words.' She returned to the top of the page and selected a dropdown arrow beside the word 'options'. This gave her the choice, among other things, of setting a maximum number of words per result. She selected two and reran the name.

'Ah, that's more like it,' she said, as the list shrunk more than twenty-fold.

'What's that?'

'If you limit it to two words, you get thirty-six results.' She ran her eyes slowly down the list. 'Four of which look a bit like Harvey,' she observed. 'Is Olny a surname?' She spelt it out. 'I know I've seen it with an E.'

'Olney's a place in Buckinghamshire,' Lawrence said. 'But have someone run it – and anything else that could conceivably be a name – through the misper database and the PNC.'

'Do you want me to include women's names? I've got Evelyn and Helen here.'

'Evelyn isn't only a women's name.'

'Really?'

'Evelyn Waugh?'

'Oh,' Rebecca nodded. She recognised the name, but she couldn't have provided any other details.

'It's also a surname, I think.'

Rebecca regarded the list in front of her for a moment before saying, 'How about initials?' She dropped her hand into her lap, looking to Lawrence. 'Jakob used a middle initial for his alter ego. What if they took a middle initial from Henry Love's original name?'

'Let's keep things simple for now,' Lawrence replied. 'Get someone to run the thirty-six combinations on that list, and we'll see where that takes us.' He slowed the car as the light ahead turned red. 'If we go down the rabbit hole of every possible permutation, we may never get out again.'

Thirteen

None of the names Rebecca had derived from the moniker Henry Love appeared on the missing persons database, but two names – Elvyn Hore and Herve Lyon – did come up in a search of the Police National Computer. They were able to quickly rule Elvyn Hore out of the running on account of his having been incarcerated in Durham Prison for the best part of a decade, leaving them to concentrate on Herve Lyon. The man in the film wasn't recognisable from mugshots on the system, because he had spent most of his time on screen hidden by a hood, and on the rare occasions his face was exposed, it was dark. One of the video technicians had spent some time enhancing a stretch of footage before applying facial-recognition technology, but, even then, was able to tell them only that Herve Lyon couldn't be ruled *out* as being the actor named as Henry Love in the credits of *In the Shadows*.

Determining whether Herve was still alive proved more challenging still. On the occasions of his two most recent arrests – both for drugs-related offences – a couple of years earlier, he had reportedly been of no fixed address. And, much as a homeless drug addict might be, as Jakob had put it the night before, *bloody hard work to direct*, he would have made for an ideal candidate if you were looking for a victim who was unlikely to be missed.

Having handed Eva the task of trying to find out more about Herve Lyon, as well as the location of *In the Shadows*'s shooting and the whereabouts of Summer Tilney, Lawrence and Rebecca had set out for the Surrey town of Ashford, where Irene was being held on remand at Bronzefield Prison. Rebecca had made an appointment with the prison for ten a.m., and by five past she, Lawrence and Irene were sitting in a small, windowless interview room. Irene looked pale and tired, but perfectly composed, her anxiety betrayed only by the way she had the sleeves of her grey jumper pulled down over her hands.

'We'd like to talk some more about what happened on the morning after Martina's party,' Lawrence began.

Irene's dark eyebrows contracted into a frown. 'Why?'

'Because I don't think you told us the full story. In fact, I think the story you've told us so far contains more than an element of fiction.'

'Why would you think that?'

'Let's just say there are a few things that don't add up,' Lawrence responded. 'So we're here to give you the opportunity to tell us what really happened.'

'I already did.'

'Really?'

'Yes.'

'Ok, well if you're not going to tell us what happened, I'm going to tell you what *I* think happened,' Lawrence replied, resting his forearms on the table and threading his fingers together. 'You weren't the one to find Tony's body. That was Jakob.' Lawrence paused for emphasis, watching Irene closely. 'He came to you on the Sunday morning to tell you what had happened, and offered – for whatever reason – to help you move the body. He allowed you to believe Tony's death was your responsibility, the result of the ketamine you'd supplied. You probably had no reason to doubt him.' Lawrence paused again. 'But in reality, the ketamine wasn't what killed Tony. Jakob did. So, in actual fact, you helped *him* to move the body.'

Irene didn't immediately respond, several different emotions crossing her face as she presumably processed what Lawrence had just said. At length, she said, her voice unsteady, 'But why would he have done that?'

'Because Tony was in a position to report him for a crime.'

Irene swallowed. She looked shell-shocked.

'He was never interested in protecting you, so I wouldn't put yourself on the line on his account,' Lawrence added.

'What crime?' Irene asked, her voice wavering. 'What did he do?'

'I'm afraid I can't go into that.'

Irene didn't respond.

'Were you really the one who found Tony on the morning after the party?'

The seconds ticked by. Eventually, Irene shook her head.

'So what did happen?'

Irene drew a deep breath. 'I woke up about eleven. I was really hungover, but I could hear the others talking downstairs, so I got up and headed down.' She raised a hand to rub her forehead. 'Then, an hour or so later, Maya and Martina left for the pub.

Jakob said he'd wait for me to get ready. After they'd gone, he told me about Tony. I lost it.' She swallowed. 'He forced some whisky down me, to try to calm me down. I'm not sure whether I calmed down or just zoned out, but once I'd stopped crying he said he could help me move the body that night. He said if we put him in the corner beyond the shed, it would probably just look like he'd passed out drunk and frozen out there. He said it happens all the time in places like Russia.' She paused. 'Then he said we ought to go to the pub so the others didn't get suspicious, and that if I couldn't face it he'd tell them I was too hungover and had gone back to bed.'

'Did you at any point question why he was offering to help you conceal a body?' Lawrence asked.

'He said calling the police wasn't going to bring Tony back, and –' she cast her eyes down before adding, in little more than a whisper, 'And that it had been his choice to take the ketamine.'

'There's a big difference between not calling the police and moving and hiding a body,' Lawrence observed.

Irene nodded. 'He said –' she broke off, closing her eyes momentarily. 'He said if I went to prison he'd never have a chance to – to –' she stopped again. 'He said *to do this*, and then he kissed me.' Irene raised a hand to cover her eyes. 'He told me he had feelings for me – that he had done for ages – and –' she gulped. 'And idiot that I am, I believed him!'

'And how did you feel about him?'

'I honestly don't know,' Irene replied, rather hopelessly. 'I was hardly in the best head space. And I was really grateful to have someone take charge.' She swallowed. 'That sounds so pathetic.' She shook her head slightly. 'I can't believe I fell for it. All this because of him.' She cast her hands around to indicate their surroundings.

'It's not all because of him, though, is it?' Lawrence responded. 'You committed a crime without Jakob's help.'

'Yeah, but I'd never have held my hands up to the ketamine if I'd known it wasn't what killed Tony,' Irene returned, bluntly. 'That was what clinched it. Thinking I'd done that was killing *me*.'

Not surprisingly, Jakob had denied having any part in moving Tony's body, and dismissed Irene's version of events, accusing her of lying. After spending the best part of an hour in an interview room with the man, Lawrence had decided to take a break and had made his way back upstairs to CID. He'd scarcely sat down at his desk when a knock came at his open office door and he looked up to see Eva standing on the threshold.

'Afternoon.'

'Hi,' she replied, advancing towards his desk. 'I've searched every system and social media network out there and I've turned up no results for a Summer Tilney who even remotely fits the bill. I tried running the name Emily Munster, as well, but that didn't net me anything useful, either.'

Lawrence sighed. 'It could be that neither is actually her real name.'

'I did wonder about that,' Eva admitted. 'I've also been through Jakob's credit card history. There's not much that stands out, but he did make a payment at a petrol station in Lochgilphead in June last year.'

Lawrence nodded, mentally trying to place the location and failing.

'There's an insane number of castles in Scotland, but I've drawn up a list of the ones in that part of the country and identified those that seem to be available for rent,' Eva went on. 'The film footage doesn't show enough for us to identify the place from the limited pictures I can find online, so either someone's going to need to go and check them out, or we're going to have to try to get in touch with the owners and see whether they recognise any of the interior shots.'

Lawrence nodded again. If he wanted to look any further into the making of *In the Shadows*, he was going to have to discuss it with his boss, Chief Superintendent Angus MacLennan. Between the fact that they had no hard evidence any crime had been committed and that Herve Lyon hadn't been reported missing, he suspected MacLennan wouldn't view it as a valuable use of resources.

'Ok, could you send that list through to me, and –'

His mobile began to ring, and he felt glad of the interruption even before he saw Rebecca's name on the screen. The verdict in Healy's trial was expected before the end of the day, so she had taken the afternoon off. It was always a tense wait to see whether their work had paid off, but never more so than today.

'Thanks, Eva,' he said, as he reached for his phone. 'Leave it with me, ok?'

She nodded, turning to go, and he accepted Rebecca's call.

'Becky. Is the verdict in?'

'Yes,' she said, over a hubbub of background noise. 'GBH. Five years.'

Lawrence breathed a sigh of relief. He couldn't honestly say it was the result he had been hoping for, but in terms of what had seemed realistic, it was the best-case scenario. Proving that Norman Healy had locked Leighton in the freezer container with the intention of killing him would have been nigh on impossible. Lawrence had no doubt that Healy had been the one to close the freezer door, but even after spending hours interviewing the man, he couldn't have said whether Healy had anticipated his actions resulting in any serious harm. That didn't change the fact that he *had* caused irreparable damage, however, and, in the absence of any clear intent, five years was the maximum sentence a judge could have imposed.

'I'm glad they managed to make GBH stick,' Lawrence said. 'How does Leighton feel about it?'

'I've no idea,' Rebecca replied. 'When we left the courtroom he said he wanted to go to the pub and talk about something else.'

'Is that where you are now?'

'Yes, we're in the Coal Hole.'

'I'll try to pop in if you're still there when I'm done. In the meantime, have one on me and I'll reimburse you tomorrow.'

'Thanks, I'm sure he'll appreciate that.'

'Ok, well I'll let you go. Keep me posted if you head out somewhere else.'

'Of course.'

Lawrence rang off, then immediately thought of a question he should have asked: whether Leighton had filled Max in on the result. He was just writing Rebecca a quick text message when Jamie appeared in his office doorway.

'Did you hear?' The young man asked, excitedly.

'About Healy?' Lawrence replied, hitting send and returning the phone to his desk. 'Yes. Becky just called.'

'Good news, huh?'

Lawrence nodded.

'Are we planning to have another crack at Jakob today?'

Lawrence smiled, guessing what Jamie was really asking was what time he might be able to join Leighton and Rebecca - and whoever else might be with them - in the pub. Between Leighton's popularity and the significance of securing a conviction against someone who had wronged one of their own, Lawrence imagined many of their colleagues would be similarly keen to join in the celebrations. Given that Jamie had been there on the morning in April when Lawrence had opened the door to the freezer container to find Leighton curled up motionless inside, Lawrence was inclined to let him join in sooner rather than later.

'I'll take care of Jakob,' he said. 'You head over to the Coal Hole.'

Jamie's eyebrows rose. 'What, now?'

'Yes.'

'Are you sure?'

'Yes. Just don't make a big song and dance about it, because I can't let everyone leave early.' He paused, then, when Jamie hesitated, added, 'Go on,' with a wave of his hand for emphasis. 'Get down the pub before I change my mind.'

Lawrence arrived home to find Elise sitting at the kitchen table working on a poster entitled SHARKS. Central to the piece of A2 paper was a large drawing of a shark turning in the water, surrounded by a scattering of what Lawrence took to be subheadings, written in Elise's scrupulously neat hand. One of these read *Sharks are Voraicous Predators*, and he wondered, not for the first time, how it was that an avid reader like Elise didn't have a better grasp of spelling. Perhaps it was the result of the ubiquitous use of computers and other devices that not only came with spell checkers, but more often that not also corrected any errors unbidden.

'Well this looks impressive,' he said, slipping off his jacket.

'It's for school,' Elise informed him, unnecessarily, as she looked up from colouring in the fish's tail fin. 'We're doing a project on endangered sea life.'

'How much sea life is in danger of being eaten by sharks?'

'Nowhere near as much as is endangered by us,' Elise returned, reproachfully, clearly not amused by the joke.

'No, I'm sure.'

'Sharks were alive before the dinosaurs,' she went on. 'They've been around for millions and millions of years, and now humans are endangering them by eating them *and* their food.'

The last few words were delivered pointedly; Elise had turned vegetarian earlier in the year and had yet to give up on trying to persuade the rest of the family to follow suit. The chances of her succeeding were slim, although she had managed to cut their consumption of meat and fish simply because Katie was loath to cook two separate meals every night of the week. Jimmy's response, much to his sister's disgust, had been to add tinned hotdog sausages to any meal that didn't contain meat. Lawrence didn't imagine Katie was any happier than Elise about this development, having studied nutrition as part of her sports science degree, but suspected she had written it off as a battle not worth fighting.

'So what else can you tell me about sharks?' He asked.

'They don't have bones,' Elise responded. 'And they hardly kill anyone. More people are killed by cows than sharks.'

'Really?' Lawrence exclaimed, wondering how much that was simply a product of the sheer number of cows on the planet. He didn't voice the thought, however, guessing it would only prompt a diatribe on the evils of beef and dairy farming.

'And selfies,' Elise added.

'What about selfies?'

'Selfies kill more people than sharks.'

'Now that I can believe,' Lawrence said, thinking that in many of those cases the word *selfies* was probably synonymous with *stupidity*. 'You will be careful when you're taking them, won't you?'

'Yes Dad,' Elise returned, with a roll of her eyes.

Lawrence smiled. 'I'll let you get back to work. It's looking great.'

'You think?' She asked, her brow furrowing as she returned her eyes to the poster.

'I do. The only thing I would change is this,' he indicated the word *voraicous*. 'I know it doesn't sound like it, but the *I* needs to come after the *C*.'

'Are you sure?'

'Yes.'

Elise sighed, reaching for the Tippex pen that lay on the table. Lawrence turned for the hallway, pondering the vagaries of the English language and wondering whether the prevalence of disorders like dyslexia varied between countries according to how intuitive the spelling of a language was. He started up the stairs, then stopped, feeling in his jacket for his notebook and wishing he had brought his laptop home. As things stood, he would be dependent on someone else to run a check of the PNC, and that would mean waiting on them for an answer. And Lawrence wasn't at all fond of waiting.

Fourteen

Rebecca had snoozed her alarm three times before she finally managed to prise herself out of bed, cursing herself for drinking so much the night before. As she made for the kitchen to start up the coffee machine, she recalled an American friend of a friend remarking on the British habit of going out for drinks after work and having nothing to eat all evening beyond the odd handful of crisps or nuts. It wasn't, in her experience, as if most of those heading for the pub at knocking-off time *intended* to skip dinner, and she wondered why it was such a common occurrence. Perhaps in other countries there were fewer establishments whose primary purpose – at least historically – was selling alcohol. The advent of the gastropub was, after all, relatively new. Rebecca's parents had occasionally taken her and her sister to the pub when they were small, and she remembered sitting in the beer garden whilst her father went to buy drinks, because children weren't permitted inside. That had been scarcely thirty years ago. Pubs, and the attendant drinking culture, had been around for centuries.

She returned to the bedroom to find Leighton sitting up in bed, the backs of his hands resting on the duvet and his fingers curled loosely over his palms. He glanced up as she appeared, his face very pale.

'Could you do us a favour?' He asked, before she had a chance to ask if he was all right.

'Sure.'

'Can you get a couple of these out?' He nodded towards the box of tablets on the bed beside him.

'I think I'm just about awake enough to manage that,' Rebecca replied, with a smile, rounding the bed. Perching on the edge, she reached for the packet and, taking in the details of what it contained, said, 'Are you really suffering today?'

'No, I just forgot to get them out in advance.'

'Do you take these every day?' She exclaimed.

'Uh-huh.'

'Is that a good idea?'

'Asking me that right now is not a good idea,' he returned, shortly.

'Sorry,' Rebecca offered, opening the box and slipping the blister pack out. She popped two capsules out of the foil and deposited them in his right palm before standing and heading for the door. 'I'll get you some water.'

By the time Rebecca had showered and dressed, Leighton was up, and was sitting on the sofa in his dressing gown with Pandora in his lap. Rebecca joined him, setting a mug of tea down on the table in front of him and taking a mouthful of her coffee, immediately regretting it when the hot liquid burned her lip.

'Thanks,' Leighton said, with a smile that looked rather forced. 'Sorry about earlier.'

'Me too. I didn't mean to give you a hard time.'

He shook his head. 'It wasn't an unreasonable question. It's just difficult to think straight when it feels like you're being mauled by a gang of piranhas.'

Rebecca smiled at the analogy. 'I had no idea it was still that bad. You sh–' she stopped herself, guessing the words *you should have told me* might come across as a criticism. 'I wish I'd known.'

He shrugged. 'Moaning about it isn't going to help. And it's not like you can do anything to change it.'

Rebecca hesitated before asking, 'Are there any medical options that might?'

'Not to fix the nerve damage, but there are other drugs that might be safer and more effective. Not to mention more practical. As things stand, I can't work and I can't drive.'

'Have you talked to the consultant about trying those?'

'She said we can look at it after they fuse a couple of these knuckles,' he replied, holding up his left hand.

Rebecca nodded, wishing she could ask when that would be without feeling as if she was interrogating him. She wondered how he would fare as and when he stopped taking opioids, suspecting that the drugs were, at least in part, responsible for his apparent ability to cope with all that had happened in the preceding six months. Presumably they were also a major factor in occupational health's refusal to sign off his return to work. Before she had had a chance to decide what to say next, he changed the subject.

'What's your day looking like?'

'Hard work unless this is magic coffee,' she replied, ruefully, reaching for her mug.

Leighton smiled. 'You need a bacon sandwich.'

Rebecca grimaced. 'Ugh, no thanks.'

'Cheese toastie?'

'Maybe later.' She sipped her drink. 'What are you going to do today?'

'Besides physio at eleven, I dunno.' He paused. 'I reckon I could use a holiday, though. I might look at booking a week away someplace warm.' He glanced her way. 'D'you fancy a last-minute break?'

'Where to?' Rebecca responded, feeling pleasantly surprised by the suggestion he wanted to spend a holiday with her.

He looked thoughtful. 'The Canaries, maybe? Have you got much leave to spare?'

'I've got plenty of leave, it's a question of when I can book it.'

'Yeah, my calendar's looking pretty full, too,' Leighton joked.

'I'll see what I can do,' Rebecca responded, glancing at her watch and taking another mouthful of coffee. 'Right now I need to get going. Can I get you anything before I head off?'

'No, you're all right, thanks.'

'Ok,' she leaned to kiss him, then stopped herself. 'Sorry. I don't suppose you want a share of my lipstick.'

'Oh, I don't know, I think watermelon punch might suit me.'

'I can't believe you know the name of my lipstick,' Rebecca replied, reaching for her handbag and getting to her feet.

'Ah, I'm a mine of useless information, me.'

Rebecca smiled. 'I'll call you later,' she said, turning for the door.

'Hang about.'

Rebecca looked back around. 'What's up?'

'You've got lipstick on your teeth.'

Lawrence normally only saw Rebecca browsing online shops during her lunch break, and hoped it was a one-off when he passed her desk shortly after nine to find her scrolling through the website of a department store. As she clicked on one of the products on the screen, he said, 'Retail emergency?'

'More like retail research,' she replied, as she turned towards him, apparently unconcerned that he had seen the web page.

'I'm sorry I didn't make it yesterday, I wasn't done until almost nine. Was it a good night?'

'Too good,' Rebecca replied, ruefully.

Lawrence smiled. 'How's Leighton feeling this morning?'

'Better than the rest of us, I expect. He still seems to be able to bounce back from a night out like a teenager. I don't know how he does it.'

Lawrence's first thought was to say *years of practice*, but he stopped himself. Given how often he had complained in the past about Leighton's fondness for long lunch breaks in the pub, he suspected Rebecca would interpret it as a criticism. 'There's no justice,' he remarked, instead.

'Sorry I'm late,' Jamie put in, wearily, as he dumped his bag on the desk opposite Rebecca's. 'My bus broke down in the bloody sticks on the way home,' he shed his coat and draped it over his chair. 'My phone was dead, so I couldn't call a cab. I didn't get in 'til after two.' Turning his attention to Rebecca, he asked, 'How was the afterparty?'

Rebecca frowned. 'Huh?'

'Huh?' Jamie mimicked, before rolling his eyes and shaking his head.

Guessing what Jamie was getting at, Lawrence decided to change the subject. 'While you two were out carousing, I managed to find Summer,' he revealed, indicating a printout from an Instagram account that he had added to the board earlier that morning. 'In a manner of speaking, at least.'

'What?' Eva exclaimed, pushing her chair back from her desk, standing and heading for the board. 'But I searched *everything*. Where did I go wrong?'

'You didn't,' Lawrence replied. 'Jakob did. He misspelt her name, which is Summer Tinley, not Summer Tilney.'

'Sneaky fucker,' Jamie remarked.

Lawrence nodded. 'I suspect it was a deliberate misdirection, but he'll no doubt argue it was a genuine error because he's dyslexic.'

'And there's no way for us to disprove it,' Jamie replied.

'No.'

'You said *in a manner of speaking*,' Rebecca observed. 'Does that mean she's dead?'

'Good question,' Lawrence responded. 'She seems to have disappeared.'

'As in gone missing, or done a runner?'

'That much isn't clear. She was originally reported missing by her live-in landlady when she didn't pay her rent and the woman couldn't get hold of her, but her phone, purse and computer were nowhere to be found, and the newsagent whose shop the flat was above reported seeing her leaving with a suitcase a couple of weeks earlier. CCTV bore that out, so no further action was taken.'

'When was that?' Eva queried.

'Early this year.'

'Some time after her relationship with Jakob ended, then.'

'According to him, at least, yes.'

'I wonder whether she ever turned up again?' Rebecca mused.

'The landlady's number is on file, if you'd like to try to get in touch with her this morning?'

'Sure.'

'Presumably she should at least be able to give us a phone number for Summer and, depending on the rental arrangement, possibly bank details.'

'Is it worth checking ANPR, as well?' Rebecca asked. 'Does Summer have her own car?'

'No,' Lawrence replied, having already thought of checking the Automatic Number Plate Recognition system. 'In fact, according to the DVLA, she doesn't even have a driving licence, so I'm not sure how she could have been the one to drive Jakob to and from their filming location. I'll be asking him about that later.'

Rebecca nodded.

'Pinning her down has to be a priority. We may well find ourselves in the same *he said, she said* situation we're in with Irene and Jakob, but there's also a chance we'll get enough to convince MacLennan to authorise an investigation into what happened during the filming of *In the Shadows*.'

'I might actually have something to break the stalemate between Irene and Jakob,' Rebecca replied, nodding towards her monitor.

Lawrence looked automatically at the screen, and, seeing the department store's website still open, he frowned. 'You're going to have to give me a clue.'

Rebecca smiled. 'Someone left a calling card,' she said, with a knowing lift of her eyebrows. 'I just didn't spot it until now.'

*****

To Rebecca's surprise, Summer's landlady, Jennifer Duncan, had held onto the bulk of Summer's belongings, which she had packed up and stored in her loft. In the wake of Rebecca's phone call that morning, the woman had helpfully brought them back down and stacked them in her minimalist lounge, where the dusty, mismatched boxes looked thoroughly out of place. As she showed Rebecca into the room, Jennifer explained that she had kept the possessions with an eye to using them as leverage should Summer ever return, in the hope of recouping the two months' rent she was owed. More than six months on, Rebecca suspected the chances Jennifer was ever going to see either Summer or her money again were slim.

A quick survey of the boxes' contents was sufficient for Rebecca to understand why Jennifer had hung onto Summer's meagre possessions; she certainly wouldn't have made much by selling what Summer had left behind. There were a few party dresses that might have been worth listing on eBay, but the bulk of what remained of Summer's wardrobe hailed from the cheaper end of the high street, and its resale value would have been minimal.

The clothing offered little real insight into Summer's personality, and Rebecca quickly moved on in search of something that might shed light on more than just her sense of style. The first box she came to was filled solely with books. These comprised a mix of fiction – almost exclusively horror – and non-fiction on subjects such as serial killers, vampires, witchcraft and the occult. As Rebecca flicked through the pages of each tome in case anything was concealed inside, she couldn't help wondering what had drawn Summer to such dark topics. Did she actually believe in witchcraft? Or was she simply intrigued by those who had in a bygone age? At a time in which you could send a message around the world in a fraction of a second and scientists could drive vehicles on Mars, Rebecca felt mystified by the idea that anyone might still believe in magic, dark or otherwise.

Jennifer hadn't kept easily replaceable things like toiletries, and, making a start on emptying out another box, Rebecca felt momentarily excited by the sight of a hairbrush, given its potential as a source of Summer's DNA. The emotion quickly turned to disappointment when she discovered the brush was completely devoid of hair; evidently either Summer or Jennifer had cleared it out. Rebecca bagged it up anyway – there was a reasonable chance someone would be able to lift skin cells from its surface – and hoped Jennifer might be persuaded to provide a sample of her own DNA to allow them to exclude her from the search.

A number of the items towards the bottom of the box had been carefully wrapped, and Rebecca felt surprised by how much effort Jennifer had gone to in packing everything, given that Summer had upped and left without a word. Beneath the tissue paper and bubble wrap were an intricately engraved silver perfume bottle that looked to be an antique, two delicate spiral candlesticks and a glass vase. The contents of a small tin with a stylised picture of a wolf on the lid might have proved a let down had it not been for the absence of hair on the brush: the tin was filled with hair bands and clips, several of which still had hairs tangled around them.

Underneath all of these was a beautiful wooden jewellery box, inlaid with mother of pearl, that Rebecca would have been tempted to buy had she come across it in a shop. Inside, it was divided into two layers. The top one, which lifted out, was occupied by various pieces of what looked to be relatively inexpensive jewellery, including several Celtic rings, a pentagram pendant on a black cord and a small snake charm. The base of the box, meanwhile, contained a strange assortment of odds and ends, among them a dried rose, what looked like a cat's claw, a string of skull-shaped beads and a stone painted to resemble a mouse. They had no monetary value and no practical use, so had presumably been of some personal significance to Summer, much like the lilac fluffy bug sticker – no longer sticky – and the threadbare hundred-year-old toy rabbit originally procured from the Oban Bunny Shop that Rebecca had at home. Those weren't things Rebecca would have moved on and left behind, and she questioned whether Summer was likely to have done as much, either. She suspected the same was true of some of the other items spread out on the table in front of her: they might not be valuable, but they struck her as precious, nonetheless. And the more she looked at the myriad belongings, the more convinced she felt that Summer hadn't disappeared of her own accord.

'I've ID'd the film's location!'

Lawrence raised his eyes from his monitor to see Rebecca in his office doorway, her expression triumphant.

'Great! Where is it?'

'Floireans Castle. It's in Argyll,' Rebecca replied, moving to sit down and sliding a photograph onto his desk. It showed an old stone building with narrow windows and a couple of unremarkable turrets; the description of the property as a *castle*, Lawrence couldn't help thinking, seemed to put it rather above its station.

'How did you identify it?'

'There was an old mobile phone among Summer's things. It didn't contain a SIM card, but there were loads of photos, including several of her sitting on the sarcophagus that features in the film. And the metadata places those pictures at Floireans Castle. It's privately owned, but they rent it out. If we can get access to the grounds to take soil samples from the chapel, we should be able to determine whether or not a serious amount of blood was spilt there. I checked, and the volume we're talking about should still be detectable years later.'

'Good to know,' Lawrence replied. 'The question is whether we can *get* access. Even if I can convince MacLennan to authorise an investigation, I think we'll struggle to secure a search warrant with what we have. Could you try to get hold of the property's owners? See if you can persuade them to let a couple of CSIs quietly check out the chapel?'

'Sure.'

'Did the phone yield anything else?'

'Oh yes,' Rebecca replied, with a meaningful lift of her eyebrows. 'It hasn't been used in over a year, but the browser history was still accessible. She was on several online forums with the username Emily Munster, the same name she used for *In the Shadows*. One, called Killer Instinx, is about fantasies involving homicide. And there's a subforum dedicated to the subject of serial killers that she was particularly active in. She had a bunch of books on that subject, as well.'

'I've never understood that particular fascination,' Lawrence admitted.

'Maybe it's down to the fact their actions are so far removed from most people's comprehension,' Rebecca suggested. 'Most of us can understand angry people killing in the heat of the moment, or more calculated crimes where people kill for personal gain or to keep something quiet. But the idea of killing for pleasure – or even sexual gratification – is a completely different ballpark.'

Lawrence nodded.

'I pulled the sites up on my computer and had a sort through. From the content of some of the posts, it's clear Summer and a few others were in contact through more than just the forums. I'm wondering whether they might have been in touch one-on-one, so I've requested a trace on the relevant IP addresses.'

'Good thinking.'

'Did Eva get anything back on the bank or phone records?'

'Yes, although nothing very promising. The phone hasn't been used since a few days after Summer was last seen. She had debit and credit cards that were in use for several weeks after that, but always for small amounts that could easily have been put through as contactless payments.'

'Figures,' Rebecca replied.

Lawrence raised his eyebrows. 'How so?'

'Some of the conversations on the homicide fantasy forum are seriously twisted,' she said. 'And Jennifer Duncan has a box of Summer's belongings that's full of things I can't see someone just abandoning. A beautiful jewellery box, an antique perfume bottle, a bunch of odd bits and bobs carefully stored despite having no intrinsic value –' she shrugged.

'So what do you think has happened to her?'

'I reckon she's become a victim of someone else's homicide fantasy.'

Fifteen

Maya's hair had changed colour since Rebecca had last seen her, and was now a mix of pastel pink, lilac and ice blue that reminded Rebecca of stripy marshmallow sweets she had been partial to as a child. Given the subtle way the hues faded in and out, it was clear the dye job had been done professionally, rather than in front of the bathroom mirror, and Rebecca idly wondered how much such a specialist style might cost. Not that she was ever likely to be emulating it; one of the few downsides of her job, as far as she was concerned, was the restrictions it imposed on hair and body art. While she had no real desire to collect earrings or tattoos – unlike a couple of her colleagues, who regularly grumbled about being required to remove multiple piercings for work – she did miss being able to experiment with alternative hair styles and colours. But, given that Maya's marshmallow tresses would be difficult for a brunette like Rebecca to achieve without a serious amount of peroxide, perhaps it was for the best.

'Gentian,' Rebecca began, resting her forearms on the interview room table and threading her fingers together. 'What does that mean to you?'

Maya's eyebrows contracted into a suspicious frown. 'It's a flower,' she answered, sounding as if she half expected to be corrected.

'A blue flower,' Rebecca went on. 'Which is why the name intrigued me when I saw it on your coffee table last week. Blue's an unusual colour for a lipstick.' She flipped open the folder that lay in front of her on the table and presented Maya with a printout of a page from the department store whose website she had been browsing that morning, and a photograph from Martina's party. The former showed a picture of a dark blue lipstick emerging from its metal case, and, below it, a large zig-zag swatch of the colour; the latter Maya, Martina and Irene. Maya's lips were scarcely visible in the photograph, in which she was posing with them clamped around a straw; had Rebecca not noticed the lipstick on Maya's coffee table the previous Friday, she might have mistaken the blue traces that were discernible for red wine stains or a trick of the light.

Maya shrugged. 'Why be dull and wear nude like everyone else?'

'Why indeed,' Rebecca replied. 'Although if you had worn something more conventional, you might have avoided leaving traceable evidence when you gave Tony mouth-to-mouth.'

'What?' Maya managed, at length, her voice sounding strangled.

'No doubt you washed it off his face, but you left some of your lipstick on one of his front teeth.' She added another photograph to the table, this one showing the blue pigment in the ridge of Tony's front tooth. 'Our forensic chemists will be able to match that to the lipstick you have at home.'

Maya swallowed, but said nothing.

'I'm sure you tried your best to revive him, but it was too late, wasn't it?'

Maya didn't respond, her eyes on the table.

'You probably assumed Jakob had already called for help. I'm sure you were shocked when it became clear he hadn't; that he didn't intend to. That put you between a rock and a hard place, didn't it? Irene's your friend. And she didn't mean Tony any harm.' Rebecca paused. 'But Jakob wasn't trying to protect Irene. He was looking after number one.'

Maya's eyes came up abruptly. 'What?'

'Situation normal, from what you've told us previously,' Rebecca went on. 'That he was concerned for someone else strikes me as a remarkable volte-face. Did it not occur to you to question it?' Rebecca gave Maya several seconds to think about this before saying, 'He wanted Tony out the way, and he knew Tony had taken ketamine that night, so he murdered him and turned the blame on Irene. You might not have stayed silent for him, but you and Irene go back a long way.'

There was a brief silence before Maya said, hesitantly, 'Was it not the ketamine that killed him?'

'Would it have made a difference?'

Tears came to Maya's eyes and she bowed her head.

'I'm guessing that's a yes.'

'I thought – I mean –' she gave up, her voice breaking.

'When did he involve you?'

Maya didn't immediately respond, her eyes on the table. Her respirations were audible. At length, she drew a long, slow breath. 'I woke up a bit after four. I was dying for the loo, so I got up and headed downstairs.' She paused. 'Jakob was coming out of Tony's room when I reached the landing.'

Rebecca had to fight to keep the look of triumph from her face. She had been wondering why Jakob had involved Maya ever since making the connection to the woman's delft blue lipstick. It seemed he hadn't had a choice.

'He looked shocked – but – I mean – you would be, if you found someone like that, wouldn't you? Then he grabbed my arm and dragged me in there. He said Tony wasn't breathing – that he'd been coming to get me, because I'm a first aider. And I tried – I *really* tried – but –' she shook her head. 'I think I knew it was too late even before I started.'

'Did you suggest calling the emergency services?'

'Of course I did!' Maya exclaimed, as if she couldn't believe Rebecca needed to ask. 'I kept asking if he'd called – and then, after –' she stopped. 'He said that reporting it wouldn't do anyone any good, it couldn't bring Tony back. I wasn't thinking straight. I wasn't even *sober*. And he just kept on and on about how it would ruin Irene's life, and – and –' she gulped. 'And I *owed* her.'

'Irene?'

She nodded.

'What did you owe her that was worth carrying something like that around?'

Several seconds passed before Maya said, her voice scarcely more than a whisper, 'She did it for me.'

Rebecca's eyebrows rose. 'Covered up a suspicious death?'

'No.' Maya drew a shaky breath. 'Nobody died. But she did cover for me.'

'Covered what, exactly?'

'A fire,' Maya revealed, her voice unsteady. 'At my granddad's church.' She paused briefly before adding, 'He was the vicar.'

'I have never torched a church,' Rebecca recalled.

'I didn't torch it,' Maya protested. 'I mean, it wasn't arson. I'm not even sure whether it was caused by a candle or a cigarette. But it was my fault we were in there.'

'*We* being you and Irene?'

'No, she wasn't there. She gave me an alibi.'

'So who were you with?'

'My boyfriend.'

'And how did you come to be in the church? Clearly it wasn't during the course of normal worship.'

'One of us had the idea of spending Halloween night in a graveyard. It sounds stupid and corny, now, but I was seventeen and it seemed daring and cool.' Maya cleared her throat. 'We went there from the pub after closing. The first couple of hours were a laugh. Ivan – my boyfriend – had a hip flask full of apricot brandy. But then it started raining – properly pissing it down – so we went into the church.'

'Was it open at that time of night?'

'No. But I knew there was a loose window latch in the vestry. We lit some candles – spread a bunch of kneelers on the floor to lie on – finished the brandy –' she shrugged. 'At some point I dozed off. When I woke up, flames were tearing up the banners hanging on the walls. Ivan tried tackling them with a fire extinguisher, but the fire had already taken hold. We had to get out.'

'Did you leave the same way you entered?' Rebecca asked, when Maya didn't continue.

'Yes. And we did try to get help. There was a phone box down the road. Ivan called nine nine nine before we legged it. But by the time the fire brigade arrived, the roof was burning, and the whole thing caved in before they could put it out.' She paused. 'I knew my granddad would be heartbroken enough to lose his church – it'd been his parish for more than twenty years – and if he'd known it was my fault –' she trailed off. 'He'd never have looked at me the same way again. And I couldn't bear the thought of that.'

Rebecca had to respect Maya's honesty in admitting it was concern for her own feelings that had stopped her from coming clean. Many people would have attempted to persuade Rebecca – and perhaps themselves – that they had simply been protecting the injured party's feelings. But it was never that simple.

'So where does Irene come into the story?' Rebecca asked.

'I went to her place straight from the phone box. My parents thought I was staying there anyway. She washed all my stuff – it reeked of smoke – and said she'd tell anyone who asked I'd been there all evening. Her folks were away overnight, and the only other person in the house was her elder brother. He used to spend almost all his time playing computer games in his room, and when I bumped into him in the kitchen the next morning he just assumed I'd been there all along.'

'Was anyone ever charged in relation to the fire?'

'No. I was terrified they might be, because I don't think I could have let someone else take the blame. The police were convinced it was someone at our school, and gave the whole sixth form a serious talking to – the headmaster added his two cents, as well – but nobody came forward, and in the end I guess they shelved the investigation. And I did try to make amends. I put all my free time into fundraising to repair the damage and rebuild the roof.' She swallowed before adding, sadly, 'My granddad never stopped telling everyone how proud he was of me. I felt like a fraud.'

'And Irene kept your secret, so when Tony died you felt compelled to keep hers.'

Maya nodded. 'She didn't mean to hurt Tony any more than I intended to burn down a church. I knew that. But I'd never have kept quiet if I'd realised his death wasn't an accident. I swear.'

Rebecca didn't respond, her feelings of triumph at having strengthened the case against Jakob tempered by the knowledge that Maya's involvement was likely to see her handed a custodial sentence. The courts always treated the offence of perverting the course of justice seriously, and, as much as Rebecca could understand why, she couldn't help feeling for someone whose misplaced loyalty was going to cost them so dearly. That Jakob had been the one to push Maya into making an ill-advised decision whilst she had been in a state of panic only strengthened Rebecca's determination to ensure that he faced the consequences of his actions. Unfortunately, Maya's and Irene's testimonies were unlikely to prove sufficient to put him away. Rebecca resolved to find something that would.

Lawrence had despatched a couple of uniformed officers to Clapham to arrest Jakob immediately after the conclusion of the interview with Maya. There was often much to be gained from leaving people to sweat for an hour or two after bringing them in, but on this occasion Lawrence had been keen to make a start as soon as Jakob had been booked in by the custody sergeant, and by 8 p.m. the two of them were sitting opposite one another as Rebecca completed the formalities for the recording device.

'Maya has filled us in on what actually happened in the aftermath of Martina's party,' Lawrence informed Jakob, once Rebecca was done. 'And how you made her an unwitting accomplice. She didn't –'

'She seriously said that?' Jakob exclaimed. 'That's bullshit! She's lying!'

'Lying?' Lawrence echoed. 'Why would she do that?'

'I don't know! Maybe she's trying to get Irene off the hook!'

'Off the hook for what, exactly?' Lawrence asked. 'We're not looking to charge Irene with anything further than supplying a class B drug. That charge will stand regardless of what happened to Tony.'

'Maya's hardly impartial,' Jakob retorted. 'If she'd had her way, she and I would be an item by now. I turned her down.'

'She's looking at a charge of perverting the course of justice. I can't imagine anyone would risk prison time to take revenge over a one-night stand.'

'Yeah, well, you don't know her. She's done some extreme shit before now.'

'That's as may be, but if that's what she was seeking to do, she would have painted a much darker picture of events. She never suggested you'd intended Tony any harm. It didn't seem to have occurred to her that you'd pulled her into the situation out of anything other than a genuine hope she might be able to do something for Tony. But you already knew he was beyond help, didn't you? In fact, you wouldn't have involved her at all had you had any choice. But she caught you coming out of his room and you had to think on your feet.'

Jakob shook his head vehemently. 'No.'

'Everything she and Irene have told us adds up. The only account that doesn't square with what we have is yours. And there's only one reason why that could be.'

'No, I mean that's not how it was.'

'What isn't?'

'What you said. About why I – involved Maya. It wasn't because –' he broke off. 'I didn't mean to hurt Tony. It was an accident.'

'Really?' Lawrence responded, disbelievingly.

'I swear.'

'So what happened?'

'When he fell on the stairs –' Jakob hesitated. 'He wasn't behind me. He'd followed me up to my room, shouting the odds, and he was out of control. He kept shoving me, and in the end I shoved him back. I was only trying to get him to back off – but he stumbled –' he trailed off with a shrug.

'Effectively, then, you pushed him down the stairs.'

'No! I didn't mean for him to fall! And if he'd not been so out of it, he wouldn't have lost his balance!'

'Right,' Lawrence returned, sceptically. 'And what happened after that?'

'It didn't seem like it knocked him out, but he was a bit dazed after. He sat at the bottom of the stairs for a couple of minutes. I asked if he wanted to lie down. I left him lying on his bed. He seemed ok. I wouldn't have left him if I'd thought he wasn't. I meant to check on him after a quarter of an hour or so, but –' Jakob sighed. 'I got distracted by Maya. And by the time I did go back –' he closed his eyes momentarily. 'I really didn't mean to hurt him, much less –' he shrugged in lieu of completing the sentence.

'If it was an accident, why cover it up?' Lawrence asked, when it became clear Jakob wasn't going to add anything further.

'You don't think I've been asking myself that every day since?' Jakob returned. 'I don't know! The whole thing was a massive headfuck! None of it seemed real. I kept telling myself it wasn't. I mean, I know I went to check he was ok, but I never really thought he *wouldn't* be.'

'So it wasn't because you didn't think people would believe you.'

Jakob sighed. 'That did cross my mind, yeah, given that Tony had been ranting at me and calling me every name under the sun the last time anyone saw him. Not that I thought anyone would believe I'd meant to kill him, but maybe that I'd belted him one, or something. But that wasn't all there was to it. My reasoning was shot.'

'Could you describe the position Tony was lying in when you found him?'

The question appeared to take Jakob by surprise, and he didn't immediately answer. 'I'm not sure I can give much of a description,' he admitted, eventually. 'I didn't switch the light on to start with, because I didn't want to wake him, and by the time I did I'd already turned him over in a panic because I *couldn't* wake him.'

'Make up your mind, did you want to wake him or not?'

'Not initially, no! But once I'd realised something was wrong, disturbing him became the least of my concerns!'

Lawrence nodded. 'You say you turned him over. Can you at least give us an idea of what position you turned him from to?'

'From his front to his back.'

'Given that you then went to get Maya, presumably you weren't certain he was dead,' Lawrence observed. 'So why didn't you call an ambulance?'

There was a long silence before Jakob admitted, 'I think deep down I knew, but I was hoping –' he trailed off with a shrug. 'None of it really makes sense in the cold light of day, but at the time –' he broke off again. 'I wasn't thinking clearly, and I made the wrong call. And once I'd started down that road, there was no going back.'

'Did you believe any of that?' Rebecca asked, rejoining Lawrence in his office on her return to CID.

'Not a word,' Lawrence replied. 'But unfortunately for us, it's all very plausible. We've no evidence to contradict what he's saying. And even if we can convince the CPS to bring charges, I think there's a good chance he'll get off simply on the basis of reasonable doubt. He did a very good job of sounding regretful when he had to.'

Rebecca sighed, dropping into a chair.

'I suspect he's had that version of events worked out as a last resort all along,' Lawrence went on. 'I hoped I might catch him out with the question about what position he found Tony in, but he was clever enough to think around that one.'

Rebecca nodded.

'And, as it stands, we've no real motive. It doesn't look as if Jakob had any involvement in the child abuse, his covert sex tapes would land him with a fine at worst, and we've no evidence *In the Shadows* is anything more than an amateur horror flick.'

'But neither of us believes what happened to Tony was an accident,' Rebecca observed. 'So unless we're wrong, there must be a motive somewhere. You don't suffocate someone without good reason.'

'We do have to allow for the possibility that we might *be* wrong,' Lawrence conceded. 'We've all been failed by gut instinct at one time or another.'

'It's not only gut instinct we're going on, though, is it? If *In the Shadows* really is just a bog-standard film, why was Jakob prepared to tell us so little about it?'

'True.' Lawrence tapped his right forefinger on his desk for a few seconds before saying, 'We need to focus on the film. Have you managed to get hold of the castle's owners yet?

'No. I'll try phoning them again.' Rebecca moved to stand.

'Thanks. After that, let's call it a day. Tomorrow morning we'll go through everything again and see where that takes us.'

Rebecca nodded.

'You never know, we might get lucky. The missing piece of the puzzle could be hiding in plain sight.'

Sixteen

Beyond the fact that his job – and so his salary – was contingent on arresting lawbreakers, it wasn't often that Lawrence saw much benefit from someone's having a criminal record. However, in Herve Lyon's case it had been key to Chief Superintendent MacLennan's decision to approve a forensic survey of the derelict chapel at Floireans Castle. On hearing that the technicians should be able to extract DNA from the soil if a significant amount of blood had been spilt there, MacLennan had given the nod on the basis that they already had Herve's DNA on file, and so stood a good chance of getting a definitive answer. Had the enterprise looked set to generate only more questions, Lawrence didn't doubt the request would have been declined.

Having been given the go-ahead on Wednesday morning, Lawrence had managed to get a forensic team dispatched to the site before the end of the day. With the time-consuming process of collecting soil and other samples contingent on the crime-scene investigators getting a positive result with the dye fluorescein – indicative of the presence of blood – Lawrence felt cheered by the news that parts of the sarcophagus and the surrounding area had fluoresced accordingly. His optimism was quickly dampened when the technician at the other end of the line added, in a strong Glaswegian accent, that there was a strong smell of fox in the vicinity, and that urine could generate a false positive. Lawrence had nevertheless prevailed upon Max to pull some strings to get the testing of the soil samples fast-tracked, and was hoping to hear back before the weekend.

In the meantime, he was focusing on trying to trace Summer. Rebecca had made an appointment with Odette Browning, one of Summer's contacts from Killer Instinx, for Friday afternoon, and they had spent much of the morning in the car en route to her home in Newcastle-under-Lyme. Odette – presumably a Swan Lake fan – had rather appropriately opted to use the name of the white swan's villainous alter ego, Odile, online. However, the mental image that the name Odile conjured up was a far cry from the dumpy and bespectacled fifty-something woman who opened the door to them at five to one.

It soon became apparent that Odette was very nervous, and her hands shook as she set mugs of coffee down on the kitchen table. Perching on the edge of the chair opposite where they were sitting, she tucked her hands under the table and regarded them expectantly.

'As I think DS Palmer mentioned when you spoke this morning, we're trying to trace a woman called Summer Tinley,' Lawrence said. 'I understand you knew her as Emily Munster.'

'Yes.'

'Did you and she ever meet?'

'No. She suggested it a couple of times, but I didn't feel very comfortable with people from that –' Odette hesitated before settling on, 'Community – knowing who I was in real life.'

Thank goodness for some common sense, Lawrence thought.

'I was only really on there because I was researching a book on serial killers,' Odette added, apparently feeling the need to justify her use of the forum. 'I'm a behavioral psychologist.'

Lawrence nodded. 'But you did give Summer your phone number, I think?'

'No, just my Snapchat details.'

'Is that the preferred means of communication between members of Killer Instinx?'

Lawrence wasn't surprised when Odette confirmed that it was. Given the nature of some of the conversations he had seen on the site, he could imagine that those authoring anything more extreme would want to use a messaging medium that didn't leave a digital trail.

'When did you last hear from Summer?'

'I don't remember the exact date, but it was in early February, because we talked about Valentine's Day.'

'What did she say about it?'

'She was talking about making a horror film called Valentine's Day. She was obsessed with snuff movies. She boasted that she'd made several.' There was a momentary pause before Odette added, hurriedly, 'I don't know whether that was true.'

'Did she ever name any of these films?'

'Yes. One was called *Water Demon*. I can't remember the others.'

'How about *In the Shadows*?'

There was a brief pause before Odette nodded. 'Yes, that rings a bell.'

'Presumably she wasn't planning to shoot the film alone?' Lawrence said. 'She must have needed an accomplice, either to do the filming or the acting.'

'She didn't go into detail, but she did mention a guy once or twice when she was talking about it.'

'Can you recall his name?'

'Miles? Milo? Something like that.'

'And have you any idea when or where she was intending to shoot the film?'

'I'm not sure about where, but I know she wanted to film the murder on Valentine's Day itself.'

'Did she say anything at all that might give us a clue to the location?'

'Well she did say something about it, but I didn't understand it, and when I asked what she meant she just sent back a skull and crossbones emoji followed by a laughing one.'

'What exactly did she say?'

'A few days before Valentine's Day, she said she was off to meet Milo – or whatever his name was – in a kite yard.'

'Kite yard?' Lawrence echoed.

'Yes,' Odette replied, before spelling it out.

Thinking of what Odette had said so far, Lawrence guessed it might have been a typo, and said, 'Did she ever mention Scotland?'

Odette's eyebrows contracted in puzzlement. 'I don't think so.'

'Was that the last you heard about it?'

'It was the last I heard from her.'

'Were you surprised when she abruptly stopped communicating with you?'

There was an uncomfortable pause before Odette said, 'A little.'

'Given the risky nature of what she was doing, I think I'd have been concerned by her silence if I were in your shoes,' Lawrence replied. 'When you didn't hear from her, did you not think it might be an idea to report it?'

'I did consider it,' Odette admitted. 'But I wasn't sure whether it was just some elaborate game she was playing to mess with my head. I didn't even know whether she was really a woman. And – ' she hesitated. 'Well, I scarcely knew her, really. I didn't imagine anyone would take me seriously. And I figured if anything had happened to her, she probably had real friends who would raise the alarm.'

*****

'What do you think she meant by kite yard?' Rebecca asked, as Lawrence turned out of Odette's street en route back to London.

'At a guess, kirk yard,' Lawrence replied. 'Kirk's the Scottish word for church. Unfortunately, that doesn't help us any. Scotland must have hundreds of churches.'

'Jamie was going to chase up Summer's phone company this morning. Their mast data should be able to point us in the right direction.'

'True, although I'm still not sure how much use that would be. I can't see many graveyards being equipped with CCTV.'

'If they've been affected by vandalism they might be,' Rebecca pointed out, before realising, aloud, 'But then I don't suppose they'd have much reason to keep the footage if nothing happened.' She sighed.

'Talking of footage, can you have someone track down *Water Demon*?'

'Sure,' Rebecca agreed, feeling in her handbag for her mobile. She drew it out to find several messages waiting, including one from her brother. He had sent a comical picture of a cat, complete with a one-line joke, and she laughed.

'The reason cats are so pissy,' she read aloud. 'Is because they're God's perfect killing machines, but they only weigh five kilos and we keep picking them up and kissing them.'

Lawrence smiled. 'Is that Leighton?'

'No, Nathan.' She dropped the hand holding the phone into her lap. 'Leighton's at Downview Prison this afternoon, visiting Miranda. I don't know how he can contemplate even giving her the time of day.'

'Maybe it's just something he needs to do to move on,' Lawrence observed. 'It's not as if he had the chance to talk to her when it happened.'

Rebecca shook her head dismissively. 'He doesn't even seem to hold her responsible! Says it was his decision to go out to the farm, as if she played no part in it!'

There was a brief pause before Lawrence spoke, and when he did Rebecca guessed he had been weighing up how to respond. 'I realise he wouldn't have crossed paths with Healy without her input,' he said. 'But he must have been aware he was taking a risk in going to the farm alone. Nobody told him to do that.'

'She knew him well enough to know he would take that risk!'

'I'm not sure she had any idea how big a risk it was,' Lawrence replied. 'We didn't find any evidence she'd been in contact with Healy. That being the case, perhaps he'd rather just give her the benefit of the doubt. By all accounts, they used to be friends.'

Rebecca sighed. 'Yes, maybe.'

'Besides, he's always tended to see the best in people. He's certainly a lot more forgiving than I am.'

'Too forgiving.'

'Would you have him any other way?'

'No,' Rebecca conceded, with a smile.

Lawrence's mobile began to ring, and he drew it from his jacket pocket and handed it to Rebecca. Seeing Eva's name on the screen, she answered it, then immediately put it on speakerphone.

'Hi Eva.'

'Hi,' she replied, her voice competing with a cacophony of background noise that led Rebecca to guess she was in a mainline train station. 'I found Herve Lyon.'

'What?' Lawrence exclaimed. 'Where?'

'A halfway house in Kings Cross. I've just spoken to him.'

'So he's alive and well,' Lawrence responded, still sounding surprised by the news. Rebecca guessed Eva's revelation had prompted the same conflicting mix of emotions she was feeling. On the one hand, the discovery that any individual was alive rather than dead was good news; on the other, had *In the Shadows* been nothing more than a fictional horror story, the chances were that the only charge they would be able to level against Jakob was that of perverting the course of justice. And none of them really believed the man was innocent of any involvement in Tony's death.

'Yes,' Eva replied. 'But here's the thing. He says he's never met anyone called Summer Tinley *or* Emily Munster. And that he's never been involved in making a film.'

By the time Lawrence and Rebecca made it back to the office, a trawl of the dark web had turned up the film *Water Demon*. Once again, Summer starred under the name of Emily Munster, and, once again, she took the part of a killer. The film wasn't as slickly made as *In the Shadows*, and, as he sat watching the climactic scene, Lawrence suspected its producer – whomever he or she was – had been less accomplished than Jakob. Given the length of time *Water Demon* had been circulating, it was clearly the older of the two, and Lawrence wondered whether in its wake Summer had actively sought a partner with the relevant skills. Almost as he was thinking this, it occurred to him that, had the murder scenes been real, finding an accomplice would have been challenging enough without the addition of any other criteria.

Meanwhile, given that several days of intensive searching had taken them no further forwards in the hunt for Summer, it seemed their chances of finding her were similarly small. Mobile phone data had allowed them to track her approximate movements in the first forty-eight hours or so after her departure from her flat in Blackheath – as Lawrence had predicted, she had travelled to Scotland – but after that the trail had gone cold. They had found no sign of her, online or off, in the ensuing months, and Lawrence was beginning to suspect Rebecca had been right, and that the woman's fascination with murder and murderers hadn't ended well.

A renewed trawl of the various databases available to them had identified no missing individuals with the name Henry Love or anagrams thereof, and Lawrence found himself once again questioning the likelihood that the rumours circulating about *In the Shadows* were nothing more than that. An obvious next step would be to circulate the best picture they could get from the film footage in the hope that someone might recognise the man involved – or that he himself might come forwards. However, unless the results from the samples collected at the castle threw up any surprises, Lawrence didn't imagine MacLennan would be in favour of expending any further resources on the investigation.

A knock at his office door interrupted his cogitations, and he glanced up to see Max standing on the threshold.

'I know what you're going to say,' Lawrence preempted. 'Herve Lyon didn't die at Floireans Castle.'

The surprise that Lawrence already knew this was briefly visible on Max's face before he said, 'No, he didn't.' He reached to pull a chair up to the other side of Lawrence's desk. 'But it looks like someone did.'

'Did they find blood?' Lawrence exclaimed.

'Quite a lot,' Max replied, as he sat down. 'And that's not all.'

'They haven't found a body, as well?'

'No. But they did manage to retrieve DNA, and that DNA belongs to a man who has been missing for the better part of eighteen months.' Max slid a photocopied picture of a smiling young man onto the desk. Beneath the image, the name *Leon Hervi* had been handwritten in block capitals. 'French Canadian. He'd been backpacking around Europe. A couple of weeks after he came to London, he told friends he'd been offered a few days work up north. That was the last anyone heard from him.'

Lawrence's excitement at this revelation was tempered by another concern. 'How did we miss this guy in our search?'

Max raised his eyebrows and held his hands out in an *I don't know* gesture.

Lawrence quickly scrawled the name *Henry Love* on a Post-it note to enable him to look at the two names side by side, and almost immediately answered his own question. 'We were one letter out,' he said. 'Jakob used a *Y* instead of an *I*.' He wondered whether the substitution had been deliberate. Even if Jakob wasn't, as he claimed, dyslexic, it would have been an easy enough mistake to make. An *I* could easily be misheard as a *Y* – particularly against distracting background noise, or over the phone. And given that Summer had featured in a film as Emily Munster prior to embarking on her relationship with Jakob, the use of anagrams had clearly been her idea, not his.

Lawrence dismissed the question with a shake of his head. How the discrepancy had come about really didn't matter in the grand scheme of things. What he needed to know was whether Leon Hervi could conceivably be the man in the film and, if so, what other evidence there might be to tie him to the enterprise and, by extension, to Jakob. Given that the information Max had just conveyed strongly suggested that the rumours surrounding *In the Shadows* were rooted in truth, Lawrence suspected he had a reasonable chance of persuading MacLennan to approve a more in-depth examination of Floireans Castle's chapel and its surroundings. He reached for the phone.

Seventeen

Thanks to a quirk of teenage logic, Lawrence had found himself walking to his son's school alone on the morning of the first Saturday in December. On the occasions he was free to spectate at football matches, it was clear Jimmy valued having his support – but that didn't mean the boy was prepared to be seen walking *to* the match with him. So Jimmy had run on ahead, and Lawrence had made the fifteen-minute walk at a more leisurely pace, feeling thankful that it was warmer than it had been on his previous visit to the school's playing fields. He felt perfectly comfortable in a wool overcoat and scarf, and, given the paucity of clouds, wished he'd thought to look out his sunglasses.

As he approached the school gates, he was surprised to see that Leighton had arrived ahead of him. Given the pathologist's chaotic timekeeping, Lawrence hadn't expected him to make it with much time to spare. He was wearing a leather jacket and his blue-and-white-striped Sheffield Wednesday scarf, and it occurred to Lawrence that he couldn't recall ever seeing his colleague in a coat. Leighton smiled and raised a gloved hand in greeting as Lawrence neared.

'Morning,' Lawrence responded, as he reached the gates.

'All right?' Leighton said, cheerily. 'Where's Jim?'

'Too cool to be seen with me,' Lawrence replied, ruefully.

'Ah, that old chestnut.'

'Hopefully I've another couple of years before Elise joins the club.'

'How's she doing? Becks said she broke her arm.'

'She's fine, thanks. Katie's taken her into town this morning to do some Christmas shopping.'

Leighton grimaced. 'Rather them than me. As far as I'm concerned, if I can't get it online, nobody wants it.'

Lawrence smiled. He had similar feelings on the subject, although he only really had to worry about buying something for Katie – by the time Christmas was close enough for him to start thinking about it, she already had almost everything else planned. With this in mind, he said, 'I think it's an excuse to go out for lunch as much as anything.'

'Ah, now you're speaking my language.'

'Although with a bit of luck, Kate might manage to find a present for Elise while they're there.'

'Does Elise not have anything in mind?'

'She's desperate for a puppy, but that's not happening,' Lawrence replied, indicating the direction of the playing fields with one hand before starting to walk. 'Even leaving aside the fact that once the novelty wore off Katie would be the one who ended up looking after it, it wouldn't be fair to have a dog when nobody's home half the time.'

Leighton nodded. 'Don't be fooled by anyone who suggests getting a kitten instead, because cats are easy,' he said. 'The only easy thing about cats is how easy they are with their affections towards people who don't pay their vet bills.'

'Did yours ever turn up?' Lawrence asked, realising he hadn't given any thought to the animal whose absence had led to the discovery of Tony's body.

'She did. Picked up right where she left off, ordering me around. If she was human, she'd be insufferable.' He paused, then added, cheerfully, 'Still, I'll get my own back next week.'

'I gather you're off to La Palma.'

'Yep.'

'Jim tells me it's the site of one of the world's best observatories.'

'He's obviously been doing his homework.'

'Well that's a first,' Lawrence joked.

'It sounds like he's interested in doing more than just going to space.'

'That's true, he's also interested in going to Florida and Hawaii,' Lawrence replied, with a wry smile. 'I need to do some research on where we can go chasing the stars closer to home.'

'The Kielder Observatory in Northumberland might be a good place to start,' Leighton suggested. 'You could fit in a holiday in the national park at the same time.'

'That sounds more like it,' Lawrence said. 'I'm all for his getting into science, I just want to be sure it's the science and not the location that's really of interest.' He paused, then asked, out of curiosity, 'What did you want to do when you were fifteen?'

'Forensic science.'

'Really?'

'Yeah. My chemistry teacher was smart enough to realise most of us weren't interested in learning about the subject for its own sake, so he found ways to apply it to the real world, including how it might be used to catch a serial killer. It made me realise there might be jobs out there that I'd be interested in doing. That hadn't really occurred to me before.'

Lawrence nodded. Conversely, the message that had been drummed into him throughout his school career was that, if you worked hard, you could have a job you enjoyed. The trouble with that approach was that, all too often, it seemed to have given people unrealistic expectations of what they could expect from adult life. In her twenties, his sister had regularly opined that she *didn't want an office job*, a remark generally prefaced with something along the lines of, 'It's all right for you, you like your job', as if he wouldn't rather be on the golf course or hiking in the Brecon Beacons. There was, he had generally replied, a reason why it was called *work*.

'And my dad thought it was a diabolical idea, which immediately made my mind up,' Leighton added.

'What did he have in mind for you?'

'Oh, I don't know, something more conventional, I expect,' Leighton replied. 'You know, signing on or dealing drugs.'

Lawrence smiled. 'Lofty ambitions.'

'And I gave all that up to come and make life difficult for you lot.'

'Well your teacher was clearly more inspiring than Jim's. The other day Jim told me chemistry is *dead*.'

Leighton gasped in mock horror. 'Sacrilege! I hope you told him to wash his mouth out.'

'I'm afraid I suggested he study a different science.'

'Ah, you can't escape it that easily. Chemistry is really just applied physics, and biology is applied chemistry. They're all wrapped up together.'

'So what's pathology?'

'Messy.'

Lawrence laughed.

'But I'm good with mess. It's my natural habitat.'

Where Leighton's desk was concerned, that was certainly true. At one time, Lawrence would have said that the pathologist's way of working – jumping from one thought to another in a seemingly random manner, often abandoning what he was supposed to be doing in order to follow up something that had just come to mind – was equally messy. But the diversions frequently bore fruit, and Lawrence had come to the conclusion that, despite appearances, Leighton probably had a comprehensive mental map of the convoluted route and multiple detours he took along the road from A to B. He might forget to do things, but he never forgot information.

His question, a fortnight earlier, about whether the SD card had been tested for DNA, had also produced results. The lab had succeeded in matching the DNA to Gareth Corcoran, providing a definitive answer to the question of how deep his involvement in the pictures' production went. But, given that they couldn't prosecute a dead man, it wasn't the result Lawrence had been hoping for. Despite several attempts to interview Harvey, the boy had remained resolutely silent, so the case against Dale was limited to the brief view of his thumb in the video, his connection to Gareth and the preponderance of child pornography at his home. Had the DNA sample been his, the chances of securing a conviction for child abuse would have been greatly increased. It wasn't all bad news, however; they had at least amassed sufficient evidence for Dale to be placed on the sexual offenders register, so he would never again be able to work with children.

Meanwhile, a diving team had succeeded in retrieving what remained of Leon Hervi from the lake in the grounds of Floireans Castle. His body had been bundled up in bin bags before being weighted down, preserving evidence that would otherwise have been lost to the watery depths. As a result, Max and his colleagues had been able to determine the man's cause of death – as in the film, his throat had been slit – and to recover DNA traces and fingerprints belonging to both Jakob and Summer.

Unsurprisingly, Jakob had denied all knowledge of the man's demise and laid the blame squarely at Summer's door, suggesting she must have dispensed with Leon after his departure from the castle. He dismissed the DNA evidence as circumstantial and attempted to explain away the fingerprints, saying he and Summer had originally transported various props, including the costumes, in bin bags, and that she had presumably reused these. Whether he would succeed in convincing a jury remained to be seen, but the evidence had been sufficient for the Crown Prosecution Service to charge him with conspiracy to murder Leon and, by extension, Tony's murder.

Despite a concerted effort to find Summer, she was still missing. Lawrence had initially wondered whether Jakob was behind her disappearance, but they had found nothing to contradict the man's assertion that he had had no contact with her in over a year. Nonetheless, Lawrence suspected that if Summer did ever turn up, it wouldn't be alive.

'You might not recognise your desk when you come back to work,' he remarked, thinking of the major effort Max had made in April to sort through and file months' worth of Leighton's paperwork.

'You mean I might be able to see it,' Leighton replied, genially. 'Yeah, I'm thinking of using the same strategy next time my filing gets out of hand.'

'Don't even joke about it.'

Leighton smiled, but didn't immediately respond, and they walked in silence for several seconds before he said, 'Given that chunks of April and May are rather hazy, I don't remember whether I ever thanked you properly.'

'There's no need.'

'There is. You're the reason I'm still here.'

Lawrence wasn't sure what to say to that. He might have been the one in a position to officially action the search on the night of Leighton's incarceration in the freezer, but it had been Rebecca and Jon, one of the other pathologists, who had convinced him it was necessary. His initial response to their concern over Leighton's absence had been that the pathologist had probably just lost track of time – and his phone. On the basis of past form, neither had seemed particularly unlikely. Lawrence remained acutely aware that, had he acted earlier, when Jon first raised the alarm, the frostbite damage might not have been so severe. Feeling awkward, he said, 'Anyone else would have done the same.'

'No they wouldn't.'

Lawrence couldn't really argue. One of his peers hadn't even let Jon finish explaining his reason for calling before telling him to stop wasting everyone's time.

'Anyway, thank you.'

'You're welcome.'

'Going forwards, I'm planning on leaving the dangerous jobs to you guys.'

'I'm very glad to hear it, although I think you may need to reset the bar if trespassing on a railway line didn't make the cut.'

'I wasn't actually *on* the line,' Leighton replied. 'And it's not as if I could have fallen all the way up the embankment, so unless there was a killer rabbit lurking in the undergrowth, the biggest risk was probably tripping over the brambles.'

'Even so. There's a reason why it's a criminal offence.'

'Yeah, I hear you,' Leighton conceded, amicably. 'I tell you what, I'll make abiding by the rules my new year's resolution. Ok?'

'Have you ever stuck to a new year's resolution?' Lawrence asked. The concept always struck him as rather incongruous. If you wanted to make a change, why hold off until a particular date? It seemed akin to waiting until a person's appraisal to raise a concern; if there was a problem, it needed to be dealt with immediately, not months down the line.

'Not that I can recall,' Leighton admitted. 'You?'

Lawrence shook his head.

Leighton laughed. 'Scratch that idea, then,' he said. 'I'm not a miracle worker. And let's face it, if you can't do it, what hope is there for me?'

A note from Sadie

Thank you for choosing to read this book. If you have enjoyed *I Have Never*, I would be very grateful if you would consider rating it, or even writing a review – just a few words can make a difference in helping to persuade others to give my books a try!

Printed in Great Britain
by Amazon

69299254R00128